MacCallister
The Eagles Legacy

D0036645

MacCallister
The Eagles Legacy

William Johnstone
with J. A. Johnstone

PINNACLE BOOKS
Kensington Publishing Corp.
www.kensingtonbooks.com

PINNACLE BOOKS are published by

Kensington Publishing Corp.
119 West 40th Street
New York, NY 10018

PUBLISHER'S NOTE
Following the death of William W. Johnstone, the Johnstone family is working with a carefully selected writer to organize and complete Mr. Johnstone's outlines and many unfinished manuscripts to create additional novels in all of his series like The Last Gunfighter, Mountain Man, and Eagles, among others. This novel was inspired by Mr. Johnstone's superb storytelling.

All Kensington titles, imprints, and distributed lines are available at special quantity discounts for bulk purchases for sales promotions, premiums, fund-raising, educational, or institutional use. Special book excerpts or customized printings can also be created to fit specific needs. For details, write or phone the office of the Kensington special sales manager: Kensington Publishing Corp., 119 West 40th Street, New York, NY 10018, attn: Special Sales Department; phone 1-800-221-2647.

PINNACLE BOOKS and the Pinnacle logo are Reg. U.S. Pat. & TM Off.
The WWJ steer head logo is a trademark of Kensington Publishing Corp.

ISBN-13: 978-0-7860-2480-3
ISBN-10: 0-7860-2480-1

First printing: April 2011

10 9 8 7 6 5 4 3 2 1

Printed in the United States of America

Chapter One

The White Horse Pub in Donuun had an island bar, Jacobean-style ceiling, beautiful stained-glass windows, and etched mirrors. Despite its elegant décor and clientele of nobles, it was primarily a place for drinking, and most who came behaved with decorum, enjoying the ambiance and convivial conversation with friends. But some, like Alexander, Donald, and Roderick Somerled, sons of Angus Somerled, Lord High Sheriff of Argyllshire, regarded their station in life not one of seemliness but one of privilege. They drank too much, considered all others to be beneath them, and behaved with little restraint.

Duff Tavish MacCallister, a tall man with golden hair, wide shoulders, and muscular arms was sitting on a stool at the opposite end of the bar from the Somerleds. This wasn't by accident; there was a long-standing feud between the MacCallister and Somerled Clans, going back to the time of Robert the Bruce. And although the killing of each other had stopped a hundred years ago, their dislike of each other continued.

Ian McGregor, owner of the tavern, was wiping glasses behind the bar and he stepped over to speak to Duff. "Duff, m'lad, I was in the cemetery the other day and I saw marked on the tombstone of one of the graves, 'Here lies Geoffrey Somerled an honest man.' So this, I'll be askin' you. Think ye now that there may be two bodies lyin' in the same coffin—Geoffrey *and* an honest man?"

Duff MacCallister threw back his head and laughed out loud. He was wearing a kilt, and he slapped his bare knee in glee. McGregor's daughter, Skye, a buxom lass with long red hair, flashing blue eyes, and a friendly smile, had been filling three mugs with ale as her father told the joke. She joined in the laughter.

Duff and Skye were soon to be married, and their banns were already posted on the church door. Most of the customers of the White Horse Pub appreciated Skye's easy humor and friendly ways and treated her with respect due a woman. But some, like the sheriff's three sons, treated her with ill-concealed contempt.

"Bar girl!" Donald shouted. "More ale!"

"You know her name, Somerled," Duff said. "And it isn't 'bar girl'."

"'Tis a bar girl she is and her services we're needin'," Donald said.

"I'll not be but a moment, Mr. Somerled," Skye replied. She had just put the three mugs on a carrying tray. "I've other customers to tend now."

"You're carrying three mugs, there be but three

of us," Donald said. "Serve us first. You can get more ale for them."

"I'll not be but a moment, sir," Skye replied.

Donald was carrying a club, and he banged it so loudly on the bar that it startled Skye, and she dropped her tray.

"What a clumsy trollop ye' be!" Donald said. "If you had brought the ale here, as I asked, this no' would'a happened."

"I told you, sir, I had other customers."

"Your other customers can wait. Be ye daft as well as clumsy? Do ye know who I am?" Donald asked.

"Donald Somerled, that is my fiancée you are talking to, and if you speak harshly to her again, I will pull your tongue out of your mouth and hand it to you," Duff said, barely controlling his voice, so intense was his anger.

"We'll be seeing who is handing who their tongue," Donald said, hitting his open hand with his club.

Duff put his mug on the bar, then stepped away to face Donald. "I'm at your service," he said.

With a defiant yell Donald charged Duff, not with his fists, but with the raised club. Duff grabbed the same barstool he had been sitting on and raised it over his head to block the downward swing of the club. The clack of wood crashing against wood filled the entire pub with a crack almost as loud as a gunshot. The noise got the attention of everyone in the bar and all conversation stopped as they turned to watch the confrontation between a MacCallister and a Somerled.

Donald raised his staff for a second try, but as he held his club aloft, MacCallister turned the stool around and slammed the seat into Donald's chest so hard that he let out a loud *whoosh* as he fell to the floor with the breath knocked from his body.

"You'll be paying for that, Duff MacCallister!" Alexander said, and even as Donald writhed on the floor trying to recover his breath, his older brother charged Duff.

Duff tossed the barstool aside, then put up his fists to meet Alexander's charge. He parried a wild roundhouse right, then countered with a straight left that landed on Alexander's chin, driving him back. With a yell of anger, the third of the Somerled brothers, Roderick, joined the fray.

Duff backed up against the bar, thus preventing either of them from getting behind him. He sent a whistling blow into Roderick's nose and felt it break, causing the big man to grab his nose and turn away from the fight. Now only Alexander was left, but he was the biggest and the most dangerous of the three. Shaking off the blow to his chin, he raised both fists, then advanced toward Duff.

The two men danced around the barroom floor exchanging blows, or rather, attempted blows. Duff learned early in the fight that he could hit Alexander at will. That was because Alexander was so big and so confident of his strength that he made no attempt to block Duff's blows, willing to take them in order to get into position to return the blow. And, he seemed to be taking them with no ill effect.

Duff, on the other hand, bobbed and weaved as Alexander tried roundhouse rights, straight punches, and uppercuts. Finally Alexander connected with one of his attempts, a straight shot that Duff managed to deflect with his left shoulder, thus avoiding a punch to his head. And, even though it was not a direct hit, there was so much power in the blow that Duff felt his left arm go numb, which meant he could no longer count on that arm to ward away any more of the big man's punches.

Duff knew he was going to have to end the fight soon, so he bobbed and weaved, watching for an opening. The opening came after Alexander tried another roundhouse right. Duff managed to pull back from it, and as Alexander completed his swing, it left the opening Duff was looking for. Duff pulled the trigger on a straight whistling right that drove his fist into Alexander's Adam's apple.

Alexander gagged, and put both hands to his throat. When he did so, Duff followed with a hard right to the chin that sent Alexander down to join Donald, who was just now getting up but showing no interest in continuing the fight.

For a long moment everyone in the bar looked on with shock and amazement. The Somerleds had a reputation for fighting, something they did frequently. And, because they were the sons of the sheriff, they never had to pay any of the consequences that others of the county had to pay when they engaged in the same activity.

They seldom lost a fight, and yet here, in front of an entire inn full of witnesses, one man, Duff MacCallister, had taken the measure, not just of one of them, but of all three, and at the same time.

"Hear, hear, let's give a hurrah for Duff MacCallister!" someone shouted, and the bar rang with their huzzahs.

"Now, gentlemen, I believe you called for more ale?" the bartender said, speaking to the Somerleds as if nothing had happened, as if he were merely responding to their request. Donald and Roderick responded with scowls and helped their oldest brother to his feet. Then the three men left.

Everyone in the pub wanted to buy Duff a round, but he had already drunk his limit of two mugs, so he thanked them all, accepting their offers to buy for him when next he came in.

"Skye, would you step outside with me for a moment?" Duff asked.

"Ian, best you keep an eye on them," one of the other customers said. "Else they'll be outside sparking."

Skye blushed prettily as the others laughed at the jibe. Duff took her hand in his and walked outside with her.

"Only four more weeks until we are wed," Skye said when they were outside. "I can hardly wait."

"No need to wait. We can go into Glasgow and be married on the morrow," Duff suggested.

"Duff MacCallister, sure and m'mother has waited my whole life to give me a fine church wedding now, and you would deny that to her?"

Duff chuckled. "Don't worry, Skye. There is no way in the world I would start my married life by getting on the bad side of my mother-in-law. If you want to wait, then I will wait with you."

"What do you mean you will wait with me?" Skye asked. "And what else would you be doing, Duff MacCallister? Would you be finding a willing young lass to wait with you?"

"I don't know such a willing lass," Duff replied. "Do you? For truly, it would be an interesting experiment."

"Oh, you!" Skye said, hitting Duff on the shoulder. It was the same shoulder Alexander had hit in the fight, and he winced.

"Oh!" she said. "I'm sorry. You just made me mad talking about a willing lass."

Duff laughed, then pulled Skye to him. "You are the only willing lass I want," he said.

"I should hope so."

Duff bent down to kiss her waiting lips.

"I told you, Ian! Here they are, sparking in the dark!" a customer shouted and, with a good-natured laugh, Duff and Skye parted. With a final wave to those who had come outside to "see the sparking," Duff started home.

Three Crowns

Duff Tavish MacCallister was the fifth generation to live on and work Three Crowns, the property that was first bestowed by King Charles II upon Sir Falcon MacCallister, Earl of Argyllshire and Laird of Three Crowns. Falcon was Duff's great-great-great-great-grandfather. The title passed on to Falcon's eldest son, Hugh, but died when Hugh migrated to America. The land stayed in the family, passing down to Braden MacCallister, who was Duff's great-great-great-grandfather. The land passed through the succeeding generations so that it now belonged to Duff.

Three Crowns got its name from three crenellated hills that, with imagination, resembled crowns. The family cemetery was atop the middle crown, where Sir Falcon MacCallister and all succeeding generations, down to and including Duff's father, mother, and only brother, lay buried. Duff was the last MacCallister remaining in Scotland.

Duff raised Highland cattle on Three Crowns. He liked Highland cattle, not only because they were a traditional Scottish breed but also because they required very little in the way of shelter, enjoying conditions in which many other breeds would perish. Cold weather and snow had little effect on them, and they seemed to be able to eat anything, getting fat on what other cattle would pass by.

Duff had read of the great cattle ranches in the American West, and how they required many cowboys to ride atop the huge herds across vast areas. But because the Highland cattle were so easy to handle, and he had only three hundred acres, Duff was able to manage his farm all alone. He did have something in common with the cowboys of the American West, though. He oversaw his herd from the back of a horse, and this morning he saddled his horse. Then, as the sun was rising, he took a ride around his entire three hundred acres, looking over his cattle. It was a brisk morning and both he and his horse blew clouds of vapor into the cool air.

His horse whickered as he rode through his small herd of cattle, distinctive with their long hair and red coloring. The cattle were grazing contentedly, totally unresponsive to the horse and human who had come into their midst.

As Duff rode around his herd, he imagined what it would be like when he had a son to help him run the farm. He and Skye had spoken often of it.

"What if our first child is a girl?" Skye teased.

"Then we shall make her a princess, and have a son."

"But if we have only girls?"

"Then I will make them all tomboys, and they will smell of cattle when they go to school."

"Oh, you!" Skye said, hitting him playfully.

Duff also planned to build a place for Skye's parents so they could live on Three Crowns with them. For now, Skye's father, Ian McGregor, enjoyed a good living running the White Horse Pub, but there would come a time when he would be too old to work. When that time came, Duff promised Skye, Ian could retire in comfort in his own house, right there beside them.

As Duff reached the southern end of his property, he saw a break in the fence. Ten of his cattle had gone through the break and were now cropping the weeds that grew on the other side of the Donuun Road. Duff slapped his legs against the side of his horse, then rode at a quicker pace until he reached the break in the fence.

"Who told you cows you could be over here?" Duff said as he guided his horse through the break and across the road. He began rounding the cattle up and pushing them back across the road toward the break in the fence. It wasn't a particularly hard thing to do: Highland cattle were known not only for their hardiness, but also for their intelligence and docile ways. He had just gotten the last cow pushed back through the break, when Rab Malcolm rode up. Malcolm was one of Sheriff Somerled's deputies.

"Your cows are trespassing on county property," Malcolm said. "You could be fined for that, you know."

"My cows were keeping the weeds down along the side of the county road," Duff said. "I should charge the county a fee for that."

"Making light of the offense does not alter anything," Malcolm said. "I saw your cows on the road. That is a violation and you could be cited."

"Cite me or ride away, Rab Malcolm," Duff said. "I'll not be listening to your prattle."

Malcolm was wearing a billyclub hanging from his belt. He lifted it from his belt, then used it as a pointer, pointing it directly at Duff.

"With your wild carryin'-ons last night, 'tis an enemy you have made of the sheriff," Malcolm said. "And in this county, 'tis not a smart thing to make the sheriff your enemy."

"Sure'n the Somerleds and the MacCallisters have been enemies for two hundred years and more. I doubt that there is anything I could have done last night that would make it more so."

"You will see," Malcolm said. "The sheriff was very angry. I've never seen him more angry."

"Be gone with ye, Malcolm. 'Tis enough of your mouth I've listened to today."

"See that your fence is mended, Duff MacCallister. I will not have commerce along this road disturbed by the likes of your cattle," Malcolm said, just before he rode away.

Because the cattle frequently pushed through the fence at one point or another around his ranch, keeping it mended was an ongoing operation. Duff had long ago acquired the habit of carrying in his saddle bags the tools and wire he would need to perform the task. He dismounted and took out his tools and wire. Duff's horse stood by patiently for the fifteen minutes or so it took to make the repair.

Chapter Two

"I'll not be playing the pipes at my own wedding," Duff said that evening at the White Horse Pub. "For sure now, and how would that look? My bride would come marching in on the arms of her father, finely dressed in her bridal gown, looking beautiful, but there is no groom standing at the chancel waiting for her. 'Where is the groom?' people will say. 'Poor girl, has the groom deserted her at the altar?' But no, the groom is standing in the transept playing the pipes."

Skye laughed. "No, I dinnae mean play the pipes at the wedding. But afterward, at the reception you could play the pipes. You play them so beautifully, 'twould be a shame if ye dinnae play them."

"A fine thing, Ian," Duff said to Skye's father behind the bar. "Your daughter wants me to work on my wedding day."

"Duff MacCallister, for you, playing the pipes isn't work. It is an act of love and you know it. Sure'n there's no' a man alive can make the pipes sing a more beautiful song than you."

"So the two of you are doubling up on me, are you?" Duff said.

"And if we need another, there's m'mother," Skye said. "For she would want to hear you play as well. Say you will, Duff. Please?"

Duff laughed. "Aye, I'll play the pipes, for how can I turn you down?"

"Best you be careful Duff, m'boy, lest you let the lass know how much power she has over you."

"Ian, do you think she doesn't already know?" Duff asked. He put down his empty beer mug, then stood. "Best I get home," he said. "Skye, would you be for stepping outside with me?"

"No need for that, Duff MacCallister," Skye said. "The only reason you want me to step outside is so I will kiss you good night, and I can do that right here."

"In front of everyone?"

Skye smiled, sweetly. "Aye, m'love. In front of God, m' father, and everyone else."

Skye kissed him, and the others in the pub laughed and applauded.

Before stopping by the White Horse Pub, Duff had picked up his mail. Not wanting to read it in the pub, he waited until he got home. Now, settled in a comfortable chair near a bright lantern, he looked through the mail.

Dear Cousin Duff—
   My name is Andrew MacCallister, and yes, we are cousins, though I'm certain that you have never heard of me. I have heard of you only

because I hired someone to research my family's past with particular emphasis on any of my family that might remain in Scotland. That brought me to you.

You and I share a great-great-great-great-grandfather, one Falcon MacCallister from the Highlands of Scotland. You might be interested to know that I have a brother named after him, and, I am pleased to say, Falcon has done the name proud.

My twin sister Rosanna and I are theatrical players, and on the fifth of April we shall be appearing at Campbell's Music Saloon on Argyle Street in Glasgow. It would please us mightily if you could attend the performance as our guest.

> *Sincerely,*
> *Andrew MacCallister*

White Horse Pub

"I thank you for the invitation, Duff," Skye said in response to Duff's invitation for her to accompany him to the play. "But 'tis thinking, I am, that you should go by yourself, for they are your kinsmen."

"And soon to be yours as well," Duff said. "For when we are married, my kinsmen are your kinsmen."

"Aye, but we aren't married yet, so they are not my kinsmen now. And they dinnae invite me. They invited you."

"That's because they know nothing about you," Duff said. "I will introduce you, then they will know you."

"I think it would be better if I dinnae go," Skye

said. "Besides, after we are married, I will no longer work for my father, so I feel I should give him all the time I can."

"Then if you won't go, then I won't as well."

"Duff Tavish MacCallister, how dare you do that to me?" Skye said. "Don't saddle me with the responsibility of you not going."

"I just meant—"

"I know what you meant," Skye said, interrupting him. "Duff, you must go to the play. I would be very upset with you if you did not. Go, then come back and tell me all about it."

"I'll do better than that," Duff said. "If you won't go to meet my kinsmen, then I shall bring them here to meet you."

Skye smiled. "Aye, now that I would like. I have read of them in the newspaper. They are quite famous in America, you know."

"Are they?"

"Aye. 'Twill be a grand thing to meet them, I am thinking."

Campbell's Music Saloon, Argyle Street, Glasgow
April 5

Duff MacCallister was a reserve captain in 42nd Foot, Third Battalion of the Royal Highland Regiment of Scotts. As such, when he arrived at the theater he was wearing the kilt of the Black Watch, complete with a *sgian dubh*, or ceremonial knife, tucked into the right kilt stocking, with only the pommel visible. He was also wearing the Victoria Cross, Great Britain's highest award for bravery.

He went inside the theater to the "will call" counter.

"The name is MacCallister. I am not certain, but I believe you may have a ticket for me."

"Indeed, I do, sir," the clerk replied. "Just a moment, please." The clerk called one of the ushers over. "Timothy, would you be for taking Captain MacCallister to the green room? Introduce him to the stage manager, Mr. Fitzhugh. He will know what to do."

"Aye," the usher said. "Come, Captain."

Duff followed the usher down a side corridor to an area behind the stage.

"I heard Mr. Service call you MacCallister. Be ye a kinsman to Andrew and Rosanna MacCallister?"

"I am told that is so, though I confess that I have never met them," Duff said.

"They are quite famous in theater," Timothy said. "We are very lucky to have them come to Glasgow to perform."

They came to a large room with chairs and sofas, also tables with tea and biscuits on them.

"'Tisn't green," Duff said.

"Beg pardon, sir?" Timothy asked.

"He said take me to a 'green room.' This room isn't green."

The usher laughed. "It's what they call the room where the actors can gather offstage. I think the first one must have been green. Now 'tis the name for all."

"Makes no sense to me," Duff said.

"Aye, nor does it make sense to me," Timothy said. "There is much about the theater that makes no sense to one who is not in the business. But 'tis a good job to have."

There were several men and women standing about in costumes and stage makeup, talking among themselves in words and phrases that were unique and exclusive to their profession.

"George was out on the apron, corpsing while we were working out the blocking. He had me so flummoxed that I didn't know whether to go stage left or stage right," a young woman was saying.

"Had it been me, I would have just given my exit line and stepped behind the backdrop," a young man said, and they all laughed.

"Mr. Fitzhugh, this is Captain MacCallister," the usher said, introducing Duff to an older, bald-headed man who was wearing square-rim glasses situated far down on his nose. He was looking at notes he had fastened to a clipboard.

"Ah, yes, Captain," Mr. Fitzhugh said. "Mr. Mac-Callister was hoping you would come. If you would wait here, sir, I shall summon him."

"Thank you," Duff said. He moved over to one side of the room, providing some separation between himself and the players in costume and makeup. He noticed that one or two of the young women seemed to be paying special attention to him, and he looked away self-consciously.

Suddenly all the conversation stopped.

"Mr. MacCallister, can I do something for you?" someone asked.

Duff looked up, thinking the person was talking to him, but saw that they were talking to another person, a man who was in his early fifties and carrying himself with great dignity. Like the others, he was in costume and makeup.

"No, thank you, relax, relax," the man said. Spying Duff, a broad smile spread across his face. "Cousin Duff, how good of you to come," he said, extending his hand.

"It was good of you to invite me," Duff replied, appreciative of the man's firm grip. "You would be Cousin Andrew?"

"I am," Andrew replied.

"Ma'am," someone said and, as they had with Andrew, all stood in respectful silence as a very attractive woman, also in costume and makeup, came into the room.

"Sister, come and meet our Scottish kin," Andrew called to her. "Cousin Duff, this is Rosanna."

Rosanna stuck out her hand and Duff bowed his head slightly, then raised her hand to his lips for a kiss.

"Oh, my! How gallant!" Rosanna said. "Andrew, do pay attention to our young cousin, perhaps you will learn a thing or two."

"Timothy?" Andrew said.

"Yes, m'laird?" the usher replied.

"Please take Mr. MacCallister to the orchestra, row five, center seat," Andrew said. He smiled again at Duff. "I may have just sown the seeds of my own disaster. That is the best seat in the house. If I stink up the stage with a poor performance, there will be no hiding it from you. The play we are presenting tonight is called *The Golden Fetter* by Watts Phillips. I do hope you enjoy it."

"Oh, I am certain that I will greatly enjoy the performance," Duff replied.

When Duff was escorted with great pomp and circumstance to his seat in the theater, he was aware of the reaction of the others when he, a Highlander in the uniform of the Black Watch, took the best seat in the house.

"Who is he?"

"Perhaps a relative of the Queen?"

"He is someone of great importance, of that we can be certain."

"Aye, he is wearing the Victoria Cross. That alone should be enough to warrant the best seat in the house."

The lights in the theater dimmed, but were brightened on the stage. Before curtain rise, the sound of a storm was heard, and as the curtain drew up a flash of vivid lightning was seen, followed by a loud clap of thunder. Onstage was the interior of a village barber's shop, fitted up with the usual paraphernalia.

Duff enjoyed all three acts of the melodrama, feeling a sense of pride in that his kinsmen were indeed the stars of the performance. After escaping many perils and dangers, Andrew and Rosanna were now the last two actors on the stage.

Andrew (as Sir Gilbert): Look up—look up, dearest! With his own hands he has broken the fetter, and you are mine now, *(embraces her)* you are mine!

Rosanna (as FLORENCE): *(as her head sinks on his shoulder)* Forever, Gilbert, forever.

The curtain came down to thunderous applause. Then it rose again so that the players could take their curtain call, in groups for the lesser players, then singly for the more principal roles. Finally Rosanna curtsied, then left the stage for Andrew, who bowed, then held out his hand to call Rosanna back so they could take the final bow together as, once more, the curtain descended.

Duff remained seated as the others in the audience began to exit the theater. He wasn't entirely sure of what was expected of him now. Was his only obligation to come and see the show? Should he go back to the green room and wait? Or would that be too presumptuous on his part?

Not until he was the only person remaining in the auditorium did he stand and start to leave. That was when Timothy appeared from the same side door Duff had gone through when he visited the green room.

"Captain MacCallister?" Timothy called.

"Aye?"

"Mr. MacCallister's compliments, sir, and he asks if you will join him in his dressing room."

Duff followed Timothy along the same path he had traversed earlier, but this time they passed through the green room, which was even more crowded now than it had been before. All the cast and the stagehands were gathered there, babbling in excitement as they came down from the exhilaration of the production. Timothy led him through the green room and down a long hall to one of two doors, each of which had a star just above the name. The sign on one door read: MISS MACCALLISTER. The sign on the other door read: MR. MACCALLISTER. It was upon this door that Timothy knocked.

"Mr. MacCallister? It is Timothy, sir. I have Captain MacCallister with me."

The door opened and Andrew stood just on the other side, his face white and shining with some sort of cleansing lotion.

"Thank you, Timothy. Come in, Duff, come in," Andrew said. "I shall be but a few minutes longer. Then perhaps you would honor Rosanna and me by allowing us to take you out to dinner."

"No," Duff said.

"No?" Andrew had a surprised expression on his face.

Duff smiled. "I was your guest for the wonderful play. Now I insist that you and Rosanna be my guests for dinner."

Andrew smiled and nodded his head. "We would be delighted," he said.

Duff watched in fascination as Andrew sat down at his dressing table and, using a towel, wiped his face clean of the cleansing lotion. Gone, also, were the dark lines that had been around his eyes, and the dark outline of his lips.

"You must wonder what kind of man would put

makeup on his face," Andrew said, glancing at Duff in his mirror.

"No, I . . ."

Andrew's laugh interrupted his response. "I know, I know, my own brothers tease me about it. But one must outline the eyes and the mouth when onstage for, next to the voice, those are the most important instruments in an actor's profession. With them, we exhibit surprise"—Andrew opened wide his eyes and mouth—"anger"—he squinted his eyes and drew his mouth into a snarl—"sadness"—he managed to make his eyes droop and his lips curl down—"and happiness." Again his eyes were wide, though not quite as wide, and his mouth spread into a wide smile.

Duff laughed, and applauded. "That is very good," he said.

"Yes, you could see it because you are here with me, in the same room and but a few feet away. Onstage, however, the audience member in the farthest row from the stage must be able to see those same reactions, and in order to do that, we must use makeup."

"I can see how that would be so," Duff said.

There was a light knock on the door and a woman's voice called through. "Andrew, are you decent?"

"Why, Sister, I am one of the most decent people I know," Andrew replied.

"That had better be more than a joke, because I am coming in," Rosanna said, pushing the door open and stepping into the room. Her makeup and costume had been removed, but she was still, Duff saw, a very attractive woman. She smiled at Duff. "Did Andrew tell you we want you to be our dinner guest tonight?"

"I told him, but he refused," Andrew said.

"What?" Rosanna replied in surprise.

"It turns out that he wants us to be his guests."

Rossana laughed. "I hope you accepted."

"Of course I did," Andrew said.

Chapter Three

After the show Duff took his two cousins out to dinner at the King's Arms restaurant.

"It is Scot you are, so Scot ye shall eat," Duff said.

"We defer to you, cousin," Andrew said.

Duff ordered a rich, Scotch broth to start the meal, then a hearty pot-roasted chicken with potatoes as the main course, and he finished it up with clootie dumplings covered in a rich custard sauce.

During the meal Andrew explained how they were related.

"Our father, that is, mine and Rosanna's, was Jamie Ian MacCallister the Third. He was captured by the Shawnee Indians in 1817 on his seventh birthday and raised among them so that he was more Indian than white. He learned the warrior's way, and when he was only nine, he shot a deer with a bow and arrow he had made himself. And if that wasn't enough, he fought off two wolves for the carcass. That earned him the name Man Who Is Not Afraid."

"Father was at the Alamo," Rosanna added. "He was the last courier Colonel Travis sent out before the final battle."

"There is a statue of him in the town of MacCallister, Colorado. The statue was made by the noted sculptor Frederic Remington," Andrew continued.

"My, with a history like that, a statue and a town of the same name, your father must have been quite a successful man," Duff said. "I'm sure you are very proud of him."

"We are," Rosanna said. "He was one of the true giants of the American West, and founder of the city that bears his name."

"His father was Jamie Ian the Second," Andrew said, continuing the narrative. "He was one of the early settlers and a successful farmer in Ohio. My great-grandfather was Jamie Ian the First, and he was truly a giant. He made the trek West with Lewis and Clark, and he became a mountain man, living and trapping on his own for many years before returning to civilization.

"My great-great-grandfather Seamus MacCallister, was a captain during our Revolutionary War. He was with Washington at Valley Forge, crossed the Delaware with him, and was at his side at the final Battle of Yorktown. In doing family research, I came across a letter written to him by George Washington in which he praises Seamus for his military skills and courage.

"My great-great-great-grandfather, Hugh MacCallister, was a captain in the service of Governor Joseph Dudley of Massachusetts during the Queen Anne War. Hugh MacCallister was the first of our family to emigrate from Scotland, and was the brother of Braden MacCallister, your great-great-great-grandfather. Both were sons of Falcon Mac-Callister, and that, my dear cousin, is where our family lines cross."

"You said in the letter that you have a brother named Falcon," Duff said.

"Indeed, we do," Andrew said. "And I hope you will forgive the familial pride, but Falcon is one of the most storied people in our American West. Have you heard of General Custer?"

"Of course, I have read much of him," Duff said.

"Falcon was with Custer on his last scout."

"But how can that be? I thought all who were with Custer were killed."

"Custer divided his forces into three elements," Andrew explained. "All who were with him were killed, that is true. But most of the other two elements survived."

"I must confess that when Uncle Hugh took the MacCallister name to America it sounds as if he, and all who followed, have done the name proud," Duff said.

"Do you know much of our mutual ancestor, Falcon?" Andrew asked.

"Aye," Duff responded. "On February 7, 1676, Fingal Somerled and his clan set out to destroy the MacCallisters and steal all their cattle. But our mutual grandfather, Sir Falcon MacCallister, Earl of Argyllshire, learned of the threat and set a trap for the Somerleds. When Somerled and his men entered Glen Fruin, he encountered a large force of men led by Falcon MacCallister. Somerled tried to withdraw, but he found his exit blocked by a strong force that Falcon had put into position for just that purpose. The Somerleds were trapped with Mac-Callisters in front and at the rear, and the walls of the glen on either side. They were completely routed, many were killed, and Fingal barely managed to escape with his life. That was the start of a feud between our two families that continues to this day."

"You mean you are still killing each other?" Rosanna asked.

"Oh, no, thankfully we have put that aside." Duff thought of the recent fight he had with Donald, Roderick, and Alexander Somerled, and he chuckled. "But we do still have our moments," he added.

"Do you know the history of any of your other ancestors?" Andrew asked.

"Oh, yes. We have kept an oral history as part of our lives, so much so that I feel I actually know ancestors whom I never met. Duncan MacCallister is an interesting ancestor, but I'm afraid my great-great-grandfather, Duncan, fought against your great-great-grandfather Seamus in your revolutionary war. He was with General Cornwallis at Yorktown. As a result, he was part of an ignoble surrender. I am proud to say, however, that he fared much better at Waterloo, where Napoleon was defeated. Duncan was a sharpshooter with the 95th Rifles, part of the Duke of Wellington's army.

"My grandfather, Alair MacCallister was a brigadier with Sir Harry Smith in India when Ranjodh Singh was defeated. My father was a captain with General Simpson during the Crimean War, at the Battle of Sevastopol."

"And you?" Andrew said.

"Ah, yes, my uniform. I am a captain in the reserves."

"You may be in the reserves now, but I know for a fact that you are not wearing the uniform of the Black Watch merely for show," Andrew said. "You took part in the battle of Tel-el-Kebir in Egypt. That is where you received the Victoria Cross you are wearing."

Duff smiled self-consciously. "You have done your homework, haven't you, Andrew?"

"I wanted to find out as much as I could about our Scottish cousin," Andrew said. "And while, admittedly, the bloodlines that connect us have grown thin with succeeding generations, I believe that the spark of kinship can quite easily be fanned into a flame of genuine friendship."

"For anyone else, the blood might be too thin at this point to claim kinship," Duff said. "But not for the MacCallisters. Sure and we are as kin as if ye were my brother." He glanced over at Rosanna. "And a more beautiful and talented sister I could scarcely envision."

Rosanna extended her hand across the table and, once more, Duff raised it to his lips for a kiss.

After they enjoyed their dinner, Duff took them to the White Horse Pub. Duff was greeted warmly by nearly every customer in the pub. Ian was behind the counter, and he smiled broadly as he saw Duff arrive with Andrew and Rosanna.

"Ian, my friend, may I introduce to you my kith and kin from New York?" Duff said.

Ian, who had been drying glasses, put the towel over his shoulder and extended his hand toward Andrew. "Sure and 'tis a pleasure to meet the

American cousins of my dear friend, and soon to be son-in-law, Duff MacCallister," he said. He looked toward Rosanna. "And what a beautiful woman you be," he said. "'Tis no wonder you are so successful in the theater."

"Are all Scots so gallant?" Rosanna said.

Ian laughed. "'Tis our way," he said.

"Where is Skye?" Rosanna asked. "I must meet my cousin's fiancée."

"She is there waiting on yon table," Duff said, pointing her out.

"Oh, my," Rosanna said. "What a beautiful young woman she is. Duff, I can see why you are so smitten with her."

"As can I," Andrew said. "What I can't see is why she should be smitten with you."

Andrew's jibe drew a laugh as Ian put mugs of ale on the bar in front of each of them.

Andrew reached into his pocket for money, but Ian held up his hand. "This is on the house," he said. "Surely I can furnish a beer to m' own cousins now, can't I?"

"Cousins?" Andrew said. He looked at Duff. "Did I not go far enough in my genealogy research?"

"We aren't cousins yet," Ian said. "But when my Skye marries Duff, 'tis cousins-in-law we shall be."

Andrew chuckled. "I suppose that is true, isn't it?"

Skye returned to the bar then and was introduced to Andrew and Rosanna.

"'Tis most pleased I am to meet such famous theater people," Skye said with a little curtsey as she greeted the pair.

"It is true that we strut and fret our brief hour

upon the stage," Andrew said. "But thus far, fame has eluded us."

"He is being modest, Skye," Duff said. "You should have seen the high esteem in which they were held by the people of Glasgow when I visited there to see their show."

"The people of Glasgow were uncommonly kind," Rosanna said. "Certainly they treated us with more deference than we deserve."

"I think not," Skye said. "I read of you in our newspaper. I have the article here." Skye reached under the bar, then pulled out a newspaper that was carefully folded to display the article that held her interest.

She began to read:

> Campbell's Musical Saloon has occasioned many theatricals and musicales of note, but rarely have the boards been so crowned as to be trod by that magnificent pair of thespians, Andrew and Rosanna MacCallister. Brother and sister they, the MacCallisters, have long been the object of attention and admiration in New York. Should one be fortunate enough to attend a performance in which these two appear, they will indeed regard the evening of entertainment as time well spent.

She put the paper down. "If the paper writes that of you, then you are truly famous."

"You read very well, young lady," Andrew said. "You would make a fine thespian yourself."

Skye blushed at the flattery.

At that moment Sheriff Angus Somerled came

into the tavern and much of the laughter and conversation grew quiet as he stood just inside the door, perusing the place with dark and brooding eyes.

"Skye, lass, see if we can be of service to the sheriff," Ian said quietly.

Skye approached the sheriff, then curtseyed. "Sheriff, may we serve you?" she asked.

Sheriff Somerled looked over at Duff, then pointed at him.

"Is it true that, last week, you fought with my sons for no reason?" he asked.

"That is not true," Duff replied.

"How can you say it is not true when with my own eyes I saw the bruises you inflicted upon them?"

"I am not saying that I didn't fight with them," Duff said. "What I dispute is that I fought with them for no reason. I fought with them because they attacked me."

"There are three of them and but one of you, yet they are the injured ones. Would you be tellin' me, Duff MacCallister, that they attacked you first, and yet you bested the three of them? Because that I am not believing."

"You should believe it, Sheriff, for Duff is speaking only the truth," Ian said. "All who were here that night will bear witness to the fact that your sons attacked MacCallister."

"Aye, Sheriff, 'tis true enough," one of the other patrons said. "Your sons started the fight."

The sheriff said nothing in direct reply, but a blood vessel in his temple began to throb, a visual display of his anger. He looked at Andrew and Rosanna.

"Are you the theater people I have heard about?" he asked.

"I don't know if, or what you might have heard of us. But it is true that we are theater people," Rosanna replied.

"Why dishonor yourselves by standing with one who is known to be a brigand?" Angus Somerled asked.

"Duff MacCallister is my cousin," Andrew replied. "Were he at the gates of hell, I would stand by him."

"You make claim that he is your cousin?"

"Aye, of the self-same blood as Falcon MacCallister, he who defeated your ancestor at Glen Fruin," Andrew said, perfectly adopting the Scottish brogue.

"*Ochh.* It is worthless you are, the lot of ye," Sheriff Somerled said as, spinning on his heel, he left the tavern.

"And it is good riddance to ye, Angus Somerled!" Ian McGregor called out after the sheriff left. It wasn't loud enough for the sheriff to hear, but it was loud enough for all in the pub to hear, and they laughed out loud.

Two days later, Duff came to Glasgow to tell his cousins good-bye.

"We have had a wonderful visit," Rosanna said. "Especially so since we met you and were able to reconnect our family after all these years. And how wonderful it was to meet Skye. She is such a delightful young lady. I am sure the two of you will be very happy."

"Thank you, I am sure we will be as well. And I

enjoyed meeting both of you," Duff said. "It was an interesting experience, finding out what happened to those of my family who went to America."

"You should come to America as well," Andrew said. "Yes, come to America after you have married, and bring your bride with you."

"Perhaps I will," Duff said. "I would like to see America, and I would like Skye to see it with me."

"But if you come, you should come to live, not just to visit," Andrew said. "You would love it in America, and Americans would welcome you. We are that kind of people."

"I have land here," Duff said. "If I were to come to America, how would I live? I have no land there."

"Land is easily acquired," Andrew said. "We have so much land in America that we give it away. It is called homesteading. All you have to do is move onto a piece of unoccupied property, work it, and file a claim. Then it becomes yours."

"Aye, that is an interesting proposition, but Skye still has her family here. I think it might be difficult to persuade her to undertake such an adventure."

"Perhaps not as difficult as you may think," Rosanna said. "Skye strikes me as a young woman with an adventurous spirit. She may want to come. But, whether you come to visit or to live, you must spend some time with us."

Chapter Four

White Horse Pub

A large banner stretched across the top of the mirror behind the bar. The banner was festooned with flowers and bore the words:

CONGRATULATIONS TO
CAPTAIN DUFF TAVISH MACCALLISTER
AND SKYE MCGREGOR

Ever since he arrived at the pub earlier this evening, customers had been coming up to him, congratulating him on the fact that tomorrow he and Skye were to be married.

"'Tis the surprise to me that after twenty days of posting banns, not one person came up with a reason why a scallywag such as yourself is nae fit to marry with the lovely and sainted Skye McGregor," one of the customers said.

"Here, here," another called and all laughed.

"'Tis teasin' you I am, Duff, for sure'n I can think

of no one better to be the groom of our fair Skye. Lads, charge your glasses," he called, holding his mug aloft.

The others rushed to have their own mugs and glasses refilled.

"To Captain Duff Tavish MacCallister, long may he live and many a fine son may he sire!"

"MacCallister!" the others in the pub shouted.

Skye wasn't here. In fact, as of one week ago, she no longer officially worked in the pub, but because her father owned it, and she had made many friends among his customers, she still came around.

"She is at home with her mother," Ian explained. "Evidently there was some last-minute emergency with the wedding dress. And if ye dinnae realize it yet, m'lad, you will soon enough—women can find more last-minute emergencies than you can ever imagine. You'll just have to put up with it and continue to love 'em."

"That I can do," Duff said.

"Tell me, m'lad, have you heard anything from your cousins since they returned to America?" Ian asked.

"I got a nice letter from them a few days ago, wanting me to thank everyone for the hospitality they were shown while they were here," Duff said.

"You got the letter a few days ago and you are only now getting around to thanking us? Pray tell, lad, what has kept you so long?"

Ian was teasing Duff because for the last three days Duff had been busy preparing for the wedding by renovating his house to make it more habitable for Skye.

"I meant to, but I got so . . ." Duff started to say,

then when he saw the wide grin on Ian's face he knew he was being teased. "I just didn't get around to it."

"Well, it was easy to be hospitable to the likes of them," Ian said. "You must be proud of them, being as they are kin, and all."

"The truth to tell, Ian, is that we are not that much kin. I had never even heard of them until Andrew sent me the letter. But they are good people, and 'tis proud I am to claim kinship with them. I very much enjoyed the time I got to spend with them while they were here."

Ian glanced up at the clock, something he had done several times over the last few minutes.

"Are you that anxious to close for the night that you have to check the clock every few minutes?" Duff teased.

"You've noticed, have you?"

"You have looked at the clock so many times 'tis a wonder you haven't looked the hands right off the face."

"'Tis wondering, I am, what might be keepin' Skye," Ian said.

"I thought you said she had gone home because of some emergency."

"Aye, but she said she was coming back to help me close. 'Tis ten-thirty already. I'll be closing at eleven."

"No doubt she and her mother found even more emergencies to work on," Duff suggested.

"Knowing m' wife and m' daughter as I do, I'm sure you are right," Ian said. "And I think I would rather her be at home than out all by herself, in the dark o' night."

Duff finished his ale and put the mug down. "I tell you what—I will walk the path from here to your house. If she is home, I will tell her to stay there. If I see her, I will walk with her back to the pub."

"Thank you, lad. 'Tis a good son-in-law you'll be makin' for thinkin' of my worry like that. I must confess it would be a comfort to me to see her come through that door now."

"I'll find her," Duff promised, and he acknowledged the good-byes of the others as he left the pub.

It was quite pleasant outside. The night air was soft and warm, but not overly so, and redolent with a faint smell of the sea, as well as the perfume of aromatic flora. From somewhere close Duff could hear an owl, and in the woods, the song of crickets.

A loud burst of laughter rolled out from the pub he had just left.

Down the street a baby began to cry.

A two-wheeled cart, pulled by a single horse, passed by. The horse's hooves echoed loudly, the wheels whispering softly on the dirt road.

"No, please, leave me be!"

It was Skye's voice, and it came from across the road from beyond the shrubbery.

"Hold your hand over her mouth," a man's voice said. It was low and gruff.

Duff thought he could hear Skye's voice again, but this time all she could do was squeak.

Duff dashed across the road, then through the line of shrubbery. Though it was dark, in the light of the full moon he could see Skye struggling with Donald and Roderick Somerled. The top of Skye's dress had been pulled down and both her breasts were exposed, the creamy white flesh gleaming in the moonlight. Donald was holding her and Roderick, with a leering grin on his face, was unbuttoning his pants.

"Let her go!" Duff shouted angrily.

Startled by Duff's shout, Donald let Skye go. Then the two men turned toward him. Recognizing him, both smiled, and both pulled daggers from their belts.

"Well now, if it isn't Duff MacCallister come like an avenging angel to rescue his woman," Roderick said.

"Aye, and himself without a barstool," Donald added.

"Or a knife," Roderick added. "We'll be settlin' our scores permanent."

"Run to your father, Skye," Duff said.

"Duff, they both have knives," Skye said. She was busy pulling her dress back up to cover her partial nakedness.

"I'll deal with them," Duff said easily. "You get yourself somewhere safe now."

"Aye," Skye said, running quickly through the dark toward the pub.

Roderick made the first move, coming toward Duff with his hand extended, the knife held low. Duff leaped adroitly to one side. Then, with the side of his fist, he clubbed Roderick on the back of his head as he slipped by him. Roderick went down and Duff reached down to pick up his knife. Now, armed, he turned to face Donald.

Donald made a swipe at him, jumped back, then made a second swipe. On his second attempt, Duff countered, driving the blade of Roderick's knife in between Donald's ribs. Donald let out a whoosh as if he had been hit in the solar plexus, then backed up with the knife still in his side. He reached down and pulled the knife out, then covered the wound with his hand as the blood spilled out between his fingers.

"You . . . you have killed me," he said, his words strained.

"You left me no choice, Donald Somerled."

Donald took a few steps toward Duff, then he fell to his knees, where he remained but a moment before falling across the prostate form of his brother.

Roderick, who was just regaining consciousness, groaned in protest.

When Duff returned to the White Horse Pub to check on Skye, he met Ian just coming out of the bar, holding a club, his face twisted in anger.

"Duff, Skye said you were in trouble," Ian said. "I was coming to lend a hand."

"Thank you. How is Skye?"

"She is inside," Ian said. "The lass is terrified. She said two of the Somerled brothers attacked you with knives. She'll be glad to see you are well." Turning, he went back inside with Duff.

Duff saw Skye sitting at the far end of the bar, with modesty restored, if not composure. She was wiping away her tears.

"Are you all right, Skye?" Duff asked.

"Oh, I was so frightened for you!" Skye said.

"Don't be frightened for me. 'Tis you I'm worried about. Are you all right?" Duff asked again.

"They were—they tried to . . ." Skye was unable to finish the sentence. "If you hadn't come along when you did, I might have been . . ."

"Wait a minute. What are you saying, girl?" Ian asked. "Did they hurt you? Because if they did." Ian put the club down and pulled a pistol out from under the bar.

"No, they did nothing," Skye said quickly. "Duff came along in time."

"It makes no difference whether he came along in time or not," Ian said. "I'll be squarin' things with them."

Ian started toward the door, but Duff held up his hand to stop him. "There is no need for you to go," Duff said. "I've already killed Donald."

Skye gasped. "You killed him?"

"I had no choice. They both came toward me with knives. It was a case of kill or be killed."

"Aye, before I left I saw that they both had knives," Skye said.

"I had better go to the sheriff to report it," Duff said. "Though I'm sure that Roderick has already made the report."

"The sheriff is not going to take too kindly to you killin' one of his own sons," Ian said.

"It was self-defense," Duff said. "The sheriff will have to know that."

"Duff, those boys have been naught but trouble their whole lives, and the sheriff well knows that, but has he ever lifted a hand to stop them?" Ian shook his head. "No, he has not," Ian said, answering his own question. "Why think you now that the sheriff will believe you?"

"I am an innocent man, Ian," Duff said. "I'll not be running like a common criminal when I know I've done nothing wrong. I'll be going to see the sheriff now."

"I will come with you to tell the truth," Skye said.

"There's no need for you to come," Duff asked.

"I'll not see my husband-to-be jailed for something he dinnae do."

"You stay here."

"Duff MacCallister, you are not yet my husband, so you've no right to tell me I can't come with you."

Ian laughed. "Best ye get used to it, lad. She is a girl with her own mind."

"All right, I'll not be fighting with you on the very night before we are to be wed," Duff said.

"'Tis a smart husband you will be," Skye said, and the others laughed.

Duff and Skye were halfway to the office of the sheriff when they saw the sheriff and three of his deputies coming toward them. Rab Malcolm, who was Somerled's chief deputy, was one of the men with him.

"Sheriff," Duff called. "I was coming to see you."

"Shoot him!" Sheriff Somerled shouted.

"No, Sheriff!" Skye shouted, jumping between Duff and the sheriff.

The sheriff and all three deputies opened fire. The flame patterns of their pistols lit up the night, and the sound of gunfire roared like thunder.

"Oh!" Skye said, and as she spun around toward Duff, he saw a growing spread of crimson on her chest. She fell to the road, and even as the sheriff and his deputies continued to shoot, he managed to pull her off the road and through the shrubbery.

"Skye!" Duff shouted, his voice racked with pain and horror at what he was seeing. "Skye!"

Skye lifted her hand to his face and put her fingers against his jaw. She smiled. "'Twould have been such a lovely wedding," she said. She drew another gasping breath, then her arm fell and her head turned to one side. Her eyes, though still open, were already clouded with death.

"No!" Duff shouted. "No!"

"He's down there!" the sheriff called.

Duff moved into the shrubbery and waited. A moment later, one of the sheriff's deputies came through the hedgerow. Duff stepped out of the shrubbery and, with his fist, landed a haymaker on the deputy's jaw. As the deputy went down, Duff took his gun and, in a rage, shot him from point-blank range.

"Gillis! Gillis, did you get him?"

Duff stepped back through the hedgerow and out onto the road. He was holding Gillis's gun.

"No, Somerled. I got Gillis," Duff shouted.

"There he is!" the sheriff shouted. "Shoot him, Rab, Nevin, shoot him!"

The three shot at Duff, and Duff returned fire. Nevin went down, and when he did, the sheriff and Malcolm suddenly realized that, in seconds, their number had been decreased by half. The two men turned and ran.

For a moment Duff considered running after them, but he gave that up. Instead, he threw the gun away, then scooped Skye into his arms to take her back to her father.

* * *

Ian was just closing up his pub when Duff pushed in through the front door of the White Horse. He was carrying Skye in his arms.

"Skye!" Ian shouted. "What happened? My God! What happened?"

"It was the sheriff and his deputies," Duff said. Duff laid Skye on the bar and Ian fell across her, sobbing loudly.

"I killed Gillis and Nevin," Duff said. "Sheriff Somerled and Deputy Malcolm ran away. I didn't go after them because I wanted to bring Skye home."

"I thank you for that, lad," Ian said.

"I'm going after them now."

"No, don't. You'd best be getting away."

"Where would I go? No matter where I go in Scotland, I'll be a wanted man," Duff said. "So I may as well get my revenge."

"No," Ian said. "I've lost Skye. I'll not be wantin' to lose you now, for 'tis my own son you are for all that my Skye didn't live until tomorrow when you would have wed. Go. Please."

"All right. I'll just stop by my place and gather a few things."

"There's no time for that," Ian said. Opening his cash box, he took out ten ten-pound notes and thrust them in Duff's hand. "Go."

"I can't take your money."

"'Tis little enough," Ian said. "Oh, and I've something else for you."

"You've given me enough."

"This be yours, already," Ian said. "'Tis something ye left here so as to be wearin' at your wedding."

Ian reached under the bar, opened a metal box, then handed an object to Duff. It was the Victoria Cross, showing a crowned lion above the crown of England, and bearing the inscription, "For Valor."

"Keep this with you, lad, wherever you go. And remember always God and the Queen."

"Thank you, Ian," Duff said. He put the Victoria Cross in his pocket, then stepped down to look at Skye's body. He stayed there for a long moment. Then he looked back at Ian. "Give me a piece of paper and a pen," he said.

Ian got a sheet of paper and a pen and handed the items to Duff. Duff began to write.

In exchange for one hundred pounds paid in full, I, Duff Tavish MacCallister, with this instrument, do transfer ownership to Ian McGregor the three hundred acres of land known as Three Crowns, to include all buildings, improvements, appurtenances, livestock, and any and all things of value.

Duff Tavish MacCallister.

"I'm beholdin' to you, Ian," he said, handing the document to Ian.

"Here, lad, you don't want to do that," Ian said, pushing the paper back.

"Ian, you and I both know I will never return to Scotland. That means my land will be confiscated by the county. Don't you know I would rather you have it?"

Ian thought for a moment, then, nodding, he took the paper. "Aye, lad, I see your point," he said.

"But know this. If ever you should return, Three Crowns is all yours."

Duff shook Ian's hand, then he went over to Skye's body. Leaning over, he kissed her on her lips. Then straightening up, he wiped a tear away.

"She will always be in my heart, Ian."

"I know, lad, I know. Now, please, be gone with you before the sheriff comes back."

Duff nodded and started toward the front door.

"No, lad, they may be out there watching. The back door."

With a final wave, Duff opened the back door, then slipped out into the night.

Chapter Five

Firth of Clyde

There were three ships on the Firth of Clyde. Two were steamships that lay anchored in the harbor. But one was tied up against the docks, and it was the *Hiawatha,* a three-masted, square-rigged, sailing ship.

There was a sailor standing watch on the dockside of the ship, which meant Duff was going to have to get onboard without the man on watch seeing him. As he considered how best to accomplish this, he saw a skiff tied up about one hundred yards down the dock.

Looking around to make certain he wasn't being observed, Duff untied the skiff, then rowed it out a short way before turning back to approach the *Hiawatha* from the opposite side. There he climbed up the side of the vessel, over the railing, then into the shadows of the ship. Finding a dark, out-of-the-way place on deck, he settled down to wait and see what would happen next.

He had almost gone to sleep when he heard the sheriff's voice.

"You, aboard! Sailor on watch! I'm Sheriff Somerled. I would have a word with you."

"I ain't done nothin' that would draw the attention of a sheriff," the sailor called back in a flat, twangy, American accent.

"Still your concerns, sailor, 'tis not yourself I am questioning," the sheriff replied. "Has a man come aboard seeking passage to America?"

Looking out from behind a large stanchion, Duff followed the conversation between the sailor and Sheriff Somerled. On the dock with the sheriff, Duff noticed, was Deputy Malcolm.

"Sheriff, this here is a merchant ship. We ain't got no passenger a'tall."

"I'm looking for a murderer. He is a big man with light hair, brawny arms, and shoulders the width of an axe handle. He would have come on only in the last few minutes."

"Like I told you, we ain't got no passengers a'tall. We got nothin' but wool, bound for New York."

"Maybe he boarded without you seeing him," Sheriff Somerled suggested.

"There ain't nobody what's come onboard, Sheriff, by that or any other description," the sailor replied. "Not while I been on watch."

"Lower the gangplank. I'm comin' aboard to see for myself," the sheriff said.

"There ain't nobody comin' onboard this here ship without the cap'n sayin' he can."

"Then do be a good man and inform the captain that Sheriff Somerled wishes to come aboard."

"I ain't wakin' the cap'n for you or nobody," the sailor said.

"Very well, I shall return in the morning and speak with your captain."

"We'll be pullin' anchor with the mornin' tide," the sailor on watch said. "Won't do you no good to come back, 'cause we won't be here."

"Come," Sheriff Somerled said to Malcolm. "The brigand cannot have gone too far. I'll see him hanged before sunrise."

Duff had stayed very quiet during the exchange and remained in place until the sheriff and his deputy were well away from the dock. Not until then did he improve his position, crawling from behind the stanchion into a tarp-covered lifeboat.

The ship was well under way when Duff awoke the next morning, lifting and falling, rolling from side to side as it plowed over the long, rolling swells of the North Atlantic. When he looked out from under the tarp, he could see the sails of the *Hiawatha* shining brilliantly white in the bright sunlight, and filled with a following breeze. The propelling wind, spilling from the sails, emitted a soft, whispering sigh.

The helmsman stood at the wheel, his legs slightly spread as he held the ship on its course. Working sailors were moving about the deck, tightening a line here, loosening one there, providing the exact tension on the rigging and angle on the sheets to maintain maximum speed. Some sailors were holystoning the deck, while others were manning the bilge pumps.

Because all were busy, no one noticed Duff when he crawled out of the lifeboat. He approached a sailor who was twisting a turnbuckle to increase the tension on a line.

"Pardon me, but where might I find the captain?"

"Lord ha' mercy, where did you come from?" the sailor asked. "And who are you?"

"I am," Duff started, then he paused in mid-sentence. "I am Captain Duff MacCallister, and I wish to speak with the captain."

"How did you get aboard the *Hiawatha*, Cap'n?" the sailor asked.

"Please. Your captain?"

"You wait here."

"Yes," Duff said. "Where else would I go?"

Duff walked over to the rail and looked back. In the distance he could barely make out the shoreline.

A moment later the sailor returned with another man whom Duff took to be one of the ship's officers.

"Are you the captain of this vessel?" Duff asked.

"I am Mr. Norton, the bosun. Who are you?"

Whereas Duff had used his reserve rank of captain with the sailor, with the bosun he was more direct.

"My name is Duff MacCallister," he said.

"Jiggs said you called yourself a captain."

"Aye, in the Scottish Reserves I am a captain. I am sorry if the sailor misunderstood. I wonder if I might speak with the captain of this ship."

"Look here," the bosun said. "How did you get onboard this ship?"

"I don't know," Duff replied.

"What do you mean, you don't know?"

Duff put his hand to his forehead. "I had a great deal to drink last night," he said. "I remember leaving the pub, then I remember nothing until I woke up on this ship this morning. Methinks some of my friends may have played a trick on me."

"I think we had best see the captain," Norton said. "Come with me."

"Aye, such was my request," Duff replied. "I would like to purchase passage to New York."

"How did you know this ship was going to New York?"

Duff had heard the sailor on watch the night before say that the ship was bound for New York, but he could not say that or he would give away the fact that he was aware last night that he was onboard.

"I don't know that you are," he replied. "I know that many of the ships that leave from the Firth of Clyde are bound for New York. I assumed that was so with this ship. Have I erred in my assumption?"

"No, we're going to New York, all right," Mr. Norton said. "Come with me."

Captain Powell drummed his fingers on the taffrail and glared down from the quarterdeck at Duff and his bosun.

"Who have we here, Mr. Norton?" he asked.

"We found him aboard this morning, Captain."

"What is your name, stowaway?" Captain Powell asked. It was obvious from the tone of his voice and the expression on his face that he was displeased with seeing Duff.

"The name is MacCallister, Captain. And 'twas not my intention to stow away," Duff replied.

"It was not your intention to stow away? Then,

pray tell, MacCallister, how is it that you are on my ship?"

"I was drinking with some friends," Duff said. He put his hand to his forehead. "I woke up on the ship this morning. They must have thought it good sport to put me here."

"It matters not how you came aboard. The point is, you are aboard, and that makes you a stowaway."

"I've nae wish to be a stowaway. I have enough money to pay for my passage, and would be happy to do so," Duff said.

"That might be good if we were a passenger-carrying ship," Captain Powell replied. "But we are not. We are a merchant ship, and you are un-wanted cargo."

"What shall I do with him, sir?" Norton asked.

"Confine him to the brig for the duration of the voyage," Captain Powell said. "When we reach New York, we will give him an opportunity to buy passage back to Scotland."

"Aye, aye, sir," Norton said. He started toward Duff, then paused, and turned back to the captain. "Cap'n, if you would permit a suggestion?"

"You may do so."

"Peters did not return to the ship 'ere we weighed anchor. We are short one man in the starboard watch. Perhaps . . ."

"You would replace Peters with the stowaway?" Captain Powell asked.

"Aye, sir, if you be willing," Norton said.

"Have you ever been to sea, MacCallister? Could you do the work of an AB?"

"I've been to sea, Captain, and fare well without

becoming sick. I have never worked as a sailor, but I learn quickly."

"From your dress, you have the appearance of a man of means," Captain Powell said. "Are you a wealthy man, MacCallister?"

"I have land and livestock," MacCallister replied, but even as he was saying the words, he realized that he would never see either again.

"Would you feel the work of an able-bodied seaman beneath a man of your station?" Captain Powell asked.

"Captain, as you have pointed out, and as I readily admit, I am a stowaway on your ship. My alternative to working, it would appear, would be to spend the entire voyage in the brig. I would consider honest labor to be far superior to that condition."

Captain Powell laughed out loud.

"Very well, MacCallister, you may work for your passage. Mr. Norton, assign him to the starboard watch. Did Peters leave his chest?"

"Aye, sir, he did."

"MacCallister, you are a bit taller than Peters, and a bit broader in the shoulders I would say. But I think you could wear his clothes. I advise you to do so, for your current attire is ill suited for the task at hand."

"Thank you, Captain," Duff replied.

"Mr. Norton, take MacCallister below, get him properly dressed, then muster the crew."

"Aye, aye, Cap'n."

It was dim belowdecks, though not entirely dark as the sun filtered down through the hatch above, falling in little individual squares of light on the floor of the deck under the fo'castle. Duff saw several men, bare from the waist up, sitting on chests or coils of rope. They looked around in curiosity as Duff and the bosun stepped into their midst.

"Men, this is MacCallister. He'll be takin' Peters's place," Norton said.

"He don't look like no sailor man to me," one of the men said. "He looks more like what you would call a gentleman."

"Whatever he may look like, he is hired on as a sailor, and a sailor he will be," Norton said. He looked toward Duff. "Get changed into working clothes."

"Aye, sir. And thank you, Mr. Norton, for providing a way for me to avoid the brig," Duff said.

"Just see to it that you do your work, for I'll not be making excuses for you to the captain," Norton said as he started back up the ladder.

After Norton left, none of the others spoke to him. The sailors were not purposely ignoring Duff, but neither were they inviting him into their circle. Duff knew from his few voyages, the most recent being to Egypt with his regiment, that a ship's crew was a close-knit group. He wasn't going to fit in right away; indeed, perhaps not for the entire voyage. But, as he told the captain, this was better than being in the brig, and it was infinitely better than hanging, which fate awaited him back in Scotland.

As Duff went through Peters's sea bag, pulling out clothes, he was very aware of their pungent odor. Steeling himself to it, he pulled on a pair of pants and a blue-and-white striped shirt. Once dressed, he looked around the fo'castle, which would furnish his quarters for the voyage. It was filled with coils of rigging, spare sails, and items of machinery, many of which were foreign to him. He saw a hammock hanging from one hook, just above Peters's kit. Looking to his left, he saw another hook and deduced that his sleeping would be accommodated by stretching the hammock from one hook to the other. He was about to stretch out to see how it worked when the hatch was opened and Norton shouted out to the men below.

"All hands on deck! All hands on deck!"

At Norton's call, the sailors made haste to climb the ladder and spill out onto the deck. Duff went up as well, and started toward the left side of the ship when he emerged on deck from the top of the ladder, but one of the sailors reached out for him.

"Here, lad," he said. "You'll be starboard with us."

"Thank you," Duff said, thankful not only for the information but also because the sailor had spoken to him.

When all had come topside, they gathered toward the stern and looked up toward the quarterdeck. There, Duff could see the helmsman still at the helm, his hands securely on the wheel spokes, his eyes staring straight ahead. The vessel was leaned over, racing swiftly before the wind, and Duff could hear the noise of the water streaming back from the bow. He could also feel the pitch and fall of the deck beneath him as it rolled with the swell of the sea. He was glad that he had been to sea before, because he was confident that he would be able to complete this voyage without getting sick.

The captain stepped up to the rail forward of the quarterdeck, then looked down at his gathered crew.

"Men, we had a good crossing coming over, and I expect an even better crossing on the return. You know me well by now, and you know that when you perform your tasks as you have been assigned, you find me a pleasant enough captain. Shirk in your tasks and, I assure you, you will find me most unpleasant indeed. Mr. Norton?"

"Aye, sir?"

"Post the watches."

"Aye sir.

"Port watch topside, starboard belowdecks."

Duff went belowdecks with the rest of the starboard watch, and when he saw a couple of them stretch out their hammocks for a nap, he decided to do the same thing.

One week at sea

If Duff thought the life of a sailor at sea would be easy, he was quickly disabused of that notion. The ship's officers found much for them to do, and while Duff initially thought it might merely be a means of making work to keep the sailors busy, he soon realized that all the work was necessary. Whenever any of the standing rigging became slack, a condition that seemed to be constant, the coverings had to be removed, tackles tended to, and tension put on the rigging until it was drawn well taut. Afterward, the coverings had to be replaced, which, Duff learned, was no easy thing to do.

Even the work caused work, because one rope could not be adjusted without requiring an adjustment to another. One could not stay a mast aft by the back stays without slacking up the head stays. In addition to the constant attention to the ship's rigging, there was greasing, oiling, varnishing, painting, scraping, and scrubbing to be attended to, plus furling, bracing, making and setting sail, pulling, and climbing. Duff found that there was much to occupy him.

"Them that sails on the steamships don't do all this work," a sailor named Kelly said.

"They ain't hardly what you would call sailors neither," Jiggs said. "Them that sails on the steamships ain't nothin' but passengers goin' along for the ride. You ain't a real sailor 'lessen you are on a wind ship. Sails, that's where the word sailor comes from."

Those who were close enough to overhear the exchange laughed, but the work continued.

As the voyage progressed, Duff discovered that the business of running the ship was much to be preferred over the long, silent hours of night watch. That was because it was during those hours of night watch when he most felt the pain of Skye's death.

More than one time he was sure that he heard her voice.

"Duff, my darling Duff, I am here. Can you not see me?"

Duff would turn with a small cry of joy and a smile on his face. But the smile would be replaced by an expression of sorrow as he realized that what he was hearing was the whisper of the wind from the sails or the murmur of water slipping by the hull, and no more.

Sometimes, too, he would see her flashing eyes in the green light of the luminescent fish that would keep pace with the ship. Such experiences were bittersweet for him. On the one hand, it kept the memory of Skye ever fresh in his mind; on the other, it kept the pain of his loss ever aching in his heart.

Toward the end of the second week at sea, the starboard watch was below when Duff heard the raindrops falling on deck thick and fast. He could also hear the loud and repeated orders of the mate, trampling of feet, creaking of the blocks, and all the accompaniments of a coming storm. In a few minutes, the slide of the hatch was thrown back, which made the noise from above even louder.

"All hands on deck! All hands on deck! Topside, me hearties, we are into heavy seas!" Norton shouted down.

When Duff reached the deck he saw, firsthand, what it was like to be running before a storm at sea. The heavy head sea was beating against the *Hiawatha* with a noise that sounded as if someone was taking a sledgehammer to the hull. On one particularly large plunge, the bowsprit dipped and poked through a large swell. The wave broke over the bow and threw its spray the entire length of the deck.

The wind was blowing with gale force as the ship crashed through the waves. Suddenly the great mainsail on the main mast ripped open from top to bottom.

"MacCallister, Kelly! Lay up to furl that sheet before it blows to tatters!" Norton called.

"Aye!" Kelly replied. "With me, MacCallister!"

The two men climbed the mast and began working on the torn sail, but no sooner had they finished with it than the topsail tore loose and began flapping in the breeze, threatening to pull away and take with it the topgallant mast, which was now vibrating like a wand.

"We'd best get to the to'sail!" Kelly said, starting to climb even higher.

Duff had not yet climbed to the topsail, even in calm weather, but he started up one side of the mast as Kelly climbed the other side. When they reached the topgallant, the wind was of near hurricane velocity, and the mountainous waves were battering against the side of the ship with the impact of a cannonball. The *Hiawatha* would be lifted by one swell, hang quivering over the trough between the waves, then slam back down into the sea, only to be caught up by another, even larger wave.

Up here, too, Duff experienced firsthand the geometric principle of fulcrum and arm. The ship was the fulcrum, the topgallant mast was the farthermost part of the arm, thus making the gyrations aloft three or four times more severe than what those on deck were experiencing.

When he reached the top, he realized that he didn't really know what he was supposed to do. Kelly realized that as well, so he called out to him, his voice thin in the howling gale.

"We have to pull in the sail! Wrap your leg around the t'gallant yard so's you can hang on!"

Duff did as Kelly instructed, and fighting hard to overcome the flapping pitch and yaw, the two men were able to pull in the loose sail, then furl it at the bottom, securing it with line.

"We can go back down now!" Kelly shouted, but at that very moment a severe roll tossed Kelly free and he started to fall. Without thinking, Duff let go with his hands, and holding himself secure only by his legs, almost as a trapeze artist, he swung his torso down and managed to catch Kelly by one hand, at the last possible moment.

The next roll of the ship pitched Kelly into the

mast and he grabbed it with both arms. Duff pulled himself back up, then grabbed the mast and scrambled back down to the deck just behind Kelly.

"Well done, lad, well done," Norton said to Duff.

Back on deck, and with all the sails furled, there was nothing left to do but ride out the storm. The deck heaved up, then fell to starboard, then dipped sharply to port. The roll to port was much longer and deeper than the roll to starboard had been, and Duff feared for a moment that it might just keep on going until the ship capsized. But his fear was unfounded as the ship slowly returned to the upright position, only to roll back to starboard again.

Finally the storm ended, and while it left the sea a dirty green, jagged looking and frothy, at least it wasn't boiling as it had been. The sky was gray with low-lying, scudding clouds that were no longer dumping rain. The deck was a shambles and men were lying exhausted on every space available, paying little attention to the wet boards. There were broken fixtures and dangling stays, but the storm sails had been replaced with the regular sails and, once more, the ship was making all good speed.

Some time later, Duff was standing at the rail looking out over the sea when Kelly came up to him, carrying two cups of coffee.

"I thought you might like a cup of coffee," he said, extending one of the cups to Duff.

"Aye, thank you, a bit of coffee might be bracing now," Duff said, accepting the cup.

"You saved my life," Kelly said.

"You would've done the same for me."

"I might have tried, but I ain't no ways near 'bout

as strong as you, so I don't know if I could have done it," Kelly said. He took a swallow of his coffee, then stared for a moment at Duff. "Did you really kill someone?" he asked.

"I beg your pardon?"

"You are the one the sheriff was looking for the night just before we left port, aren't you? I was on watch. The sheriff said you killed someone."

"How do you know I'm the one he was talking about?"

"You came aboard that night. I don't know how you did it. I sure didn't see anyone, but that must have been when you done it."

"Yes, I came aboard that night," Duff admitted. "I borrowed a skiff, came up alongside opposite the pier, then climbed up."

Kelly chuckled. "I thought it might be something like that. Who did you kill?"

"I killed two of the three men who killed my fiancée," Duff said.

"I'll be damned. Killed your fiancée, did they?"

"Yes."

"Then they needed killin'," Kelly said.

"Indeed they did."

Kelly took another swallow of his coffee. "I'm glad you did it. And don't worry none about it, because your secret is safe with me, MacCallister."

"I appreciate that."

Duff's feat in grabbing and saving Kelly's life gave him entrée into the close-knit bond of the crew, and for the remaining voyage, he was treated as one of their own.

* * *

By the time they reached New York, Duff was an accomplished seaman. He went aloft with the rest of them to reef the sails on orders. He climbed down over the side to hang but inches above the water to apply pitch to the side. He holystoned the deck. He performed every task assigned cheerfully and ably. Now, as the ship sailed into New York Harbor, he was standing on the mizzen mainsail yard as the ship was met by a tugboat. With all sails furled, and forward propulsion being provided by the steam-powered tugboat, they were brought up snug against one of the piers. There, from the pier, small lines, attached to huge hawsers, as big around as a man's arm, were thrown up to sailors fore and aft on the ship.

"Make lines secure, fore and aft!" Captain Powell called.

The sailors, fore and aft, looped the hawsers around the on deck stanchions.

"Lines secure, fore and aft, aye, sir!" Norton called back

"Drop anchor!"

The windlass let the anchor down as the crew scrambled to check watches and see who had won the pool on the exact time the anchor would drop.

The *Hiawatha*, its crew, and Duff MacCallister were in the United States of America.

Chapter Six

New York

The paymaster from Red Ball Shipping Lines came aboard the *Hiawatha* within an hour of its dropping anchor. They were also visited by merchants from the city, tradesmen who met all the arriving ships, as anxious to relieve the sailors of their pay as the sailors were anxious to spend it.

Duff welcomed the clothing merchant and bought three pairs of striped trousers. Two pairs were dark blue with black vertical stripes, and one pair was brown with blue vertical stripes. The pants were held closed at the waist with decorative buttons. The three shirts were all white, with detachable collars and cuffs. Thus supplied, he put on a pair of trousers and a shirt, then packed his other clothes in the sea bag that Kelly had given him.

"Will you be shipping over, MacCallister?" Kelly asked. "It was fine sailing with you."

"I will confess to you, Kelly, that it was an experience I appreciated more than I thought I would," Duff replied. "But I think I'll stay ashore for a while."

"MacCallister," Norton said. "The cap'n wants a word with you before you leave. He said to send you to his cabin."

"The cap'n's cabin?" Kelly said. "I've been sailing man and boy for fifteen years, I've never been in the cap'n's cabin."

Captain Powell's cabin took up most of the area under the quarterdeck, stretching from side to side and back to the stern where a spread of windows let in the light. There was a large bed, a desk, and a chart table. He was standing at the chart table using a compass and ruler on the chart that was before him.

Duff knocked, lightly, on the door to the cabin.

"Come in, Mr. MacCallister," Captain Powell said. Looking up, he smiled when he saw what Duff was wearing. "Now I must say, that is more befitting a gentleman than the clothes you have been wearing for the last three weeks. Buy it from the clothing merchant, did you?"

"Aye, sir, I felt I no longer had the right to Peters's clothes."

"Mr. MacCallister, I kept a close eye on you during this voyage. You had an inauspicious beginning, sneaking on board as you did." He paused, waiting for some response from Duff. "I'm glad to see that you aren't refuting me. You did stow away, did you not?"

"Aye, sir," Duff admitted.

"Yes, well, as I say, you had a most inauspicious beginning, but, a most commendable voyage. You did not shirk your duties. You performed them with a skill that one would expect from a much more experienced sailor, to say nothing of your saving Kelly's life.

"I watched the men around you as well. And while it is often difficult for a new sailor to break into a crew, tight-knit as they tend to be, the men liked and respected you. I'm told that when you came aboard, you introduced yourself to Jiggs as Captain MacCallister. Are you a captain, Mr. Mac-Callister?"

"Aye. I am a captain—that is—I was a captain in the 42nd Foot, Third Battalion of the Royal Highland Regiment of Scotts. It is the regiment we call the Black Watch."

Captain Powell smiled, and nodded his head. "Yes, I knew you were officer material. I think, with my recommendation, you could ship out again for Red Ball as a ship's officer. Serve as a warrant or lieutenant for a few cruises, then you could one day command your own ship. What would you think about that?"

"I think it is very flattering, and I believe you would be most kind to make such a recommendation, Captain, but I do not think the sea is for me. I think I will stay on dry land for a while."

"I shall not try to change your mind," Captain Powell said. "But just know that if you ever have a desire to go to sea again, look me up. I will be happy to sponsor you."

"I appreciate that, Captain, more than I can say."

When Duff returned to steerage to pick up his bag, the other sailors stood, respectfully.

"Here now, what is all this?" Duff asked.

"Is it true that you are to be a ship's officer?" Kelly asked.

"No," Duff said. "Now why would I leave the fo'castle?"

Kelly smiled broadly. "Fine lad that you are, I knew you were one of us."

"Well, not entirely," Duff replied. "If I were to ship out again, it would be with you men, for I've served with no finer group of men anywhere. But, it's ashore for me. I want to see some of America."

"Then perhaps you'll have dinner with us tonight at the Port of Call," Kelly asked.

"I would be honored," Duff said.

The Port of Call restaurant was less than a block away from the docks. The sign in front was a wooden representation of a three-masted schooner. The bill of fare exhibited its international flavor by offering cuisine from a dozen countries, from Moo Goo Gai Pan to *Avocat et Oeufs à la Mousse de Crabe,* from kidney pie to Southern fried chicken.

There was a kaleidoscope of sound inside as sailors from a dozen countries carried on spirited conversations in their own languages. Everything was going well until a big Frenchman was walking by the table of the sailors from the *Hiawatha.* Just as he drew even with the table, Dowling, one of the *Hiawatha* crew, chose that moment to stand up so that he could go relieve himself. He pushed his chair back into the path of the Frenchman, and the French sailor stumbled but did not fall.

"Oh, beg your pardon, mate, I didn't see you coming," Dowling said.

"*Cochon Américain typique, aussi aveugle que vous êtes stupide,*" the Frenchman mumbled.

"*Vous êtes des ceux qui sont aveugles et stupides. Mon ami s'est excuse, mais vous êtes trop le rustre pour être gracieux,*" Duff said.

The Frenchman had called Dowling a blind, stupid pig, and Duff had responded by saying that Frenchman was the one who was blind and stupid, and too much the boor to accept an apology. The Frenchman's eyes grew large when he heard Duff speak.

"Yes, I speak French," Duff said.

The Frenchman started to walk away and Duff turned his attention back to his friends at the table. A moment later Kelly yelled, "MacCallister, look out!"

Duff turned just in time to see that the Frenchman had picked up a chair and had the chair raised high, preparatory to bringing it down on Duff's head. Duff rolled off his seat just as the Frenchman brought the chair crashing down on the table, breaking the plate Duff was eating from and sending food flying.

Shouting in anger for having missed, the Frenchman raised his chair again and turned toward Duff. From the floor, Duff sent a whistling kick into the Frenchman's groin. The Frenchman dropped the chair and grabbed himself, doubled over with pain.

While he was still doubled over, Duff leaped up from the floor, grabbed the Frenchman by the scruff of his neck and the back of his shirt, then started across the floor with him, moving him toward the door. One of the waiters saw what had happened and what was now happening, and he opened the front door, just as Duff pushed the big Frenchman through it. The Frenchman fell forward, his face landing in a pile of horse apples.

When Duff went back into the restaurant, everyone inside stood and applauded, even including the other Frenchmen.

"Claude is—as Americans would say, a sorry son of a bitch," one of the French sailors said. "It is about time someone gave him his due."

When Duff returned to the table, he saw that his broken plate had been replaced with a new, fresh serving of haggis, taties, and neeps.

"I don't know how you can eat that," Kelly said. "But the waiter brought you another serving, on the house."

Duff awakened the next morning to the sounds of the city. Just outside the window of his hotel he heard a train going by on an elevated track. From the street, five stories below, he could hear the clip-clop of horses' hooves and the ringing sound of iron-rimmed wheels rolling on the paved road. Getting out of bed, Duff moved to the window to have his first real look at New York. With five- and six-story buildings on either side of the street, he felt as if he were looking down a canyon.

The street was filled with pedestrians and vehicles, hundreds of people strolling to and fro, and dozens of large freight wagons, omnibuses, elegant carriages, buckboards, and surreys. In addition to surface traffic, there was also an elevated railroad and a spiderweb maze of telephone, telegraph, and electric lines. His room had electric lights, and the notice on the dresser proudly proclaimed that telephone service was available in the lobby.

Duff had heard of a telephone, but he had never seen one, and wasn't exactly sure how one would work. But after getting dressed, he walked down to the lobby to see how one went about using the phone.

"What number do you wish to call?" the desk clerk asked.

"Well, I don't know," Duff replied. "I don't know what you mean by number. I wish to call a person."

"Sir," the clerk explained patiently, "if that person has a telephone, the telephone will have a number. You must know that number in order to put your call through."

"Oh," Duff said. "I'm afraid I don't know the number."

The clerk took some pity on him then, realizing from his accent that he wasn't local.

"If you know the person's name, we can look up the number," the clerk said.

"Look up the number? How does one do that?"

"There is a book called a telephone book. Every person and every business that has a telephone has their name listed in that book, along with the number you need in order to call them. Like this," he added. The clerk took a phone book from beneath his desk. "Now, what is the name of the person you wish to call?"

"His name is Andrew MacCallister," Duff said

"Andrew MacCallister? Do you mean the famous actor?"

"Yes, he is an actor."

The clerk had opened the telephone book, but now he closed it. "Perhaps you had best find someone else to call," the clerk said. "Andrew MacCallister is a very famous man. I seriously doubt that he would be up to taking a telephone call from a stranger."

"But we are nae strangers," Duff insisted. "We are kinsmen."

The clerk's interest perked up. "Kinsmen, you say? And your name would be?"

"MacCallister," Duff said.

"The self-same as the actor?"

"Aye, kinsmen we are."

"Then, in that case, I will look up the number for you."

The clerk found the number, then told it to Duff. "The number you want to call is 8178." He handed the receiver to Duff, and Duff looked at it as if unsure what to do with it.

"Hold it to your ear," the clerk explained. "When the operator comes on, tell her 8178."

"Number please," a woman's voice asked.

Duff took the receiver from his ear and held it up to his mouth. The desk clerk laughed. "Not here—here," he said, pointing to the little transmitter. Duff nodded, and leaned into the transmitter. "Eight-one-seven-eight!" he shouted.

"Sir, it is not necessary for you to speak so loudly," the operator replied.

"Oh. I'm sorry."

"It's all right, many do," the operator said.

A moment later Duff heard a voice in his receiver. It was tinny, but he recognized it as Andrew's voice.

"Cousin Andrew! This is Duff MacCallister," Duff said.

"Duff, you are in New York! How wonderful!" Andrew said. "Where are you?"

"I'm at the Abbey Hotel."

"Wait in the lobby. I will send a carriage for you."

Half an hour later, as Duff disembarked from the carriage in front of Andrew's apartment building, his cousin came out to greet him.

"How much do I owe you?" Duff asked the carriage driver.

"You owe me nothing, sir. It has been paid for," the driver replied.

"Duff, it is so good to see you," Andrew said, extending his hand in welcome. Duff started to pick up his sea bag, but Andrew signaled the doorman and the doorman called to someone inside. A young man hurried out of the large apartment building and picked up the bag.

"To your apartment, Mr. MacCallister?"

"I don't have an apartment," Duff replied.

"He means me," Andrew said with a chuckle. "You aren't the only MacCallister here."

"Right, I suppose not," Duff said.

"Yes, Jimmy, take it up to my apartment," Andrew said. Then to Duff, "Come, I'll show you where I live. I'm on the top floor; I have a wonderful view of the city."

Duff followed Andrew into the building and started toward the stairs.

"No, this way," Andrew said.

"I thought your place was on the top floor."

"It is, and it is too far to climb the stairs. We shall take the elevator."

Duff had been in an elevator only one time before, and that had been when he visited Glasgow. As he recalled, he did not particularly like the experience, but he said nothing to Andrew as they stepped into the elevator cab.

"Julius, this is my cousin, Duff," Andrew said to the uniformed black man who was the elevator operator.

"It is nice to meet you, sir," the elevator operator said with a deep, resonant voice.

"It is good to meet you as well."

After the brief elevator ride, they stepped across the hall where Andrew opened a door, then welcomed Duff inside. The apartment was large and expensively decorated. But the most appealing feature of the apartment was, as Andrew had stated, the "magnificent view" of the city. Because of the height of Andrew's apartment building, much of the city could be seen, all the way down to the docks, where Duff could see both steamships and sailing ships. He was able to pick out the *Hiawatha*, just by her topgallant, and he felt a strange sense of attachment to it, as if it were his last connection to Scotland, and by extension, to Skye.

Andrew walked over to the wall and removed the telephone from the hook. "Eight-three-two-five, please," he said. Then, "Rosanna, he is here. Yes. We will have lunch together."

Hanging up the phone, he turned back to Duff. "I hope you don't mind that I invited Rosanna to have lunch with us."

"No, not at all. I will be delighted to see her again."

"How long can you stay in America?" Andrew asked.

"I'm never going back."

Andrew's expression showed his surprise at the answer. "But your fiancée," he said.

Duff was quiet for a moment.

"Skye?" Andrew asked, the word softly spoken because he perceived that, for some reason, the name was painful to Duff.

"Skye is dead, Andrew," Duff said. "She was murdered."

"Oh, Duff, I am so sorry," Andrew said. "Do they know who did it?"

"Yes, and the ones who did it have already been executed." Duff did not say that he was their executioner.

"I am glad that they have paid for their crime. And I am glad that you have come to America. I think making a fresh start will be good for you."

"I believe so as well."

"We'll have to find a place for you to stay," Andrew said. "And, will you be looking for a job?"

"Aye. I've some money, but I dinna know how long it will last."

"Good, because I know just the job for you."

With an introduction provided by Andrew, Duff began working backstage at a major theater. He was a skilled carpenter, and he had the ability to analyze complex problems and solve them quickly. Within a month, he became a stage manager, an important and most prestigious job. And now that he was securely employed in America, he decided it was time to write to his friend Ian McGregor to tell him that all was well.

> Duff MacCallister
> 200 West 48th Street
> New York, NY

Ian McGregor
The White Horse Pub
2 Elway Lane
Donuun, Scotland

Dear Ian,

My heart is still heavy with grief from the death of my beloved Skye, the more so because I was unable to be there for her funeral. But while I was not there in person, I was there in spirit and I know that, even as she sleeps in the arms of our Lord, she is aware of the undying love I have for her. I know too that at the time of her funeral she was surrounded by those who loved her most, and I take comfort from that.

On the night I left Scotland, I secured passage on a ship bound for New York. I did so by way of working as a crew member during the voyage. It was very hard work, but the very difficulty of the work helped me to deal with the pain of losing the one who was the center of my life. I take respite in the fact that our dear Skye returned my love with equal vigor, though I shall never understand how one as unworthy as I could have won the love of such a wonderful woman.

I am now living in New York and have gone to work in the theater, the position secured for me by my cousin Andrew. We are in "pre-production" as they say, for the play "The Highlander." I am told that it was inspired by the visit of my cousins Andrew and Rosanna to Scotland. Of course, Andrew and Rosanna are the principal players of the production.

I hold the most gratifying position as stage manager. The play will take place in the Rex, an elegant and ample theater which is on West 48th Street at Broadway. You may find this interesting, Ian. The Rex theatre is lit entirely by electricity, the installation personally supervised by the inventor Thomas Edison.

Please write to me and tell me how you are doing. With shared sorrow for the loss of our dear Skye, I remain,

> *Your friend,*
> *Duff MacCallister*

Chapter Seven

Postmaster Desmond Henry walked into the office of the Lord High Sheriff Angus Somerled, clutching an envelope to his breast. Deputy Rab Malcolm looked up at him.

"Postmaster Henry, may I help you?"

"I would like to speak with the sheriff, please."

"What do you want to see the sheriff about?"

"That would be between me and the sheriff," the postmaster replied.

Deputy Malcolm made a guttural sound deep in his throat, then stood and walked into the back office. He returned after a moment with the sheriff.

"What is this about, Henry?" Sheriff Somerled asked.

"Is there still a reward being offered for anyone who can tell you where to find Duff MacCallister?" Henry asked.

"A twenty-pound reward, yes. Do you know where he is?"

"Let me see the twenty pounds," Henry demanded.

Sheriff Somerled nodded at Deputy Malcolm, and Malcolm walked over to a file, opened a drawer, and took our four five-pound notes and handed them to the sheriff. Postmaster Henry reached out for them, but the sheriff pulled his hand back.

"Where is he?"

"Well, that's just it, Sheriff. I will tell you where he is, but you will nae be able to do anything about it. 'Tis out of your jurisdiction, he is."

"Where is he?" Sheriff Somerled asked again.

"He is in New York."

"New York? You mean he is in America?"

"Aye."

"Then he did get on the ship that night," Somerled said, hitting his fist into his hand. "I should have gone aboard to look for him. How do you know he is in New York?"

"He wrote this letter to Ian McGregor," the postmaster said, showing the envelope to the sheriff. "It has his return address on it. Two hundred West Forty-eighth Street, New York, New York."

"How do we know he is still there?" Deputy Malcolm asked.

"Because he has a job there," the postmaster said. "It is clear that he plans to stay for a while."

"How do you know that?" Sheriff Somerled asked.

"I steamed open the envelope and read the letter," Postmaster Henry said. "I made a copy of the letter before I returned it to the envelope."

"Let me see your copy."

"That will cost you another twenty pounds," Henry said.

"I could arrest you for opening someone else's mail," Sheriff Somerled warned.

"You could. But you may not find another postmaster who is as willing to cooperate with you as I have always been."

"Yes, for profit," Somerled said.

"One has to make a living, Sheriff. The postal service pays so little."

Somerled stroked his chin for a moment, then nodded at Malcolm. "Get him another twenty pounds," he said.

Deputy Malcolm got another twenty pounds and gave it to the postmaster who, in return, gave the sheriff a folded piece of paper. "I printed it clearly so you should have no trouble reading it," the postmaster said.

Somerled took the piece of paper, opened it, and began reading eagerly.

"If you will excuse me, I have business to attend to," the postmaster said. "I must deliver this letter to Mr. McGregor."

Because Somerled was reading the letter, he made no response to Henry, who left after carefully putting the money in the inside pocket of his jacket.

"Anything interesting, Sheriff?" Malcolm asked.

"How would you like to go to America?" Somerled asked.

"I've always wanted to visit America," Malcolm replied.

"I'll be sending you, along with Roderick and Alexander. And I'll be putting you in charge, knowing how hotheaded and irresponsible my two boys are."

"You'll be tellin' them I'm in charge, will you not, Sheriff? For without hearing from you, I think they may not listen."

"I will tell them and they will listen," Sheriff Somerled said.

"Sheriff, ye have no jurisdiction in America. When we find MacCallister, how do you want me to deal with him?"

"Deal with him? There will be no dealing with him," Sheriff Somerled said. "I'll be for wanting you to kill him."

Malcolm smiled. "It was hoping, I was, that you would say that. Gillis and Nevin were good friends of mine. I will take pleasure in avenging them."

"'Tis for them you be seeking vengeance, and 'tis for their brother that Roderick and Alexander will be doing the same. Don't let me down, Malcolm. I want Duff Tavish MacCallister killed, and when he dies, there will be no more MacCallisters in Scotland. The two hundred and more years our clans have been at war will come to an end."

Aboard the Cunard steamship Etruria

The young lady's name was Miriam Phelps, and she was from one of New York's wealthiest and most fashionable families. This was not her first transatlantic voyage, though it was the first one she had made alone, and she was now coming back from a grand tour of Europe.

Roderick and Alexander Somerled met her in the first-class dining room, and she had flirted outrageously with both of them. Malcolm had watched with interest how she was playing the brothers against each other. He knew that it was all a game to her, a means of diversion for a very wealthy young woman at whose feet the whole world lay.

"Alexander, Roderick, Roderick, Alexander," she said in a singsong voice. "I swear, you are both so handsome and so fascinating, that I don't know which of you I want to give the most attention. What is a girl to do?" She smiled flirtatiously, then turned and walked away from them, glancing once back over her shoulder.

They had been at sea for five days when, early in the morning as Malcolm was asleep in his stateroom, he felt someone's hand on his shoulder.

"What?" he said with a start as he jerked awake.

"Malcolm."

Malcolm saw Alexander sitting on the side of his bed, his eyes gleaming wildly and a look of panic on his face.

"Wake up, Malcolm. Wake up," Alexander was saying.

"I am awake," he said. "What is it? What is going on?"

"We need some help."

"Who needs help?"

"I do. So does Roderick."

"What do you mean you need help? You need help with what?"

"Maybe you had better come to our stateroom," Alexander said, referring to the cabin that he and his brother were sharing.

"What time is it?"

"It's about three o'clock."

"In the morning?"

"Aye."

"What are you doing, waking me at this hour?"

"Please, Malcolm, get dressed and come with me," Alexander said. "We need your help."

"Yes, you keep saying that."

Although Malcolm dressed quickly, Alexander kept urging him to hurry. Finally, when he was fully dressed, he left his stateroom and followed Alexander down the corridor, feeling, not only the gentle roll of the ship, but also feeling and hearing the vibration of the steam engine.

"Alexander, what . . ."

"Shhh," Alexander hissed, laying his finger across his lips.

When they reached the stateroom shared by Alexander and Roderick, Alexander tapped, lightly, on the door.

"Who is it?" a muffled voice called from the other side of the door.

"Roderick, open up."

The door opened, swinging inward, and Alexander and Malcolm stepped inside. Roderick closed the door quickly.

"What is it? What is this all about? What's going on, and why is it so dark in here?"

"Turn on the light," Alexander said.

The *Etruria* was equipped with electric lamps, so it required but the flick of a switch for the dark to be pushed away.

"She is over there," Roderick said.

"She? Who is—what the hell?" Malcolm gasped.

Lying on one of the two beds, her arms and legs

askew, her dress torn asunder to expose her naked body, her face blue, and her eyes bulging, but with her final expression of terror still discernable, was Miriam Phelps.

"My God," Malcolm said, speaking in quiet shock. "You killed her?"

"We had to, don't you see?" Roderick asked.

"No, I don't see. What do you mean, you had to?"

"She was naught but a tease," Alexander said. "First she said she wanted Roderick, then she said she wanted me, but it was a tease, all along. We brought her here, we gave her a chance to—be with one of us."

"We even said we didn't care which one," Roderick continued. "She could be with Alexander, and I would watch. Or she could be with me, and Alexander would watch."

"But she didn't want to be with either one of us, so . . ."

"You raped her?"

"Aye," Roderick said.

"Which one of you?"

"Both of us," Alexander said.

"But I think she actually wanted it," Roderick said.

"What makes you think that?"

"Because she dinnae scream," Alexander said. "No' with either one of us."

"But afterward, she said she was going to report us," Roderick added.

"And we could nae let that happen," Alexander said.

"So, we, uh—we . . ." Roderick pointed to the

girl's twisted and bruised body. He didn't finish his sentence. He didn't have to.

"So, what do you want me to do?" Malcolm asked.

Roderick and Alexander looked at each other before Alexander spoke. "Tell us what to do now," he said.

Malcolm sighed, then stroked his chin. "We've got to get rid of the body," he said.

"How?" Roderick asked.

"How? We are on a ship in the middle of the ocean," Malcolm said. "We'll throw her and her clothes overboard."

"See, Roderick? I told you that Malcolm would know what to do."

"Look out in the passageway, make certain there is no one there," Malcolm said. "There is an opening at the end of the passageway. We can go there to drop her over the side."

When the coast was clear, the three men took Miriam's body out of the cabin, then to the end of the corridor where, as Malcolm had pointed out, there was a railing that was open to the sea. They dropped the body overboard, then turned around just as a sailor was walking by.

"Ha!" the sailor said. "Feeding the fishes, are you?"

"What?" Roderick asked, startled by the question.

"That's what we say when one is seasick and throwing up over the rail. He is feeding the fishes."

Malcolm laughed. "Yes, that's a good one," he said. He put his hand on Roderick's shoulder. "I'm afraid my friend isn't that good of a sailor."

"Nothing to be ashamed of," the sailor said. "I've seen all of my shipmates get seasick at one time or another. Ask the galley for an orange," he called back as he continued on whatever mission had brought him on deck. "I've always found that an orange helps."

"Thanks," Roderick replied.

Because Miriam was traveling alone, her absence was not noticed immediately. It was two days before another young lady, who had befriended her, reported her concern over not having seen her. The captain authorized her cabin to be entered, and they found it empty. A thorough search of the ship turned up no sign of her, and the captain, reluctantly, concluded that she must have fallen overboard.

From the *New York Sentinel*:

New York Debutante Lost at Sea

TERRIBLE TRAGEDY HAD NO WITNESSES

A terrible tragedy occurred on board the RMS *Etruria* during its voyage from Glasgow to New York. Miss Miriam Phelps, daughter of Edward Phelps, wealthy owner of the New York Bank for International Investment, was lost at sea during the ship's transit. Miss Phelps was seen by many at dinner in the First-Class dining salon on Wednesday of the week previous, and by two guests who saw her later that night outside her cabin door.

First-Class passengers have their own deck, a large roomy area affording the more affluent the privacy necessary to protect them from unwanted contact with those passengers who transit via steerage. The First-Class deck is complete with shuffleboard and reclining chairs, and often passengers will, if the night is particularly pleasant, visit the First-Class deck to view the stars, or just to watch the luminescence of the water breaking white along the hull of the ship. It is thought that, perhaps to enjoy the deck in complete privacy, or perchance in an attempt to get some fresh air to combat a bout of *mal de mar*, Miss Phelps decided to visit the deck and, getting too close to the rail with no one to express caution or extend assistance, she fell overboard.

With nobody to hear her plea for help, the ship sailed on, leaving the poor woman floundering helplessly in its wake. Miss Phelps, 21, was a graduate of Smith College and is remembered by her classmates as a woman of talent, beauty, and generosity.

"Ha," Roderick said after reading the newspaper. "Did you read this in the newspaper? They think she fell overboard."

"We got away with it," Alexander said.

"This time," Malcolm said. "You were lucky. You might not be so lucky next time. So my advice to you is, stay out of trouble."

"Our father may have appointed you in charge of us while we are looking for MacCallister," Roderick said. "But he dinnae put you in charge of our personal lives."

"Nor do I want to be in charge of your personal lives," Malcolm replied. "But I am in charge of finding Duff MacCallister and dealing with him. And until that is accomplished, anything that might get in the way of our finding him comes under my purview."

"All right, we'll go along with what you say until then," Alexander said. "But after we take care of MacCallister, you are no' in charge of us anymore."

"The first thing we need to do is find the Rex Theater," Malcolm said.

"When we find the theater, let's get us good seats," Roderick said. "I like watching plays. Alexander, do you remember the play we went to in Edinburgh?"

"Aye, that was a good play," Alexander replied.

"We will find the theater," Malcolm said, "but we will nae put ourselves into position where he might see us."

"Do you mean we will have to sit in the very back row?"

"We won't sit in any row," Malcolm said.

"What do you mean? How are we going to see the play if we don't sit in any row?"

"We are not going to see the play," Malcolm said. "We will wait outside until the play is over and the audience has left. It will be dark in the auditorium then, so we will be able to sneak in without being seen."

Chapter Eight

ROSANNA (as LADY MARGARET): *(sitting on the ground of Castle Carrick, cradling Andrew's, as Lord Dumbarton, head in her lap)* Oh, noble Lord, were that I a man, that with claymore and dirk I could have joined you in your noble fight. You won, noble knight, you won, for all those of the evil clan of Hutchins are now dead. Ahh, but the sad thing is that, even in your final victory, you gave your life. *(Takes Lord Dumbarton's claymore sword and holds it over her head)* And with that sainted, but Pyrrhic victory, I vow by all that is holy to keep the name Lord Dumbarton forever in my heart.

(Curtain closes)

The theater erupted with applause and cheers. Duff stood in the wings where he could see both the actors on the stage, and the audience, all of whom were now on their feet. It had been Duff, in his capacity as stage manager, who signaled the curtains closed, and now he brought his hand down again.

"Curtains open," he hissed loudly enough for the stagehands to hear him, but not so loudly as to be heard by those in the audience.

The curtains opened again and all the secondary players rushed out to take their curtain call, their appearance onstage in inverse order of the significance of their roles. Finally, the last curtain call had been taken, the curtains closed, and the troupe gathered backstage.

"Wonderful performances from all of you," Andrew said, congratulating all the actors and actresses. "We will meet here tomorrow at six, one hour before curtain rise. Don't be late."

The actors, still up from their performance, laughed and exchanged comments on the play as they headed for the dressing rooms to get out of costume and makeup.

"Oh, Julie, you were just wonderful," one of the "nobles" said to the beautiful young woman who played the daughter of the Laird Carrick. "I have been in the theater for five years now, and have never seen an actress who, in her very first role onstage, performed it with such mastery."

Duff chuckled to himself as he overheard the conversation. The young lady was certainly adequate to the role, but he knew Phillip Cain to be a notorious "ladies' man," and he knew that he was using flattery to attain his goal.

"Duff, will you be taking dinner tonight with

Rosanna, me, and some of the others?" Andrew asked.

"I would like to, Andrew, but I think I will stay and work on the forest flats. I noticed during the play that they were not holding their position as well as they should."

"Very well," Andrew said. "But if you finish earlier than you suspect, please join us at Delmonico's."

"I shall," Duff replied.

Duff waited until all the actors and stagehands were gone. Then he made certain that all the house lights were turned off and the backstage lights were on. He looked up at the flys to examine the flats that were used for the forest scene and saw at once where the problem lay. Lowering one of the flats, he took it to a work area offstage and placed it across two sawhorses. All he would have to do is adjust the frame to take out the warp.

Across the street from the theater, Malcolm, Roderick, and Alexander watched as the patrons left the theater. The theatergoers were talking about the play they had just seen.

"I swear, Rosanna MacCallister just gets more beautiful as she gets older."

"It's all makeup. I'll bet she isn't that pretty."

"Makeup can't make you more beautiful. It just enhances what is already there."

"I liked the fight scene in the second act. It looked so real."

"Of course it looked real. It's called acting."

* * *

"When are we going in?" Alexander said.

"When we are sure that everyone has left," Malcolm said.

"They're all gone now. You can tell that."

"Don't get so anxious. We need a plan," Malcolm said.

"We have a plan. He killed our brother, and we are going to kill him. That is our plan," Alexander said.

The lights outside the theater went off.

"Now," Alexander said, starting across the street. "Let's go."

"Wait, it won't take a minute to come up with a plan as to how we are going to do this," Malcolm said.

"I don't want to wait another minute. I want to kill him now," Alexander said.

By now the three men were under the marquee and all the way up to the double doors that opened into the lobby.

"It's locked," Roderick said when he tried the door.

"I'll take care of that," Alexander said. He took out a pocketknife, opened it, then slipped it in between the doors. It took no more than a couple of seconds for him to overcome the lock and open the doors.

"Quiet," Malcolm whispered as he closed the doors behind them.

"What if he is already gone?" Roderick whispered.

"He hasn't gone. There are lights on back there,

see?" Alexander said. "And he's the stage manager, which means he would be the last to leave."

The three men moved quietly through the darkened theater until they reached the stage. Then, climbing onto the stage, they stepped through the curtains and crossed the stage before moving into the backstage area.

That was when they saw Duff working on something with a plane.

Duff leaned over to see if he had leveled the edge of the flat.

"Duff MacCallister, we have come for you," a familiar voice said from the darkness.

The voice was familiar, because it was the voice of Alexander Somerled.

Startled at hearing Alexander's voice here, in America, Duff turned toward the sound, but saw nothing in the darkness. He was at a disadvantage, because while Alexander was cloaked by the darkness, he was well lighted.

"Alexander Somerled," Duff said. "Have you come alone?" Duff moved away from the flat to the properties locker. Alongside the properties locker was the light control panel.

"I am with him," Roderick said.

"And so am I, Deputy Malcolm," a third voice said.

"Deputy Malcolm, is it?" Duff replied. "Well, you have wasted a trip, Deputy Malcolm, for you have no jurisdiction here. You cannot arrest me."

"It is not for to arrest you we have come, Duff MacCallister, but to kill you," Alexander said.

Reaching his hand up to the light control panel, Duff turned off the backstage lights. As soon as the theater went dark, he grabbed the claymore sword, the same sword Andrew and Rosanna had handled onstage. And though it was used as a prop, it was a real claymore sword, fifty-five inches in overall length, with a thirteen-inch grip and a forty-two-inch blade.

"What the hell, where did he go?" Malcolm asked.

"Where is he?" Roderick asked.

"Shoot him!" Alexander shouted. "Shoot him!"

"Shoot where?" Roderick asked.

Duff picked up a vase and tossed it through the darkness to the opposite side of the room. When it hit the floor, it broke with a great crash.

"Over there! He's trying to get away! Shoot him! Shoot him!" Alexander yelled at the top of his voice.

All three men began to shoot in the direction of the sound of the crashing vase. The flame patterns of the muzzles illuminated the room in periodic flashes, like streaks of lightning.

The flashes of light enabled Duff to come up behind them.

"Here I am, boys," he said.

The three men turned toward him, but with a mighty swing of the great claymore sword, Duff decapitated the two Somerled brothers. Malcolm, who had managed to avoid the blade, pulled the trigger of his pistol, but the hammer fell on an empty chamber. He turned and ran.

Duff heard the side door open and close. He waited for a long moment, listening to see if Malcolm had actually left or if he had just opened and closed the door, pretending to leave. When he heard nothing, he turned the lights back on.

The two decapitated Somerled brothers lay on the floor, their heads a few feet away. Alexander's head was looking up; Roderick's head was face-down. There was a great deal of blood surrounding the two bodies and Duff knew that he was going to have his work cut out for him tonight.

The first thing he was going to have to do was get rid of the bodies. He did that by putting both bodies and their heads in a pushcart that had been part of the properties of a previous play. Dropping their guns in there as well, he pushed the cart down the alley for at least a full mile away from the theater before dumping the bodies behind a trash container.

Returning to the theater, he worked for the rest of the night cleaning the bloodstains from the floor and the cart. It was nearly dawn by the time he went home to change clothes and wash up.

When he returned to the theater the next day there was no sign of the grisly event that had happened the night before. The show went on as usual with the audience just as appreciative, and the players and theater company blissfully ignorant of the fact that two men had been killed in this very place.

It was not until the next day that the newspaper carried a story of the fate of Alexander and Roderick Somerled, though as yet the two men had not been identified, so the author of the story could only surmise as to who they were and what had happened.

From the *New York Herald:*

A Most Ghastly Find

The bodies of two decapitated men were found yesterday morning in the alley behind Gimlin's Pawn Service. The two heads were found with the bodies, but officials are uncertain as to which head belongs to which body.

Charles Gimlin, proprietor of the shop behind which the bodies were found, notified the police after he discovered the bodies while taking out the trash. He says they were not there on the night before, and he is certain that he has never seen either of them. No one has yet identified the two bodies and the police say there has been no missing persons report filed that could account for the men.

One theory advanced is that they may be sailors only recently arrived and, looking for some nefarious activity, found themselves in Chinatown. Two pistols were found with the two bodies, and the theory thus advanced suggests that while in Chinatown the two men were intemperate in their behavior and in so doing made enemies of a Celestial. It is well known that a Chinaman, being heathen, will, when provoked, often cut off the head of the person who has offended him.

Police say that this being the most probable event, this case will in all likelihood never be solved as no Chinaman will tell on one of their own, and to White men, nearly all Celestials look alike.

Duff spent the next two days anticipating the return of Deputy Malcolm. He realized that the fact that Malcolm did not return right away did not mean he wasn't going to come back. Finally, after the paper came out, Duff made up his mind. He could not stay here any longer, for to do so would endanger not only Andrew and Rosanna but the entire theater company.

Duff had no choice now; he was going to have to leave. He didn't want to run; he liked this job. And if the danger was only to him, he would not have run. But he had already seen what had happened to Skye—she was an innocent victim who was killed only because she was too close to him.

He had no wish to see something like happen again. That's when he told Percy Fowler, first assistant to the stage manager, to ask Andrew and Rosanna to meet him in the sets storeroom.

"You wanted to see us, Cousin Duff?" Andrew asked. Rosanna was with him.

"Yes."

"Well, couldn't we have picked a more comfortable place to meet?" Andrew asked. "The green room perhaps? Or my dressing room?"

"I think here is better," Duff said. "What I have to say isn't for anyone's ears but the two of you, and I would not burden you with it if I did not have to."

"Burden us?" Rosanna asked. "Burden us with what?"

"With the real truth of why I came to America."

"I thought you said it was because Skye had been killed," Andrew said.

"Aye, that is true," Duff said. "She was killed by the sheriff and two of his deputies, Gillis and Nevin."

"But I don't understand," Rosanna said. "Why would the sheriff and his deputies want to kill such a lovely young girl?"

"It was not she they intended to kill, but me," Duff said. "Earlier in that same evening, I happened upon two of the sheriff's sons, Roderick and Donald, as they were attacking Skye with the intention of having their way with her. I interrupted their scheme and, in the fight that followed, killed Donald.

"After I took Skye back to her father, I vowed to turn myself in to the sheriff and plead self-defense. Skye, wonderful girl that she was, and truly in love with me, accompanied me so that the sheriff might hear the truth of the events. She did this because she knew that Roderick would have told his father a much different story.

"While on the road to the sheriff's office, we were set upon by Sheriff Somerled and Deputies Malcolm, Gillis, and Nevin. Without so much as a by your leave, they began shooting at us, and the bullets struck and killed Skye. In a rage, I killed both of the deputies, but the sheriff and Deputy Malcolm ran from me. I then stowed aboard a ship and made my way here."

"And here you shall stay," Andrew said, "for if ever there was a killing that was justified, this was it."

"Aye, and I would have been happy to stay here for a long time. The work is good, and the company is most agreeable," Duff said. "But two nights ago, the sheriff's other two sons and another deputy found me here."

"But what? How? How did they find you?" Andrew asked.

"I have no idea."

"Where are they now?" Rosanna asked. "Well, never mind that, they have no authority here. And we can secure a good lawyer for you who will help you defend yourself."

"The situation has grown more complicated," Duff said.

"In what way?" Andrew asked.

"Perhaps you read the article in the paper this morning of the two bodies found in the alley some distance from here?"

"Yes," Andrew said. "You are talking about the two men that were killed in Chinatown."

"'Twas not Chinatown where they were killed, but right here," Duff said.

"Here where?" Andrew asked, confused by Duff's comment.

"Here, in the theater. The two men are Roderick and Alexander Somerled. They and Deputy Malcolm confronted me here in the theater on the night I stayed to work on the flats. They came not to arrest me, but to kill me, and they began shooting. I managed to turn out the lights and with the advantage I had in the darkness by knowing the theater, I was able to turn the tide on them. I killed the Somerled brothers, but Malcolm got away. Then, in order that I not get anyone in the theater in trouble, I moved their bodies. But as I think about it, I know that isn't enough. Somehow Deputy Malcolm traced me here, and he can come again, and that would put the two of you in danger."

"Don't worry about that. We will face the danger together," Andrew said. "It is not as if we have never faced danger before."

"No, I must leave. I have brought enough hurt to people that I love as it is. I will bring no more."

"Where will you go?" Andrew asked.

"I don't know. It doesn't matter. I will just go."

"He can go to Falcon," Rosanna said.

"Yes!" Andrew replied enthusiastically. "I don't know why I didn't think of that myself. Duff, you must go find our brother Falcon. If there is anyone in the world who can help you now, it would be Falcon."

"I thank you kindly, but I've nae wish to bring my troubles to anyone else."

"Don't be silly, everyone brings their troubles to Falcon," Rosanna said. "He thrives on it."

"Trust me, Duff, he will welcome you with open arms. And I will write a letter of introduction for you."

"Where would I find him?" Duff asked.

Andrew smiled. "In Colorado. Oh, have you money?"

"I have some money that I brought with me, and I am owed two weeks' salary from the production company," Duff said. "But I hesitate to wait for it."

"You need not wait. I know how much is due you. I will pay you now," Andrew said. "Come to my dressing room, I will give you the money and the letter of introduction."

"And," Rosanna said.

"And?"

"Don't you remember? The Black Watch thing?"

"Oh, yes," Andrew said. "We were going to wait and present this to you at the close of the production of *The Highlander*, sort of a thank-you reward for a job well done as stage manager. But, if you are leaving now, we may as well give it to you."

Duff followed Andrew and Rosanna to Andrew's dressing room. There, Andrew gave Duff the one hundred dollars he had due in wages. Then he removed the contents of a box. It was the uniform jacket and kilt of the Black Watch, complete with a *sgian dubh*, or ceremonial knife.

"We thought you might like to keep this with you," Andrew said.

Duff nodded, then put his hand on Andrew's shoulder. "'Tis family ye are, and family ye will always be," he said. "I thank the both of ye, for all that ye have done."

Percy Fowler was hiding behind the flats. He had no idea why Duff MacCallister wanted to speak to Andrew and Rosanna, but if by listening to their conversation he could realize some advantage for himself, he would do so. As soon as he brought the MacCallisters into the storeroom, he moved quickly so as to be out of sight, and here, he heard every word they said.

Percy had been working in this theater through five previous productions, and he had been told that, with the next production, he would be elevated to the position of stage manager. That didn't happen when Duff MacCallister arrived. Both Andrew and Rosanna had insisted that their cousin be given the job, and because they were highly regarded by the producer of the play, their request was honored. Percy had been angered by being cut out of a job that was rightly his, but there was nothing he could do but accept it, for he knew of no other occupation that paid as well.

Now he was privy to some very secret information, information that he might find some way to turn to his advantage.

Chapter Nine

Carrying a box of doughnuts he had just purchased, Deputy Malcolm knocked on the side door of the Rex Theater. He had to knock several times before the door was answered by a stagehand.

"If you're here to buy tickets, you must go to the front door," the stagehand said.

"Are you the man in charge of the theater?"

"No, I'm just a stagehand."

"Who is the man in charge?"

"That would be Mr. MacCallister."

"The actor?"

"No, the stage manager. Except, wait, he ain't in charge no more. He left for some reason. The man in charge now is Percy Fowler."

"Then he is the one I should see."

"See about what? Mr. Fowler is a busy man. I can't just go lettin' anyone in off the street to see him."

"It won't take but a moment. I have a delivery of pastries," Malcolm said.

"Pastries? What sort of pastries?"

Malcolm opened the box to let the stagehand see.

"Doughnuts," the stagehand said. "Why didn't you say you had doughnuts? I'll take them."

"No, I have been told to take them directly to the stage manager."

"I can't do that."

"Very well, I shall return the doughnuts."

The stagehand looked around, then stepped back into the theater. "Follow me," he said. "You can wait in the green room."

Malcolm followed the stagehand into the theater, past the rows upon rows of empty seats, then through a small door that led to an area behind the stage.

"This is the green room," the stagehand said. "Wait here, I'll get Mr. Fowler for you."

"Thank you."

The stagehand started to leave, but he turned back toward Malcolm and took a doughnut from the box.

A moment later a rather short and nearly bald man came into the room.

"Reid said you needed to see me."

"Actually, I wanted to see Mr. MacCallister."

"He's no longer here."

"Do you have any idea where I might find him?"

"You're not American are you? You sound just like Mr. MacCallister. What are you, Scottish?"

"Yes, I am, actually."

Fowler looked at the box of doughnuts Malcolm was holding.

"You didn't come here to deliver doughnuts, did you? You came here to find MacCallister."

Malcolm smiled. "I'm afraid you have divined my

secret. Aye, 'tis to find Duff MacCallister that I have come."

"Why do you want to find him?"

"Why, the man is a good friend from Scotland. I thought perhaps that two people from the same county in Scotland, here in New York at the same time, should have a bit of a meeting."

"Is he your friend? Or have you come to arrest him for the murder?" Fowler asked.

The smile left Malcolm's face and his eyes narrowed. "You know about that, do you?"

"I know that he killed two men here," Fowler said.

The tone of Fowler's voice convinced Malcolm that he would be able to work with him.

"Aye. MacCallister is wanted for murder. And so tell me, m'lad, how is it that ye be knowin' about that?"

"I know," Fowler replied, without directly answering Malcolm's question.

"The reason I am lookin' for him, is I've been sent by himself the sheriff to deal with the matter," Malcolm said.

"Were you one of the three who came for him last week?" Fowler asked.

"You know of last week?"

"I know that before he left Scotland, Duff Mac-Callister killed one of the sheriff's sons and two of his deputies. And I know that last week, when you and the sheriff's other two sons came for him, Mac-Callister killed them both," Fowler said.

"Aye, that is true. I was here with the sheriff's last two sons."

"Why is it that you want to go after him? It sounds to me as if he is too dangerous a man to pursue."

"I will be ready for him this time. If I find him."

"I imagine the sheriff back in Scotland must want him something fierce," Fowler said.

"Aye, that he does, seein' as how MacCallister has killed all three of the sheriff's sons."

"How badly does the sheriff want him?" Fowler asked.

"What do you mean?"

"I know where MacCallister is," Fowler said. "And I could make that information available to an interested party if the price is right."

"I see. And how is it that you know where he is?"

"I overheard him talking to his cousins. They discussed where he should go. Would that information be worth anything to you?"

"Would you not be willing to share it for the satisfaction of knowing it is the right thing to do?" Malcolm asked.

"Yes, I will have the satisfaction of knowing that it is the right thing to do. But I would also appreciate the reward. There is a reward, is there not?"

"Have you not been rewarded enough by being promoted? 'Tis true, is it not, that you would nae have the job of stage manager if MacCallister had not run off?"

"That is true," Fowler said. "But with my new position comes new obligations. Financial obligations. You are in need of information, I am in need of some money. Perhaps we can work something out between us."

"You want money." It wasn't a question, it was a statement.

"Yes."

"I could see my way to giving you five pounds," Malcolm suggested.

"Five dollars? Do you mean to tell me that all the sheriff is willing to give to find the killer of his three sons and two deputies is five dollars?"

"I said five pounds, not five dollars. If you took the five pounds to the bank and made a currency exchange you would get twenty-five dollars."

"I'll be needin' more than twenty-five dollars," Fowler said.

"Ten pounds. That would be fifty dollars."

"I want a hundred dollars," Fowler demanded.

"I'll not give you a hundred dollars. The offer is fifty. Take it or leave it."

"You'll not find MacCallister without my help," Fowler insisted.

"If you know where he has gone, there will be others who know as well. Perhaps someone who knows the value of money and will give me the information for five pounds."

"All right, all right," Fowler said. "You go to the bank, convert your money into dollars, then come back and see me," Fowler said. "When you do, I'll tell you where Duff MacCallister has gone."

"Wait here, I will be back shortly," Malcolm said. He turned to leave, with the box of doughnuts still in his hands.

"Leave the doughnuts," Fowler said.

"Beg your pardon?"

"The doughnuts," Fowler repeated, pointing to the box.

"Ah, yes, the pastries. Of course." Malcolm put the box on the green room table, then left.

As luck would have it, the Commercial National Bank was but a very short distance from the theater. There, Malcolm changed all his British currency to American. He also opened an account there.

Returning to the theater, he found Percy Fowler waiting for him outside.

"Do you have the money?" Fowler asked.

"I do. Shall we go inside?"

Fowler looked around furtively. "No," he said. "I think it is best we do our business out here. I don't want anyone to see me talking to you. Give me the money."

Malcolm counted out fifty dollars in five-dollar bills. Fowler took the bills, folded them over, then stuck them in his pocket.

"He went to Colorado," Fowler said.

"Colorado? Isn't that a state? Can't you be more specific than that?"

"He has a cousin there, named Falcon MacCallister. I am given to understand that Falcon MacCallister is a name that nearly all in Colorado will recognize. I think if you go to Colorado, then start inquiring about Falcon MacCallister, you will find your man soon enough."

"All right," Malcolm said. "I will do that. But if I go to Colorado and find that I am on a wild duck chase, I'll be coming back to settle with you. And you, I know where to find."

Fowler chuckled. "Goose," he said.

"What?"

"It is a wild-goose chase. But I'm not sending you on one. MacCallister did go to Colorado, and if you can find Falcon MacCallister, you will be able to find Duff MacCallister."

After leaving the theater, Malcolm went to the transatlantic cable company, where he paid fifty cents a word to send a message back to Sheriff Somerled. He wrote it several times, but tore up the message each time until he had it worded exactly as he wanted, giving the maximum information with the least possible words. Then, once he was satisfied with it, he gave it to the clerk.

The clerk counted the words.

"Nineteen dollars," the clerk said.

Malcolm counted the words.

Alexander and Roderick have both been killed. MacCallister has escaped to Colorado. I anticipate no trouble in finding him, but I will require two hundred pounds to be sent by return cable so that I may pursue.

Malcolm

"I thought my name was free."

"No, sir. We charge for every word we dispatch," the clerk replied.

"Give it back to me. I am going to rewrite it.

Alexander and Roderick dead. MacCallister escaped. I know where he has gone. Require two hundred pounds by return cable so that I may pursue.

"Are you going to attach your name to the message?" the clerk asked.

"There is no need. He will know who it came from."

"Very well, sir. Your total is twelve dollars."

Scotland—Donuun in Argyllshire

Sheriff Angus Somerled gasped as he read the words in the telegram that was given him by the young messenger.

"Dead? Both of them? But what happened to them? He dinnae say."

"Beg pardon, sir?" the messenger, who was scarcely over fourteen years old, said.

"When did this message arrive?"

"I dinnae know, sir. Mr. McGinnis, he just gave it to me a few minutes ago. Is it bad news?"

"You mean you dinnae read it?"

"I dinnae read it, sir, for 'tis nae my job to read the messages what come in."

Somerled returned to town with the young messenger, then went into the telegraph office.

"'Tis sorry I am for your loss, Sheriff," McGinnis said. "Will ye be wantin' to send a response?"

"Aye," Somerled said and he quickly scrawled out a note.

How did boys die

It was the next day before Somerled got a reply.

KILLED BY MACCALLISTER STOP SEND MONEY STOP

New York

Malcolm had been using the Commercial National Bank of New York as his address, and when he called a day later to inquire as to whether or not he had received a cablegram, a smiling teller presented him with it.

TWO HUNDRED DOLLARS IS NOW ON DEPOSIT AT
COMMERCIAL NATIONAL BANK OF NEW YORK STOP
YOUR TASK REMAINS THE SAME STOP INFORM ME
SOONEST UPON CONCLUSION STOP
SHERIFF ANGUS SOMERLED

Malcolm read the cablegram, then looked up at the teller. "Is this right? Has the money been put in my account?"

"Indeed, it has, sir. You now have quite a tidy sum of money." The teller looked at a book and ran his fingers down the figures. "Yes, sir, you have one thousand two hundred and seventeen dollars and fifty-one cents."

"Good. I want to withdraw."

"Yes, sir," the eager teller said. "How much money do you want to withdraw?"

"I want all of it," Malcolm said.

The smile on the teller's face was replaced by a look of confusion. "All of it, sir?"

"Aye, all of it."

"But, sir, if you take all the money, it will close your account."

"Aye, that's what I want, a closed account."

"Very good, sir," the teller said. He filled out a form, then slid it across the counter to Malcolm.

"If you would sign this, sir?"

Malcolm signed the form, gave it back to the teller, and the teller counted out all the money as he passed it across to Malcolm.

"That is a great deal of money to be carrying on your person, sir," the teller said. "Do be careful with it."

"I intend to be," Malcolm replied.

From the bank he took a hansom cab to Grand Central Station, where he bought tickets to Denver, Colorado.

"Ha," he said to himself as he took a seat in the cavernous waiting room to wait for his train. "Duff MacCallister, you are going to be one surprised man when you see me."

Chapter Ten

Three days earlier, Duff had left New York via the New York Central Railroad. The train traveled along the Hudson River for a while, then passed through Buffalo, Cleveland, and Toledo, and finally, Chicago. At Chicago, he changed from the New York Central to the Illinois Central, which took him south to St. Louis. There he boarded the Missouri Pacific Railroad to Kansas City, paralleling the Missouri River across the state. At Kansas City, he realized that his clothes seemed out of place with the type of clothes worn by most of the men here, so he visited a clothing store to update his wardrobe. Here, he bought three pair of blue denim trousers, a pair of boots, and three six-button shirts, one red, one white, and one blue.

The store had a hardware department including a gun store. Duff wandered through the gun store and though he initially was drawn by curiosity only, he saw a display of Enfield Mark 1 Revolvers.

British Enfield Revolver
Sidearm of British Officers
and the Royal Canadian Mounted Police.
You can own this fine weapon
for only $20.00

This was the pistol Duff had carried during his military campaign in Egypt. He was familiar with it, and particularly liked the potency of its bullets, which were slightly over .47 caliber. When he picked the piece up, its heft and balance felt familiar to him.

"You know anything about that gun, Mister?"

"Aye, I know a bit," Duff replied.

"Here now, and are you English?"

"Scottish."

"Well then, maybe you do know something about it. To tell the truth, we just got an order in. Most of the folks comin' through here are buyin' Colts, Remingtons, Smith and Wesson. Ain't nobody bought one of these yet. Are you lookin' to buy it?"

"I don't know."

"If you buy it, I'll throw in a box of ammunition."

"Make it three boxes, and I'll also buy a belt and holster for it," Duff said.

A broad smile spread across the storekeeper's face. "Mister, you got yourself a deal."

An hour later, with his newly purchased clothes, gun, holster, and ammunition packed away in his sea bag, the same one that Kelly had given him when he left the *Hiawatha*, Duff boarded a Kansas and Northern Railroad train bound for Omaha. There, he made the final change of trains, boarding a Union Pacific train called the *Western Flyer.* He found the name of the train amusing, for while the Eastern trains had averaged a swift forty miles per hour on the open track, the *Western Flyer* proceeded along at the leisurely pace of from sixteen to twenty miles per hour.

While at the station in Omaha he bought a book called *Williams Pacific Tourist and Guide Across the Continent.**

The book had an entire page of testimonials and endorsements, including a review from *Publishers' Weekly* that declared it to be among "the very best efforts ever issued," with a "richness and completeness in illustrations, information and description that can only be realized by an examination of the work."

The slow, steady pace of the train traversing over long, straight rails made it easy for Duff to read.

Colorado is an empire of itself in enterprise, scenic beauty and abundance of pleasure resorts. In 1870, few or none of these were known, and towns were small in number and population. Since that time, it has become a center of great railroad activity, has grown in wonderful flavor as an attractive region for summer travel; and as a country for health-giving and life-giving strength, it has drawn thither thousands who have made it their permanent home.

Looking through the window, Duff could almost imagine that he was at sea, so vast was the expanse

*Published by Henry T. Williams, New York, 1876.

of gently undulating prairie, the grass waving rhythmically in the breeze. And, as if he were at sea, his view extended, uninterrupted, all the way to the horizon.

He saw three horsemen come toward the train. They rode alongside, not only keeping pace with the train, but often racing ahead, then dropping back. They took off their hats and waved them overhead. It looked as if they were shouting as well, but Duff could not hear them above the noise of the train.

"Oh, look, Sally!" said a young woman in the forward part of the same car in which Duff was riding. "They must be cowboys!"

"How exciting!" the other young woman replied, and they raised the window and began waving, flirtatiously, at the three young riders. Duff was certain that there must be other young women on the train, providing the same inducement to the cowboys, and he smiled, then turned his attention back to the book.

> Cowboys are, as a class very rough fellows, with long hair and beard, wide-brimmed hats, best fitting boots they can buy with large spurs jingling at their heels, and a small arsenal in the shape of revolvers strapped to their waists with a careless appearance.

Odd, Duff thought, that at the very moment he was seeing cowboys, he would be reading about them. A second glance at the three young riders bore out the comment in the book, that they would be armed, for all three were wearing holstered pistols.

He returned to the book.

Their chief pleasure is in a row; their chief drink is straight whiskey, and they usually seem to feel better when they have killed somebody. Houses of prostitution and tippling saloons follow close in their wake.

They are generous to their friends, dividing even the last dollar with a comrade who is broke, treacherous and vengeful to their enemies and human life is but little account with them. Their life is one of constant exposure and very laborious. They are perfect horsemen—usually in the saddle sixteen out of every twenty-four hours. Many have died with their boots on, and many more will perish the same way. Living violent lives, they often meet with violent deaths. The community in which they live, and the country generally, will be better off when their kind is gone.

As there was no dining car on this train, as there had been on the trains east of Omaha, it made regularly scheduled stops for meals, the first stop being North Bend, Nebraska.

As the train began slowing, the porters moved through the aisles of each car making the announcement.

"Folks, we are in North Bend. We'll be here for an hour and a half. If you're hungry, best you buy somethin' to eat, here."

North Bend was a thriving town with several stores, a hotel, lumberyard, and grain elevator.

Meals were served in the depot restaurant for one dollar, which Duff had learned, was the standard fare for all meals west of Omaha. The meal was ham and fried potatoes, which also seemed to be standard fare.

Next door to the Union Pacific Depot was the Occidental Saloon. Not wanting to fight the crowded lunchroom, and in no mood for the standard ham and fried potatoes, Duff stepped into the saloon, hoping they would also serve food of some sort.

"Yes, indeed, we serve food," the bartender said. "Lots of folks come in here from the train 'cause they don't like the crowds."

"And would ye be for tellin' me what sort of fare can one get here?"

"You're a foreigner, ain't you?"

"Aye, from Scotland."

"Yes, sir, I thought it was somethin' like that. I can tell by your accent."

"What can I get to eat here?"

"Chicken an' dumplin's is what you can get here. And it's a might tastier than the ham an' taters you get over at the railroad depot."

"Then I shall have that, and a beer if you please."

"Yes, sir, dumplin's and a beer comin' right up."

Duff had never eaten chicken and dumplings before, nor had he ever even heard of them. But, despite the, to him, rather unappetizing appearance, he actually enjoyed them.

He had just finished his meal when he heard the sound of a loud slap, followed by a woman's cry.

"Whore!" a man's guttural voice shouted. "Keep your finger out of my drink! Ain't no tellin' where that whore finger of yours has been."

"Please, sir, I did not put my finger in your drink."

The man slapped her a second time. "Don't you be lyin' to me, whore. I seen you stick your finger down into the whiskey when you was bringin' it over to me. You stuck your finger down into it, then you stuck your finger into your mouth, tryin' to suck the whiskey offen it."

Duff had a sudden flashback to his Skye, remembering how sometimes she had to deal with rude and abusive customers. That recollection made him feel a sense of concern for this woman. He was sitting at a nearby table, and he picked up his napkin and dabbed at his lips, then got up and walked over to the table where the big, bearded man was bullying the serving girl.

The bully had called her a whore, and that might be true. The woman was provocatively dressed, much more so than she would have been if she were only a serving girl. She might have been quite attractive at one time, but the dissipation of her profession had drained her of any natural beauty. In addition, her features were marred by a disfiguring scar that caused one eyelid to droop. That same scar continued below her eye and hooked in toward her nose.

Duff was certain that the disfiguring scar was not the result of an accident. Her left cheek was now red and already swelling from the two slaps she had just received.

"I beg your pardon, friend," Duff said as he stepped up to the table.

"What the hell do you want?" the bully asked.

Duff picked up the glass of whiskey. "'Tis wonderin' I am, if this be the drink that offends ye?"

"Offends ye? Ye?" the bully replied. "What are you, some sort of preacher? That's Bible talk, ain't it? Ye and thou—that kind of talk?"

"Aye, but 'tis also the language of my native country. I am Scottish."

"Yeah, well, tell me, Mr. Scottish Man. What the hell are you doin' interferin' with somethin' that ain't none of your concern?"

"I thought perhaps I could buy you a new drink, since you think this one has been tainted."

"Tainted? Yeah, that's what it's been all right."

Duff took out a dollar and handed it to the serving girl. "Lassie, would you be so kind as to bring another drink for the gentleman?"

The girl took the dollar, went over to the bar to buy another drink, then brought it and the change back.

"I want no change. 'Twould please me for you keep it for your trouble," Duff said.

The young woman smiled, and because the smile was genuine, it softened the features of her face.

"There you go, sir. Enjoy your drink," Duff said.

The bearded man tossed the drink down in one swallow, then looked up at Duff. "What are you goin' to do with that one?" he asked.

"Oh, I'm going to give this one to you as well," Duff said.

Smiling, the man reached for the drink, but he, and everyone in the saloon now watching, gasped in surprise when Duff tossed the whiskey into the bearded man's face.

"Why, you son of a bitch!"

The bearded man pulled his pistol from his holster and pointed it at Duff. But, calmly, Duff put his left hand down over the pistol, holding it in such a way as to prevent the hammer from coming back and the cylinder from turning.

Duff made a fist of his right hand and clubbed the bearded man on the jaw. The blow knocked him unconscious, and as he fell from the chair, he loosened his grip on the pistol so that it came out in Duff's left hand.

"Damn! Did you see that?" someone asked.

"Shaw ain't goin' to like that when he comes to," another said.

"Don't look like he's goin' to come to all that soon."

Duff walked over to the bar, emptied the pistol of all its bullets, then dropped the gun and the bullets into the fullest spittoon. That done, he looked over at the young woman whose face, like the face of everyone else in the saloon, wore an expression of shock.

"And will ye be all right, lass?" he asked.

"I—uh—yes. I will be fine. I can't believe a stranger would come to my rescue as you did. Thank you, very much."

"*Och*, dinnae worry yourself, lassie," Duff said, slipping into a strong Scottish brogue.

Duff heard the train whistle blow. The passengers had been told that the train whistle would blow ten minutes before it left the station.

"That's my train," he said. "Best I go, now. Barkeep, please tell your cook for me that the cock and pastry was quite delicious."

"Cock and pastry?"

"He means the chicken and dumplings," the serving girl said.

"Oh, yes, I will tell her," The bartender replied.

Aware that everyone was still staring at him, Duff left the saloon and walked back down to the depot. The depot platform was crowded, not only with the passengers who were getting back on the train but with several of the citizens of the town who had come just for the excitement of watching a train arrive and leave.

The fireman had banked the fire during the stay, but had re-stoked it in preparation for their departure. The train was alive with sound, from escaping steam to the gurgling of water in the boiler.

"Board!" the conductor called and he smiled and touched the brim of his hat as Duff stepped aboard.

"You gave the bully what was coming," the conductor said. "Good for you."

Duff looked at him in surprise.

"I was there, I saw everything. You didn't notice me, because I took off my coat and hat." He laughed. "I can't eat ham and fried potatoes every meal, either."

Chapter Eleven

Duff had just settled in his seat on the train when he saw the woman from the Occidental Saloon come onboard. She looked around the car for a moment, then seeing Duff, came back to his seat. He started to stand, but she held out her hand.

"Don't be troubling yourself, Mister, I won't be bothering you," she said. "I just wanted to thank you again." She held up her ticket. "I'm going on to Central City. There's nothing here for me now, and I've got a friend there."

"You gave up your job?"

The woman smiled. "Mister, in my line of work, jobs are easy to come by," she said.

The train whistle blew two long whistles, then the train started forward. As the slack in the couplings was taken up, the young woman, still standing in the aisle beside Duff's seat, was thrown off balance and would have fallen had Duff not caught her.

"I'm sorry," she said. "I'll go find a seat somewhere and be of no further bother."

"Nonsense, you are no bother," Duff said. "Please, sit here."

The woman sat down, not on the seat beside him, but on the seat across, facing him.

"My name is Belle," the woman said. Then with an uncomfortable smile, she shook her head. "No, it isn't. That's just the name I use when I'm working. My real name is Martha. Martha Jane Radley. I don't know why I told you my real name. I never tell anyone. I would not want it to get back to my pa that I am a soiled dove."

"Soiled dove? I don't know the term."

"Soiled dove is what we, that is, girls who are on the line, call ourselves."

"On the line?"

"I am going to have to come right out and say it, aren't I?" Martha said. "I don't just serve drinks. I am also a prostitute."

"I see."

"I came west from a small town in southeast Missouri," she said. "I thought I could make it on my own, but it is very hard for a woman, alone, to find honest employment. Out of desperation, I drifted into prostitution. You can't be just a little bit of a prostitute—you either are, or you aren't. And I am. I was told that it would be easy work, and I would make a lot of money."

"*Och*, but it isn't what you thought, is it?"

"You got that right, Mister. The saloon gets most of the money, and as for easy work"—she put her fingers to the scar on her face—"there is nothing easy about dealing with drunken cowboys when they get frustrated because they can't— uh—perform."

"Yes, I saw an example of that back in the Occidental Saloon."

"That was Clyde Shaw," Martha said. "He isn't the one who cut me, but he does like to slap the girls around a bit. You haven't told me your name."

"Oh, please forgive me, lass, I apologize for my lack of manners. The name is MacCallister. Duff MacCallister."

"Mr. MacCallister, believe me, you have nothing to apologize for."

Duff chuckled. "If that were but true," he said.

"MacCallister. Are you kin to Falcon MacCallister?"

"Aye," Duff said, surprised to hear Falcon's name mentioned. "He would be my cousin. 'Tis surprised I am to hear ye say his name! How is it that ye know him?"

"I know who he is, but I don't know him. I've never met him," Martha said.

"Then, how can it be that ye know who he is, if ye've never met him?"

"Don't you know?" Martha replied. "Falcon MacCallister is well known throughout the West. Why, there have been books written about him, as well as his famous father."

"He has a brother and sister who are famous as well," Duff said. "They are actors upon the stage in New York."

"Really? I didn't know that. Oh, how I would love to visit New York someday. And go to a play. And see all the sights. Have you been to New York, Mr. MacCallister?"

"Aye."

"If I ever get to visit New York, I will never leave," Martha said.

Duff and Martha continued their visit for the four hours it took to travel from North Bend to Central City.

"I had a true love once," Martha said. "But his father was a very wealthy man and he wanted his son to marry the daughter of a wealthy man. My pa was a preacher man and he barely made a living from it. Leo, that was my beau's name, came to see me the night before he was to get married. He wanted me to still be there for him after he got married. He said he would set me up with a house and would come see me when he could. I got very angry with him for asking me to do something like that. I wanted to know what kind of woman he thought I was. The truth is, I wanted to do it, but I was afraid to. Something like that would have killed my pa. So, I left home, rather than stay there and take a chance that I might take Leo up on his offer."

Martha made a sound that might have been a chuckle. "I was too good to be a kept woman—but now look at me. I am a whore."

"We cannot always direct the paths our lives will take," Duff said. "We can only but go where life leads us."

"If you mean we have no control over our own lives, you've got that right," Martha said. "Take you, for example. You said you are from Scotland, but here you are in America. Did you plan to come here?"

Duff shook his head. "I had no such plans."

Duff told Martha about Skye, and that she had died on the day before they were to wed. He did not tell her how she died, nor did he tell her of his own actions after she died. But he did tell Martha how deep his love was for Skye and how much he grieved for her.

Duff's tale left Martha in tears, and she reached across the space that separated them and put her hand on his shoulder.

"Mr. MacCallister, you are a good and decent man," she said. "You are as good and decent a man as I have ever met. I hope that you can find peace in your heart. And I hope that someday you can find a woman who is worthy of your love."

Duff had welcomed Martha's company while she was on the train, for the conversation helped pass the time on the long journey. As the train continued west, Duff stared through the window at the vast, open, and featureless plains, interrupted occasionally by small, strange-looking houses that appeared to be made of the same ground from which they rose. That idea was confirmed when he asked the conductor about them, and was told that they were sod houses, built by cutting sod from the ground. They passed through places like Elm Creek, Plum Creek, and Oglala, and he was once again alone with his thoughts. Being alone with his thoughts was not all that pleasant, for he could not get that last picture of Skye from his mind.

Skye lifted her hand to his face and put her fingers against his jaw. She smiled. "'Twould have been such a lovely wedding," she said. She drew another gasping breath, then her arm fell and her head turned to one side.

* * *

Duff shook his head to clear it of such thoughts, then continued to stare through the window at the boundless, grassy plains. On the one hand, there was nothing to see; on the other, there was almost a grandeur to the vast openness and desolation, a vastness of solitude without a tree, river, bird, or animal of any kind.

As they approached the mountains, now a purple line far to the west, the plains began to change. The grass was greener and the wildflowers more profuse and more colorful. Finally, the isolation, the rhythmic motion of the car, the drone and clack of the wheels as they passed over each rail section, and the comfort of his seat caused Duff to drift off to sleep.

Duff was cold. It had surprised him when he first arrived in Egypt to learn that the desert could get cold at night. Part of the chill, he realized, might be the task that lay before him. The Egyptians had set up their defenses at Tel-el-Kebir. The desert around Tel-el-Kebir was extremely flat, so any approach by the British would easily be spotted. As a result, the British decided to march across the desert by night and attack the Egyptian positions at dawn. The British army was guided by Commander Wyatt Rawson, naval aide-de-camp to Lieutenant-General Wolseley. Calling upon his experience as a navigator, he plotted their course across the desert as if they were at sea, using the stars to guide him. The army reached their destination, then moved into position silently.

As a captain, Duff MacCallister was the commanding

officer of one of the companies in the 42nd Foot, and once they were in position, he visited with his troops, calming them, preparing them for the battle that was to come.

"Captain, will we hear the pipes?" Private Kirk asked.

"Aye, lad, the pipes will play."

"Pity the man who hears the pipes and was not born in Scotland," Kirk said.

Although many of the men were visibly nervous, none seemed so frightened as to be unable to perform his duty, and after visiting every one of his men, Duff returned to the front of his company.

"'Tis a good officer ye be, visitin' with the men like that," First Sergeant Wallace said.

"'Tis easy to be a good officer when I have good men and good NCOs, First Sergeant," Duff replied.

"Captain MacCallister? Where is Captain MacCallister?"

Duff heard his name being called in the darkness, and he recognized the voice of Colonel Groves, the commanding officer of the regiment.

"I am here, sir," Duff called back.

Groves materialized in the dark and Duff saluted him.

"Captain MacCallister, General Wolseley has chosen our regiment to lead the attack, and I want your company on point. Is your company up to it?"

"Aye, Colonel," Duff replied. "If it's killin' o' the enemy you be wantin', we are the lads that can do it for you."

"Hear, hear," those soldiers who were close enough to overhear the conversation said.

"Very well, Captain, move your men into position and begin the attack," Colonel Groves ordered. "The rest of the brigade will move forward on your signal."

"Thank you, Colonel, for affording us this honor," Duff said.

"'Tis an honor well earned," Colonel Groves replied.

At exactly five a.m., as the high skirling sound of bagpipes could be heard all across the desert, Duff ordered his men forward. With fixed bayonets, they rushed the Egyptians. The predawn darkness was illuminated by the flash of a thousand and more rifles. Bullets whizzed by Duff's ear, some of them so close that they made popping sounds. Men to either side of him screamed in pain or fell silently as they were hit. All the while, above the bang and whiz of rifles and bullets, above the deep-throated yells of men in desperate battle, could be heard the sound of the pipes.

The charge continued until the British and Egyptian lines melded. The British soldiers were armed with Martini-Henry rifles, to which were attached bayonets, and they made frightful use of them until their blades were running red with the blood of the hapless Egyptians, who had no bayonets and thus were ill equipped for the hand-to-hand fighting that developed.

Duff, driven by adrenaline, leaped over the parapet and into a trench filled with Egyptian soldiers. Because he was an officer he was armed not with the Martini-Henri Rifle but with the Enfield Mark 1 pistol. Using his six-shot revolver, he killed six of the ten Egyptians who were in the trench. The other four, without regard to the fact that Duff was now out of ammunition, leaped out of the trench and ran.

The pipes were still playing, but one of them seemed badly out of tune and Duff could hear none of the drone pipes but only the high, screeching whistle.

* * *

The high screeching whistle awakened him, and sitting up in the dark car, Duff realized that it was not the pipes he was hearing, but the whistle of the train. He was not in North Africa, he was in America, on a train going mile after mile after endless mile. Just how large was this country anyway? He had no idea America, or anyplace in the world, could be as large as this magnificent country was.

Closing his eyes, he drifted back to sleep, but this time, thankfully, it was deep and dreamless.

After days of passing through towns that were so small they scarcely deserved to be called a town, his arrival in Denver proved to be a most pleasant surprise. Every other town since St. Louis was so small that the engine and last car of the train, while at rest in the depot, stretched nearly from one end of the town to the other. For the most part they had been windy, desolate-looking places with low, featureless buildings. But Denver was actually a city, with buildings of brick and stone, or wood that was painted and glistening in the sun. The depot was a large, three-story building, huge and impressive, and other trains either sat in the station or arrived and departed on tracks that fanned out in all directions like the spokes on a wagon wheel.

From Denver, Duff would board his final train, the one that would take him to the town of Mac-Callister. But he learned, when checking the schedule, that the train to MacCallister would not leave until nine o'clock the following morning. Duff was going to have to find a hotel room for the night—but the thought of spending the night in Denver was not daunting. In fact, he was looking forward to it.

"I'm sorry, sir," the hotel clerk said. "But we are completely filled."

With a frustrated sigh, Duff ran his hand through his hair. "This is the third hotel I have been to, and not one with a vacant room. Is it always this difficult to find lodging in this city?"

"I am afraid that you have come at a bad time, sir. Our state legislature is in assembly, and legislators from all over the state have come for the session. That always fills the hotels. I doubt there is any hotel in the city with a vacant room."

"Very well," Duff said. "I suppose I can try to make myself comfortable in the depot."

"I know where you might find a room, though being a gentleman as you are, it might not be a room that would be to your liking."

"Sure'n where would that be?" Duff asked. "I'm that tired that 'twould not take too fancy a room to suit me tonight."

"Many of the saloons have rooms upstairs. You might inquire at one of them."

"A saloon then? Aye, I will try."

The bartender was pouring the residue from abandoned whiskey glasses back into a bottle when Duff stepped up to the bar. He pulled a soggy cigar butt from one glass, laid the butt aside, then poured the whiskey back into the bottle. Duff winced as he saw what the bartender was doing, but he wasn't here to drink, he was here to find a room.

"What will it be, friend?" the bartender asked.

"I'm told one might find a room here," Duff said. "Have you a room to let? Or have I been misinformed?"

"No, you ain't been misinformed. You want it with, or without?"

"With or without what?"

"Are you kidding me, Mister? With or without a woman."

"I have no wish to share my room with a woman."

"The room will be six dollars."

"Six dollars?" Duff replied in surprise. "That's quite expensive, isn't it?"

"If the girls used the room for their customers, we could make three, maybe four times that," the bartender said. "Six dollars, take it or leave it."

Duff had been on the train for a week, and the thought of a real bed, in a non-moving room, was very attractive to him. He nodded.

"Very well, I will pay the six dollars."

The bartender held out his hand, and when Duff gave him the money, he said, "It's upstairs."

"Which room?"

"It doesn't matter," the bartender replied.

"The key?" Duff asked.

The bartender laughed. "Key? What makes you think there is a key? There ain't no key. Just go on in. If there's a man and woman in there, then just keep openin' doors 'till you come to one that is empty."

"I see."

"You might try the first one to your left up at the

head of the stairs. That's the room Suzie normally uses, and I see her over there in the corner, so like as not, that room is empty."

"Thanks."

The room the bartender had suggested appeared empty, but Duff couldn't be sure until he turned on the light, a single incandescent bulb that hung down from the long cord. He saw that it was, indeed, empty. With the light provided by the electric bulb, Duff made a closer examination of the room.

The room had one high-sprung, cast-iron bed, a chest, and a small table with a pitcher and basin. On the wall was a neatly lettered sign that read: "WE EXPECT OUR GUESTS TO BEHAVE AS GENTLEMEN." Duff placed a chair under the doorknob to act as a lock. Then he opened the window and saw that his room looked out over the street.

It was a busy night. In addition to the clanging bells and puffing steam of arriving and departing locomotives, he could hear the voices of scores of animated conversations spilling through the open windows and doors of the town's buildings. Leaving the window open to catch the evening breeze, Duff turned out the light and climbed into bed, gratified to find that it was actually quite comfortable.

Within moments, Duff was asleep, and again he dreamed.

The regiment was back in Scotland, and in formation. The pipes and drums were playing as Lieutenant-General Wolseley stepped to the front.

"Adjutant," General Wolseley said. "Summon the honoree."

"*Captain Duff Tavish MacCallister, front and center!*"
The adjutant shouted.

*Duff, who was standing at the rear of the formation,
marched to the front, then halted in front of Lieutenant-
General Wolseley and saluted.*

"*Read the citation, Adjutant,*" *Wolseley said.*

The adjutant, also a captain, began reading. "*Attention to orders. Know all ye present by these greetings that
Captain Duff Tavish MacCallister of the 42nd Foot,
Third Battalion of the Royal Highland Regiment of
Scotts, is, for intrepidity and performance of his mission,
above and beyond the call of duty, by the Queen, awarded
with his nation's highest award, the Victoria Cross.*"

When Duff awakened the next morning, he
opened his sea bag and looked at the clothes he had,
those he had bought in New York, those he had
bought in Kansas City, and the uniform of the Black
Watch that Andrew and Rosanna had given him. He
thought it strange that twice, during this trip, he had
dreamed of his time in the army. Perhaps it was because he knew that he had this uniform with him,
the last vestige of his life before America.

Selecting the clothes he would wear for this last
part of his trip, he got dressed, packed the rest
away, then left the saloon for the walk to the depot.
When he arrived, the train for MacCallister was sitting on the track, ready to go.

Chapter Twelve

North Bend, Nebraska

"A beer, barkeep, if ye dinnae mind," Rab Malcolm said. He had come into the Occidental saloon while the train was stopped long enough to allow the passengers to take their meal.

There was a big, bearded man standing at the far end of the bar, and when he heard Malcolm give his order, he looked around quickly.

"Hey, you!" he called. "Where are you from?"

Malcolm picked up the beer, took a swallow, then wiped some of the foam off his lips before he turned to face the man who called out to him.

"I am from Donuun, though it be none of your concern," he said.

"Would that be Scotland?"

There was a strong overtone of belligerence in the questioner's voice, and though Malcolm recognized it, he had no idea why. He took another swallow of his beer before he replied.

"Aye, I'm from Scotland."

"What the hell? Are we being overtook with

people from Scotland? You're the second one to come through here in the last week."

"The other Scot—would he be a big man with broad shoulders, light-colored hair, blue eyes?"

"Yes, that's what the bastard looked like, all right."

"I take it you dinnae make friends with him?"

"Friends? If I ever see the son of a bitch again, I'll shoot him on sight."

"Barkeep," Malcolm said. "Would you be for servin' my new friend another drink?"

Malcolm slapped a coin on the bar. The bartender picked it up, then poured another whiskey for the big, bearded man.

"Why did you do that? And why did you call me your friend? I don't even know you."

"The name is Rab Malcolm," Malcolm replied. "And in Scotland we have a saying. The enemy of my enemy is my friend. The man you have developed such a dislike for is Duff MacCallister. Duff MacCallister is my enemy. Did you mean it, when you said you would shoot him on sight?"

"Damn right, I meant it. Uh, that is, unless you are the law."

Malcolm smiled. "As it so happens, I am the law. And as it also so happens, Duff MacCallister is wanted by the law. So you would not be incurring trouble on my behalf if you were to shoot him."

"Well, that's good to know."

"What is your name, friend?"

"The name is Shaw. Clyde Shaw."

"Be ye gainfully employed, Mister Shaw?"

"Say what?"

"Do you have a job?"

"Oh, uh, no, not at the moment. I was workin'

down at the livery, but I got into a fight with the boss's brother-in-law, so I got fired."

"Do you seek employment?"

"Yeah, I reckon so. I reckon it depends on what it is, and if it'll pay anything."

"Suppose I hire you as my deputy, Mr. Shaw. You can help me hunt down MacCallister."

"Hunt him down? I don't know. You bein' from Scotland and all, maybe you don't know how big this country is. Hell, he could be anywhere between here and California."

"*Och, mon*, but I know exactly where he is going."

"You do? Where?"

"He is going to Colorado, where he intends to look up a kinsman of his, named Falcon MacCallister."

"Falcon MacCallister?" Shaw replied.

"Yes. Do you know him?"

"I've heard of 'im. Hell, near 'bout ever'one in the West has heard of 'im."

"What have you heard of him?"

"He s'posed to be about the best with pistol there ever was. Better'n Wild Bill Hickock, they say."

"Maybe when he was younger. I am told that he is nearly fifty years old now," Malcolm said. "How fast can an old man be?"

"I don't know. Like I say, I've never met him. Onliest thing is, I've heard of him."

Malcolm made a waving motion with his hand. "It doesn't matter anyway. Duff MacCallister is the one who is wanted by the law. He is the one we are going after, and I dinnae think you will have to worry about him. I know the man, and I know he has no skill with the pistol."

"You'd hire me, you say?"

"Aye. As my deputy."

"And what would that pay?"

"I'll give you twenty-five dollars now, and seventy-five when the job is done," Malcolm said.

"I ain't all that good with cipherin'. How much is that?"

"That is one hundred dollars. And, I will buy all the meals along the way."

Shaw held up his glass. "Drinks, too?"

"When it is appropriate," Malcolm said.

Shaw tossed his drink down. "Mister, you just hired yourself a deputy."

Onboard the Colorado Eagle

"MacCallister! MacCallister! We are coming into MacCallister!" The conductor called it out repeatedly as he passed through the car, then he left by the back door to continue on through the train.

Duff sat up in his seat and ran his hand through his hair. He could feel the train slowing and as he looked through the window he saw the buildings of the town. This town was not that different from all the other small towns he had passed through for the last week, except for one very notable exception. The train passed by a life-sized bronze statue mounted on a cement pedestal. A large plaque attached to the pedestal read:

James Ian MacCallister.

Soldier, Statesman.

OUR FOUNDER.

"Folks, this is MacCallister," the conductor said as he came back through the car a moment later. "We'll only be here for fifteen minutes, so if you leave the train and this isn't your destination, don't wander too far."

This town that bore Duff's surname was the final stop of his six-day journey from New York. It was here that he would look for his kinsman.

Duff had thrown his sea bag in the overhead bin, and as soon as the train squeaked to a complete and rattling stop, he stood up and pulled the bag down. As he started toward the front of the car he saw a young woman with a small child at her side, struggling to retrieve her bag from the overhead bin.

"Here, lass, would ye be for allowin' me to get your grip for you?"

The young woman smiled at him. "Yes, thank you," she said.

Duff took her bag down, then, carrying it and his own sea bag, followed her out of the car.

The arrival of trains in MacCallister was still enough of an event to draw several citizens out, for no other reason than to see the trains arrive and depart. Falcon reread the telegram as he stood on the depot platform.

OUR SCOTTISH COUSIN DUFF MACCALLISTER WILL
ARRIVE IN MACCALLISTER ON THE MORNING TRAIN
ON SATURDAY AUGUST 7 STOP PLEASE MEET HIM
AND EXTEND ALL HELP HE MAY NEED STOP
LETTER TO FOLLOW STOP
ANDREW

Only three people stepped down from the train: a man, a woman, and a child. The man was carrying two bags and the woman was talking to him, suggesting to Falcon that it was a husband and wife.

"Ruby! I'm here!" a man called, and the woman took one of the bags from the man who had stepped down from the train with her. Then, with a broad smile, she started toward the one who had called out to her. The child, with his arms spread wide, ran to the man to be scooped up in his arms.

The man who had stepped down from the train now stood on the depot platform for a long moment, looking around as if not quite sure what to do next. Behind him the train seemed something alive, the relief valve releasing steam in great, breathing puffs, the water in the boiler gurgling, the overheated axle terminals and wheel bearings snapping and popping as they cooled. Falcon knew then, without a doubt, that this would be Duff Mac-Callister.

Duff saw a big man coming toward him. There was a slight resemblance to Andrew, though the man coming toward him was much taller and more muscular. In fact, the man in size and body proportion was almost a mirror image of Duff himself.

"You would be—" he started to say, but he was interrupted.

"Duff MacCallister?"

"Aye, Falcon, I am Duff MacCallister."

Falcon and Duff extended their hands at the same time. The grip was firm and friendly.

"Help! Someone help me, that man took my reticule!"

The shout came from an old woman who was about to board the train. Looking toward her, Duff and Falcon could see a man clutching the woman's purse as he ran toward his horse.

"Excuse me, sir," Duff said, grabbing a polished cane from someone nearby. The man wasn't using the cane as an aid to walking, but as an affectation to his suit, vest, tie, and bowler hat.

"Here, what do you mean?" the man sputtered angrily.

Duff threw the cane at the running thief, aiming it at his legs. The cane hit the man between his legs while he was in full stride, and it had the effect of tripping him. He fell clumsily to the ground, losing his grip on the woman's purse.

Duff ran to him and, grabbing him by the scruff of the neck, jerked him to his feet. Falcon was right behind Duff, and he picked up the purse, then returned it to the woman who had lost it.

"Thank you, sir," the woman said.

Falcon smiled. "I'm not the one you should be thanking," he said. "There's your hero." He pointed to Duff.

With his right hand, Duff was holding his thumb and forefinger tight against the back of the would-be thief's neck. In his left hand, he was holding the cane he had "borrowed."

"Your cane, sir," he said to the well-dressed man who had, involuntarily, made the contribution. "I appreciate the loan."

"I didn't exactly loan it to you," the man said. He

chuckled. "But I must say you gave us all a show with it."

"I assume there is a constabulary in this town," Duff said to Falcon as he came up to him.

"We have a sheriff, Amos Cody," Falcon said. "Come, we'll pay him a visit."

"Leggo my neck," the would-be thief said. "You're hurtin' me."

"You can let go if you want to," Falcon said. "He won't go away."

"How do you know?"

"Because if he tries to run away, I will shoot him," Falcon said easily.

Sheriff Amos Cody was sitting at his desk looking through a pile of wanted posters when Falcon, Duff, and Duff's prisoner came in.

"Stand there and don't ye be movin' without the sheriff's permission," Duff said.

The young sheriff looked up. "What have we here?" he said. Then, seeing Falcon, he nodded. "Good mornin', Mr. MacCallister."

"And how would ye be knowin' m'name?" Duff asked.

Falcon chuckled. "You aren't the only MacCallister in the room, Duff."

"Aye, 'twas foolish o' me to respond. I'll be for beggin' your pardon, Sheriff."

Still smiling, Falcon saw the confused expression on the sheriff's face, so he made the introduction.

"Sheriff, this would be Duff MacCallister. He is my cousin, and he is from Scotland."

"I'm pleased to meet you," Sheriff Cody said. "And what have we here?"

"I don't know the black heart's name, but 'tis a thief he is. He stole a lady's purse," Duff said.

"Oh, I know his name all right," Sheriff Cody said. "Hello, Stripland. Welcome to MacCallister."

"My name ain't Stripland. I don't know what you're talkin' about."

"Really? Well now, that's funny, because I just saw a dodger with your likeness on it." Sheriff Cody shuffled through the pile of wanted posters until he found the one he was looking for. He held it up and looked at the woodcut on the poster, then compared it to the thief Duff had brought in. "Here it is," he said. "George Stripland. It seems that you robbed a stagecoach last month. And here you stole a woman's purse. That's quite a comedown for you, isn't it? From robbing stagecoaches to stealing a woman's purse?"

"I didn't hurt nobody," Stripland said. "I'm hungry. I was just tryin' to get enough money to get me somethin' to eat."

"Don't worry. We feed you well in here," Sheriff Cody said. "Ain't that right, Dillard?"

An old, bald, and toothless man was standing behind the bars in one of the four cells at the back of the room. The other three cells were empty.

"Whooowee, you sure got that right, Sheriff," Dillard said. "Didn't I just tell you this mornin' I didn' want you to turn me loose 'till after I et? Come on in here, sonny, me'n you will have dinner together." He laughed a high-pitched, cackling laugh, slapping his knee in glee.

"In there," Sheriff Cody said.

"Sheriff, you ain't goin' to put me in jail with that old coot, are you?" Stripland asked.

"No, sir, you get your very own cell," Sheriff Cody said, putting his hand on the prisoner's arm and escorting him to the back. There, he pushed Stripland into an empty cell, closed the door, and locked it behind him.

"Well, if you have that blaggard well in hand, we'll be goin'," Duff said.

"Not so fast," Sheriff Cody said. Sitting down at his desk, he pulled out a book and began writing. Tearing the page out, he blew on the ink to dry it, then handed it to Duff. "Here is a draft for two hundred and fifty dollars, reward for bringing in George Stripland. You can take it to the bank and they will cash it for you."

"Two hundred and fifty dollars? Just for bringing the blaggard in?"

"Sorry it isn't more," Sheriff Cody said.

Duff smiled broadly. "'Tis plenty enough, and you have my thanks."

"It's about dinnertime," Falcon said as they left the bank a few minutes later. "Shall we find a place to eat?"

"Dinner? My word, what time is it? I know the time changes as one travels west, but is it evening already?"

Falcon chuckled. "Out here it is breakfast, dinner, and supper," he said. "This is our noon meal."

"Noon meal. Aye, I am a bit hungry. But I'll be buyin' if you don't mind."

Falcon laughed. "Just because you've got all that money, there's no need for you to be spending it all that quickly. I thought Scots were thrifty."

"*Och*, lad, we're beyond thrifty, we're cheap," Duff said. "But it's thankful I am to you, and to your brother and sister for takin' in one who is so distant in kin that it can barely be traced. So I would appreciate it if you would let me buy the lunch."

"All right, and I thank you for it," Falcon said. "This is your town, what do you recommend?"

"I would suggest the City Pig."

"Sure'n I hope there is something on the fare other than fried ham and potatoes," Duff said.

"I know what you mean," Falcon said. "I've taken several trips to New York. On the trains east of Kansas City they have dining cars so you have a little more choice, but on all the restaurant stops west of Kansas City the food can get pretty tiresome. But, the City Pig is a good restaurant, the best in town, I believe, and I think you'll like it."

"I don't suppose they'd have haggis and neeps," Duff said.

Falcon laughed and waved his hand dismissively. "Lord, I would hope not," he said. "I may be Scottish, but if I have to prove it by eating that, I'll turn Irish, or English, or even French."

"So you know what it is?"

"Oh, yes. I know what it is. I tell you what, suppose you let me order for the two of us."

"Aye, that might be the best way."

Norman "Hog Jaw" Landers was standing behind the counter when Falcon and Duff stepped in through the door.

"Gracious, Falcon, who's that fella with you?" Landers asked. "He's as big as you are. I swear, the two of you together could block out the sun."

"Hello, Hog Jaw. This is my cousin, Duff, fresh

from Scotland," Falcon said. "And he just got off the train, so I hope you have a lot of food back in your kitchen, because we are going to make a run on it."

"Oh, I think we can handle it," Hog Jaw said. "We've got a big joint of beef we've been cookin' since before daylight. I tasted a bit of it a while back and it melted in my mouth."

"All right, we'll have roast beef, mashed potatoes, green beans, biscuits, and lots of gravy," Falcon said.

"I'll get them started," Hog Jaw said as he walked into the back.

There were about a dozen other diners in the restaurant, and all of them greeted Falcon as he led Duff to a table in the corner at the extreme back of the room.

"Sit there," Falcon said, pointing to one of the chairs. "I'll sit here, and because we are in the corner of the room, we will each have a wall to our back."

"Is it your habit to always have a wall at your back?" Duff asked.

Falcon nodded. "Yeah. Wouldn't be a bad thing for you to follow, either."

"But everyone in town seems to know you. You have a lot of friends."

"I also have a lot of enemies. And even when you are with friends, you never know who might come up behind you. Bill Hickock told me that, once, and if he had paid attention to his own advice, he might still be alive."

"You knew Wild Bill Hickock?"

"I knew him," Falcon said.

"I'm told that you are as well known as Hickock was, and that you are as good with a pistol."

Falcon chuckled. "Andrew tell you that, did he?"

"Aye, but he was only the first," Duff replied. "I heard from many others as well."

"You are new to America and new to the West," Falcon said. "You don't want to believe everything you hear. People in the West—I don't know, maybe it's because we tend to be a little isolated from the rest of the world—but people tend to exaggerate."

"I've no way of knowing if all I have heard of you is true," Duff replied. "But, cousin, I have heard of you."

Falcon smiled. "Then do me a favor, and believe only the good things you have heard."

Duff chuckled and nodded. "Aye, that I can do."

"Now, Duff, what's your story? What brings you out here?"

Chapter Thirteen

Denver

Rab Malcolm and Clyde Shaw stood on the brick platform of the Union Pacific Railroad Depot. The platform was filled with people, arriving and departing passengers, as well as the townspeople who were here to greet arriving passengers or to see off departing family or friends.

"Well, we are here in Colorado," Shaw said. "Now what?"

"I suggest we locate the nearest pub. It has always been my experience that one can find out much information in a pub."

"What is a pub?"

"I'm sorry," Malcolm said. "I believe you would call it a saloon."

"A saloon? Yeah, now you are talking my language," Shaw said as a broad smile spread across his face.

"What do you mean I am talking your language? 'Tis English, isn't it? That's what I've been speaking all the while."

"No, I just mean . . . never mind. Let's go find us a saloon."

The first saloon they came to was Aces and Eights, and it identified itself by a hand of cards showing black aces and eights, and a red nine of diamonds. It also had its name painted in red, outlined with gold, as well as a large, cut-out beer mug depicting a full mug of beer with a high, foamy head.

Inside the saloon, behind the bar, was a glass-enclosed box on the wall. Inside the box was the same hand of cards depicted outside the building, black aces and eights, and a nine of diamonds. The center card, the nine of diamonds, had a bullet hole in it, and underneath was a professionally painted sign.

ACTUAL HAND OF CARDS

held by

WILD BILL HICKOK

when he was murdered by Jack McCall.

"Is that real?" Shaw asked, pointing to the hand.

"Indeed it is, sir," the bartender answered. He was wearing a low-crown bowler hat, a striped shirt with detachable collar, and with the sleeves held up by garters. He had a full, handlebar moustache. "Our proprietor bought it from the owner of the Number Ten Saloon in Deadwood."

"Well, I'll be."

"What will it be, gents?" the bartender asked, as he smoothed his moustache.

"Whiskey, neat," Malcolm said.

"I'll have one as well."

The bartender served them. Malcolm tossed his whiskey down, then turned his back to the bar and called out loud.

"Gentlemen, I am Rab Malcolm, deputy sheriff of county Argyllshire in Scotland. I am in pursuit of a felon by the name of MacCallister and would greatly appreciate any information anyone might give me."

"Mister, you wouldn't be talkin' about Falcon MacCallister, would you now?" one of the saloon patrons asked.

"Aye, 'tis possible that the man I seek would be with Falcon MacCallister, being as the two men are cousins."

"Mister, from what I've he'erd tell of him, Falcon MacCallister is as good a man as God ever put on this here earth. Even iffen I know'd whereat you could find him, I don't think I would let you know."

"That was a waste of time," Malcolm said, grumbling as they left the saloon.

"Yeah, well, I reckon you are a real smart man. I mean, bein' as you are a foreigner and all, but you sure didn't go 'bout that right," Shaw said.

"You have a better way of securing information than asking for it?"

"Well, no, you got to ask for it," Shaw said. "It's just that you ain't goin' to get nowhere askin' the way you was."

"What do you mean?"

"I don't know how you do it in Scotland, but

here you don't just shout it out like that. You have to kind of sneak up on it."

"Sneak up on it?"

"Yeah, sneak up on it," Shaw said. "You know, get the feller into a conversation, then you ask."

"All right," Malcolm said. "Suppose we let you do the talking at the next pub."

"Saloon," Shaw corrected. "And that's another thing. The saloon we was just in is too highfalutin. We need one that's more down to earth, so to speak." He pointed to one that had a totally different exterior. Unlike the Aces and Eights, there was no false front to this building, no cutout, or even a drawing of a mug of beer, and no beautifully lettered and brightly painted sign. This one had crudely lettered words scrawled in whitewash across the front of the unpainted building. The name of the saloon was The Black Dog.

MacCallister homestead

The house was filled with people and they were all MacCallisters, either by blood or name. Falcon's brothers Jamie Ian, Jr., Morgan, and Matthew were there with their wives, along with his sisters, Joleen, Megan, and Kathleen, and their husbands. They were already in the house when Falcon and Duff arrived. Falcon introduced them to Duff.

"My word, I had no idea I had so many cousins in America. All of you, plus Andrew and Rosanna."

"What you see here are just a few of us," Joleen said. "This house isn't big enough to hold all of us."

"How many are there?"

"One hundred and three."

"Soon to be one hundred and four," Matthew said. "You forgot Mirabelle."

"I didn't forget her, Matthew. I know she is pregnant," Joleen said. "But the question was how many are there, not how many will there be."

The others laughed.

"Tell us, Cousin Duff, how are Andrew and Rosanna doing?" Megan asked. "We see them so seldom now that they are famous in the New York theater."

"They are doing well. When I left New York they were the principal players in a play called *The Highlander.*"

"*The Highlander*? What an odd name for a play. What does it mean?"

"It refers to someone who lives in the Highlands. It is rather like calling an American who lives in the West a Westerner."

Duff answered many more questions: how he met Andrew and Rosanna, and about his family back in Scotland, though, as he explained, he was the only one left.

"With my departure, there is not one MacCallister left in all of Scotland, or if there be, they are cousins so distant that they are not known by me."

"What brought you to America?" Jamie Ian asked.

"Andrew and Rosanna invited him," Falcon answered quickly, with a glance toward Duff cautioning him not to go any further with the answer. Falcon was now aware of all the details of Duff's flight, first to New York, and then from New York to Colorado.

The rest of the family had brought food, and they had an enormous dinner that evening. Then, as the ladies cleaned up from the meal, the men gathered in the parlor for drinks and cigars.

"The drink is fine," Duff said. "But I've never caught on to smoking."

"Ahh, it's a nasty habit anyway," Matthew said.

"Jamie, Morgan, Matthew, it was more than a mere invitation from Andrew and Rosanna that brought Duff to America," Falcon said.

Jamie took a puff of his cigar and nodded. "I thought it might be," he said.

"What was it?" Morgan asked.

"I'm going to let Duff answer," Falcon said.

"I've killed a few men," Duff said.

"Haven't we all?" Jamie Ian replied.

"What do you mean by a few?" Matthew asked.

"Five. Well, more if you count those I killed in war. But five that I killed were my own countrymen."

"I take it they needed killin'," Jamie Ian said. "Or else you wouldn't be telling of it so easily."

"One of the men I killed, the son of the sheriff, was trying to rape Skye. And because he was the son of the local sheriff I decided to go to the sheriff to tell him my side of the story. Skye would not have it any other way but that she go with me, being as she was a witness. But on the road we were met by the sheriff and three of his deputies. Before I could say a word to explain the situation, and to tell them that I was voluntarily coming to the sheriff's office, they began shooting. They were shooting at me, but they killed Skye. I killed the two deputies."

"Who was Skye?" Matthew asked.

"Skye was my fiancée."

"I thought as much," Morgan said.

"Then I was right," Jamie Ian said. "The sons of bitches needed killin'."

"I was still in Scotland when I killed those men, but knew that the sheriff was never going to let it go to trial. And without Skye's testimony as to what happened, I would not have been able to prove that the killing was justified, even if it had gone to trial. I knew that I was going to have to leave the country, so I boarded ship that very night and worked my passage to America."

"You said you had killed five men. That's only three," Morgan said.

"Aye, there is more to the story," Duff said. "Once I arrived in America the sheriff sent his other two sons and his remaining deputy after me—not to arrest me, but to kill me. They caught up with me in the back of the very theater where Andrew and Rosanna were appearing. I killed the sheriff's other two sons, but his deputy escaped."

"If he's got any sense, he's on his way back to Scotland now," Jamie Ian said. "You've certainly shown that you can take care of yourself."

"I wish I could believe that," Duff said. "But I know this fellow, Rab Malcolm. He is evil incarnate, but there is a thoroughness about him that, were he to apply it to more noble pursuits, would be admirable. There is no doubt in my mind but that he is still here, probably recruiting more men for his nefarious scheme."

"So you think he is still here?" Matthew asked.

"Aye, more than likely he is still in New York. That's why I left New York. I was afraid that if he tried again it might be dangerous for Andrew and

Rosanna, and I have no wish to get them involved. Andrew suggested that I come here."

"Which I think was a good idea," Falcon said.

"What are you going to do now?" Morgan asked.

"I'm going to find some way to make a living," Duff said. He smiled. "I've already made two hundred and fifty dollars, just since arriving here today."

"You have made two hundred and fifty dollars in one day? I would say that is a good day's wages. How did you come by it?" Morgan asked.

"It was easy. I turned over to the sheriff someone for whom a reward had been posted," Duff said.

"Wait till you hear how it happened," Falcon said, and he proceeded to tell the story of Duff "borrowing" a cane and using it to trip up a thief.

"And here is the best part," Falcon said. "You know who he borrowed the cane from?"

"No idea," Jamie Ian said.

"I'll give you a hint. The man he borrowed the cane from doesn't need it to walk."

"Ha! You are talking about Toots Nelson, aren't you?" Morgan said. "He's always so prim and proper. I would love to have seen his face."

"It was something to behold all right," Falcon said. "But the expression on Stripland's face when he went ass over elbow was even better."

The men were still laughing when the women, their work in the kitchen completed, returned.

"What's so funny?" Joleen asked.

A moment later, after hearing the story of Duff using a cane to trip up a purse snatcher, the women were laughing as well, and they were still laughing as they left the house and climbed into the various conveyances for the trips back to their own homes.

"Good-bye, Duff, and welcome to Colorado!" Kathleen called.

"Good-bye!" the others called, and Duff and Falcon responded in kind.

As the teams pulled the surreys and buggies away, Duff stood for a long moment at the front door watching. Noticing a contemplative look on his face, Falcon asked about it.

"Is anything wrong?"

"No, there is nothing wrong. 'Twas thinking, I was, what a wonderful family ye have, Falcon Mac-Callister," Duff said.

"You are thinking of Skye, aren't you?"

"Aye, and the family we would have had."

"These people, my brothers and sisters, and my brothers- and sisters-in-law, are your family, too," Falcon said.

"I much appreciate your sharing them with me."

"It's not my doing, cousin. It's a fact of life. But I can understand your thinking about Skye. We've all lost people that we love, Duff," Falcon said. "But we go on with life."

"And I will as well," Duff said. "Though I've no idea as to what my new life will be."

"What did you do in Scotland?"

"I had land. I raised cattle."

Falcon laughed.

"What is it?"

"You are a cattle rancher. There's no need for you to have a new life," Falcon said. "You'll have your old life; you'll just be having it in a new place."

"I don't know how it is in America. But in Scotland, one needs land to be a rancher."

"You can homestead."

"Homestead. Aye, Andrew mentioned something about that, but I'm not sure what he was talking about."

"It's an easy way of getting land," Falcon said. "All you have to do is file on it, build on it, and live on it for five years."

"That sounds good."

"I'll tell you what, cousin. We'll go into town tomorrow and find the best place for you to go, to file on some land."

Duff smiled. "Ha. I'll be an American landowner. Imagine that."

Chapter Fourteen

When Duff and Falcon went into town the next day, Duff was fascinated with how busy it was. The sign at the depot that gave the elevation of MacCallister as 8,750 feet also gave the population as 956. But Duff believed there were at least that many people moving about, walking up and down the planked sidewalks, crossing the crowded street, moving in and out of the stores, and riding on horseback or in wagons, surreys, and buggies. He commented on it.

"That is because we are the only town for several miles around," Falcon replied. "Many of the people you see live out in the country on farms and ranches, or in some cases, as prospectors and miners. They come into town about once a week and when they do, it is a big occasion for them. This is Saturday, that is their day to come into town.

"Let's go in here," Falcon suggested.

The painted sign on the glass window in front of the building read:

MacCallister Monitor

It was the newspaper office, and inside was the smell of ink, fresh-cut paper, and oil to keep the press operating smoothly. A somewhat overweight man, wearing a green visor, was sitting at a desk, selecting type from the type boxes as he composed a story. He looked up as Duff and Falcon entered the building.

"Falcon!" the editor greeted them with a broad smile. "How good to see you. I was just about to look you up."

"Look me up for what?"

"I wanted to get your story about what happened at the depot yesterday when a through passenger tripped up George Stripland by throwing a cane at his feet. Was it really Toots Nelson's cane?"

"Yes."

"I wonder what made the man decide to use a cane in such a way."

"Why ask me, when you can get it straight from the horse's mouth?" Falcon replied.

"What do you mean?"

"Larry, this is my cousin from Scotland, Duff MacCallister. Duff, this is Larry Fugate, editor of the *MacCallister Monitor*, as good a newspaper as you will find between the Mississippi River and the Pacific Ocean."

"'Tis a pleasure to make your acquaintance, Mr. Fugate," Duff said.

"Good to meet you as well," the editor said. He turned back to Falcon. "What do you mean, getting my story from the horse's mouth?" he asked again.

Falcon chuckled. "I just introduced you to the horse, so to speak."

"It was you?" Fugate asked Duff. "You are the one who threw the stick at the thief?"

"Aye."

"Well, then I shall need the full story from you."

"There is no story to tell," Duff said. "He snatched the lady's purse and commenced to run, I borrowed a gentleman's bat and hurled it at him with an unexpected degree of success."

"Ha," Fugate said. "Something there is that tells me that the success of your maneuver wasn't all that unexpected."

Despite Duff's reticence, Fugate managed to get the story from him, though his reluctance to be self-aggrandizing made it necessary for Falcon to introduce a few comments here and there to add the necessary color.

After the interview, Falcon called upon the newspaper editor for a favor.

"Larry, suppose a fellow wanted to homestead some land. Where would be the best place to go?"

"You mean here in Colorado?"

"Colorado, yes, that would be fine, but it isn't necessary. We are looking for the most available, as well as the best quality of land for raising livestock."

"Oh, well, in that case, if you don't just have to be in Colorado, Wyoming would be the best place, I think."

"Wyoming?"

"Yes. Up there they are so eager to have settlers that when you homestead, the territory of Wyoming will make additional land available."

"Where in Wyoming?" Falcon asked.

"Oh, just about anywhere in Wyoming. You could practically throw a dart at the map and settle wherever the dart hits. But of course, you would want the land to be fertile and well watered, so that does somewhat limit your possibilities."

"What about Cheyenne?"

"Cheyenne? Yes, I think Cheyenne would be a good place to start."

"Then what do you say, cousin, that we take a trip to Cheyenne in a couple of days?"

"I would not want to put you out any," Duff said. "'Tis not necessary that you come."

"Nonsense. You are still new to the country. I'm sure I can be of some assistance to you. Besides, I would enjoy the trip."

"Then your company would most assuredly be welcome," Duff said.

It was Falcon's routine to drop in at the post office anytime he was in town, and this morning the postmaster handed him a letter.

"It is addressed to Duff MacCallister, care of you," Pleas Terrell said as he handed Falcon the letter. "It's from your brother in New York."

Falcon took the letter from Terrell. "Thank you. This is my cousin, Duff MacCallister, the man to whom the letter was addressed. Duff, this is Pleas Terrell, our postmaster."

"'Tis an honor to meet you, Mr. Terrell," Duff said.

"Will you be with us for a while, Mr. MacCallister? The reason I ask is because if I should get any further mail addressed to you, I shall know what to do with it."

"I shan't be here for too much longer. But if you

should receive another letter for me, please feel free to give it to Falcon."

"Thank you, that is how I will handle it, then," Terrell said.

From the post office they went to the City Pig Restaurant, and there, as they waited for their meal to be served, Duff read his letter.

Dear Cousin Duff,

I hope this letter finds you, for I am writing to impart some information that I believe to be of great importance to you. Percy Fowler, whom you will remember as one of the stagehands, has betrayed a confidence. As a result, Fowler has lost his position with the theater. However, it is an act of closing the door after the horse has left the barn for I have learned, upon good authority, that Fowler provided information to Deputy Sheriff Malcolm from Argyllshire County in Scotland. Malcolm has learned that you are in Colorado and I am certain that he will be coming out there to find you, so please be on the lookout for him.

"The Highlander" continues to run with naught but glorious accolades from the newspapers. The "New York Tribune" said of Rosanna: "Rosanna MacCallister portrays Lady Margaret in the play 'The Highlander,' and such a luminary is she that Mr. Edison's electric lights, by which the theater is illuminated, are scarcely needed. Miss MacCallister brightens the stage by her mere appearance." I report this to you in all great pride of my twin sister's accomplishments, though I dare not say this to Rosanna, lest her head grow too large.

With regards and affection from your American cousin, I remain yours faithfully.

Andrew MacCallister

"The New York newspapers speak well of Rosanna," Duff said as he finished reading the letter.

"They always do," Falcon said as he spread butter on a biscuit. "They praise Rosanna and Andrew alike, and I agree. I have seen them perform and think it is more than mere brotherly pride that makes me believe them to be players of great talent."

"'Tis no mere brotherly pride, for I have seen them, too, and they are very good."

"What else did my brother have to say?"

Duff hesitated for a second before he responded because he didn't want Falcon to think that he would be asking for help in dealing with Deputy Malcolm. Then he thought that to hold back anything Falcon's brother may have said would seem impolite, so he passed the letter across the table.

Falcon read it quickly, then glanced up at Duff.

"This man, Malcolm, would be the deputy who came for you in the theater?"

"Aye."

"Then Andrew is right, we should be on the lookout for him."

"I thank ye kindly, Falcon, but this isn't your battle."

"Duff, do you really think this deputy will come after you by himself?"

"I don't know," Duff answered, though not too convincingly.

"He will find as many men as he can," Falcon said.

"But how will he be able to recruit so many?" Duff asked. "He knows no one in America."

"He knows that you have come to join me," Falcon said. "He will use that as his means of recruiting. Believe me, Duff, he will be able to round up an army just by collecting men who want to see me dead."

"*Och*," Duff said, hitting his forehead with the palm of his hand. "I did not think of that. I left New York so no' to bring danger to Andrew and Rosanna, and here, I have brought it to you instead. I am sorry."

"Don't be sorry," Falcon said. "I've been in danger before. And this may be a good way of bringing my enemies out."

After they ate, they went to the depot, where they bought tickets to Cheyenne. They would leave on the train the next day, then change trains in Denver for the northbound to Cheyenne. After making their travel arrangements, Falcon took Duff around the town, introducing him to the sheriff, the doctor, and several of his friends. They participated in a game of horseshoes, in which Duff did poorly, and a game of darts, which Duff won handily.

Then they went to the saloon, where Duff was introduced to Argus Fincher, the saloon keeper.

"You're Scottish?" Fincher asked.

"Aye."

"I've something to show you," Fincher said.

Fincher went into the back room, then reappeared a moment later, gingerly carrying something.

"Pipes!" Duff said. "Sure an' I haven't heard that sweet sound since I left Scotland."

"Can you play the bagpipes, Duff?" Falcon asked.

"Aye, and would I be Scot if I couldn't?"

"How did you come by this, Argus?" Falcon asked.

"A couple of years ago a drummer sold them to me for ten dollars," Fincher said. "I thought I might learn to play them, but they are the devil's own device. I can barely get a sound from them."

"May I?" Duff asked, reaching for them.

"What is all that sticking out of the bag?" Fincher asked.

"This is the tube you blow into in order to inflate the bag," Duff explained. "This is the chanter. You move your fingers over the holes in the chanter to play the notes. And these are the drones, two tenor and one bass."

Duff took the bag, inflated it, then began to play. At first the strange sound coming from the instrument surprised the others in the saloon, but then they heard the melody, sweet and harmonious over the steady thrum of the three drone tubes.

When Duff finished the impromptu concert, every person in the saloon applauded. He thanked them, then handed the pipes back to Fincher.

"No, sir," Fincher said, holding his hand out. "That thing belongs to someone who can play it. You keep it."

"I can't do that," Duff said. "But I'll buy them from you. How much did you pay for them?"

"Ten dollars."

Duff took out a ten-dollar bill and handed it to the bartender.

"Thank you," Fincher said.

"No, Mr. Fincher. Thank you."

"Play us another tune, would you, Mr. MacCallister?" one of the saloon patrons asked.

"I'll play for you, 'Scots Wha Hae,'" Duff said. "That means, 'Scots Who Have.'"

Duff played the song, a stately slow melody, then afterward he spoke the words.

> *"Scots, who have wi' Wallace bled,*
> *Scots, whom Bruce has often led,*
> *Welcome to your gory bed,*
> *Or to Victory.*
> *"Now's the day, and now's the hour:*
> *See the front of battle lour,*
> *See approach proud Edward's power—*
> *Chains and Slavery.*
> *"Who will be a traitor knave?*
> *Who will fill a coward's grave?*
> *Who will base as be a slave?*
> *Let him turn and flee.*
> *"Who for Scotland's king and law*
> *Freedom's sword will strongly draw,*
> *Freeman stand, or Freeman fall,*
> *Let him follow me."*

That evening Duff and Falcon sat on the front porch of the old MacCallister homestead. It was on this porch that Kate Olmstead, Falcon's mother, had died. And now she and Falcon's father lay buried twenty-five yards away.

The two men sat far into the night, exchanging

stories. Falcon said that he could understand the killing rage Duff felt after Skye was killed. His own wife had been kidnapped and murdered, and Falcon went after and killed those who were responsible. He also told of his father and mother, how they had met when very young and run away together, how he was mentored by an old mountain man who was called simply Preacher. He also told of his own, as well as his father's adventures in the American Civil War.

Duff spoke of his own father, Brigadier Duncan MacCallister, a career soldier in India, where Duff had spent much of his childhood. Brigadier MacCallister was at Lucknow, in command of 855 men, when it was besieged by over 8,000 rebels. He held them off until relieved by Major General Havelock. Though Duff had earned a commission, he had not made a career of the army. He did serve in Egypt for a while, and he told Falcon his own experiences at the battle of Tel-el-Kebir. He also told of his time at sea.

"They are a breed in and of themselves, these men who sail before the mast," he said. "Good men who have only each other for company."

In the dark vault of night, a golden meteor streaked across the sky.

"That was Skye, saying hello to me," Duff said.

"The meteor was Skye?"

Duff chuckled. "Every time Skye saw a meteor, she would say that it was the soul of some departed loved one saying hello. I laughed at her then, but find some comfort from it now. She spoke to me many times while I was sea."

Duff almost told of hearing her voice in the wind

and seeing her eyes in the fluorescent flash of fish, but he knew that Falcon wouldn't understand. Every time it happened, he had passed it off. But now he wondered—could it be true? Could it have actually been Skye, speaking to him? Was that golden streak across the sky Skye? Or was it merely a dead rock falling to earth from outer space?

"I guess you think that is crazy," Duff said.

"No, I don't. Not at all," Falcon replied, his answer surprising Duff. "The Indians have a much better connection to nature than the White man. And Indians believe, strongly, in such signs. And I know better than to question them."

The two men sat in silence for several minutes, though it was hardly silent around them. Night insects whirred and clicked, in a nearby pond frogs croaked and sang, and in the distance a coyote howled. The windmill answered a freshening breeze and the blades began to spin. The leaves of the nearby aspen trees caught the moonbeams and sent slivers of silver into the night.

There was no need for the two men to talk any further; they had already shared with each other their pasts, or enough of what they thought was important. They had taken the measure of each other, and had found it acceptable and reassuring. Now they could sit confidently in each other's presence, content in their own musings and comfortable in the developing friendship that went beyond the remote familial connections. And yet, though the blood they shared of the original Falcon, great-great-great-great-grandfather to both was small indeed, that seed of kinship was still there.

"I wonder if he is looking down at us now," Duff

said. He purposely did not identify the "he" he was talking about.

"I expect he is," Falcon said. "I have thought many times about the fact that I have his name. I hope he is proud of that. I know he is looking down now and proud that two of his grandsons, though so far separated by distance and time, have come together."

Falcon knew exactly what Duff had meant. And Duff wasn't in the least surprised.

Chapter Fifteen

Denver

If the outside of The Black Dog had been rudimentary, the inside was even more so. Whereas the bar at Aces and Eights had been polished mahogany with a brass foot rail and customer towels hanging from rings spaced no more than five feet apart on the front of the bar, the bar of The Black Dog had no such amenities. It was made of the same kind of wood as the rest of the saloon: wide, unpainted and weathered boards, filled with knotholes and other visible imperfections.

There was no mirror behind the bar to reflect the many varieties of whiskeys, tequila, wines, and aperitifs. There were no bottles of any kind visible, for the bar served only one kind of whiskey and one kind of beer. There were no brass spittoons, though there was a bucket sitting at each end of the bar. Perhaps half of the tobacco chewers and snuff users took advantage of the buckets. The rest spat upon the floor, and the floor was filled with old expectorated tobacco quids and stained with squirted snuff juice.

A bar girl came over to greet them, her smile showing a mouth of broken and missing teeth.

"Would you gentlemen like some company?" the girl asked.

"If I wanted some company, I would pick someone better lookin' than you," Shaw said.

"Honey, if that's the case, you are going to have to go somewhere else, 'cause there ain't no one better lookin' than me in the Black Dog," the girl said. She turned and walked away from them.

"This place is a disgrace," Malcolm said, wrinkling his nose in disgust.

"What does that mean?"

"It means it is a disgrace to pubs and taverns the world over."

"Yeah, well, maybe so. But this here is the kind of place we're goin' to find the men we're a' lookin' for," Shaw said.

Even as the two men were taking their seats at an empty table, a drama was playing out before them. It had started before Malcolm and Shaw had entered the saloon.

"I don't want any trouble with you, Pogue," a man, standing at the bar said. The speaker was a big man with wide shoulders, powerful arms, and big hands. His appearance was in direct contrast to the person he was addressing, a man he had called Pogue.

Pogue was slender of build, with long hair, a thin face, and a badly misshapen nose. The nose was more than misshapen, it was flat on his face, and turned up at the bottom with nostril openings so pronounced that they almost looked like a pig's snout.

"Well, you got trouble with me, Gentry," Pogue replied. Snorted would be a better way of saying it, for the words came out in a wheezing, grunting sound. "You should'a never butted in between me'n my whore."

"She ain't your whore, Pogue, she's anybody's whore who will pay her. Hell, as ugly as you are, Pogue, you should already know that. The only way you'll ever get a woman to pay any attention to you is by payin' them," Gentry said.

"If I'm the one payin' the whore, then that means she's my whore."

"Yeah, that's the whole point. You hadn't paid her nothin' yet. That means she don't belong to you, and if I want to talk to her I can."

"Stop it, both of you," a nearby bar girl said. "I don't belong to either one of you."

"You stay out of this," Pogue said to her. He turned his attention back to Gentry. "I reckon there's only one way me'n you's goin' to settle this." Pogue smiled, though the smile did nothing to alleviate the repulsiveness of his features. "We're goin' to have to fight it out."

"Fight it out?" Gentry laughed. "Pogue, you don't want to fight me. You're so scrawny and weak, I'd near 'bout break you into little pieces first time I hit you."

"Oh, I ain't talkin' about that kind of fightin'," Pogue said. "I'm talkin' 'bout makin' this here fight permanent. I'm going to give you the chance to draw ag'in me."

"Don't be a dumb fool. I ain't gettin' into a fight over a whore. Like I told you, I don't want no trouble."

"And like I told you, you already got trouble. Now I'm tellin' you, again, to draw."

Gentry turned toward Pogue. He was holding a glass of whiskey in his hand.

"Go away, little man, before I come over there and break your neck." Suddenly Pogue pulled his pistol and fired. A little mist of blood sprayed from Gentry's earlobe, and he dropped the glass, then slapped his right hand to his ear.

"What the hell? Are you crazy?"

Pogue put his pistol back in his holster as quickly as he had drawn it.

"Draw," Pogue said again.

"I ain't a' goin' to draw ag'in you."

Again, Pogue drew and fired. This time he clipped Gentry's left ear. Gentry let out a cry of pain and slapped his hand to his left ear.

"Next time it will be a kneecap," Pogue said.

With a yell of rage and fear, Gentry made an awkward stab for his pistol. With the macabre smile never leaving his face, Pogue waited until Gentry made his draw and even let him raise his gun.

For just an instant, Gentry thought he had won, and the scream of rage and fear turned to one of rage and triumph. He tried to thumb back the hammer of his pistol, but his hand was slick with his own blood, and the thumb slipped off the hammer. He didn't get a second try because by then Pogue had drawn his own pistol and fired.

As the bullet plowed into Gentry's chest, he got an expression of surprise on his face. Then his eyes rolled up and he fell, dead before he hit the floor.

"You killed him!" the bar girl Gentry and Pogue had been arguing over shouted.

"Hell, yes, I killed him," Pogue replied. "He threatened me."

"He threatened you? How did he threaten you?"

"He told me he was goin' to break my neck."

"That's right," one of the other men said. "I heard him say that very thing."

"Is there anyone here who didn't see him draw first?" Pogue asked.

"No, sir, you give him plenty of opportunity," yet another saloon patron said. "You not only let him draw first, you was goin' to let him shoot first."

"I want all of you to remember that," Pogue said.

"Surely, he will not get away with that," Malcolm said to Shaw, speaking quietly.

"Yeah, he will. All the law will ask is who drew first."

"But he clearly goaded the other man into a fight."

"They was already a' fightin' when we come in. The killin' didn't commence until that Gentry feller drawed on him," Shaw said.

It took about three minutes before a couple of Denver policemen arrived, wearing the blue uniforms, domed hats, and huge badges of their profession.

"What happened here?" one of the police officers asked.

Everyone began speaking at the same time, and one of the policemen had to hold up his hand to call for quiet.

"One at a time. I'll start with you," he said, pointing to the bartender. "Who shot this man?"

"I did," Pogue said, before the bartender could answer. "If you want to know anything about what happened here, all you got to do is ask me."

"All right, I'll start with you."

"This here fella drawed on me," Pogue said. "I didn't have no choice but to defend myself."

"Are you saying he drew first?"

"That's right," the bartender said. "I'll vouch for Pogue on that. You can see the gun is still in Gentry's hand."

"Anyone else have anything different to tell?"

"I . . ." the girl who had been the subject of the fight started to say, but she stopped when Pogue glared at her.

"What?" the policeman asked.

"I was just going to say that Pogue is right. Mr. Gentry drew first."

The two policemen spoke to each other quietly for a moment, then the spokesman of the two turned back to Pogue.

"From all we can determine, this was a case of self-defense. I reckon it doesn't have to go any further than this. But, barkeep, we are going to keep an eye on this place, and if too many things like this happen here, we are going to close you down. Do you understand that?"

"Yes, sir, I understand," the bartender replied.

"What did I tell you?" Shaw asked after the two policemen left.

"You were right. I never would have believed you, but you were right."

"Seems to me like this man Pogue would be someone we might want to recruit," Shaw suggested.

"Yes," Malcolm said enthusiastically. "See if he will come talk to us."

Shaw got up from the table, walked over to speak to Pogue, then brought him back.

"Pogue, this here is Deputy Sheriff Malcolm," Shaw said.

Pogue was startled by the introduction. "Deputy Sheriff? You didn't tell me nothin' 'bout him bein' a deputy sheriff." Pogue looked directly at Malcolm. "Look here, you got nothin' on me. A policeman has already been here."

"Oh, I'm not a local deputy, I have no jurisdiction here," Malcolm said. "Pogue, is that your Christian name, or your surname?"

"It's my name," Pogue answered without being more specific. He wheezed when he talked.

"I watched your—shall we call it performance? You seem to be quite accomplished with a pistol."

Two men were, at that moment, picking up Gentry's body and putting it on a litter.

"Put him in the wagon, I'll drive him down to the undertaker," someone said. There was considerably more attention being paid to the disposition of the body than to the conversation going on between Malcolm and Pogue.

"I'm good enough," Pogue replied.

"Have you ever heard of a man named MacCallister?" Malcolm asked.

Pogue's eyes squinted. "Yeah, I've heard of Falcon MacCallister. What about it?"

"Do you think you are as good as he is?"

"I may be. Why are you askin'?"

"Mr. Malcolm has a bone to pick with MacCallister," Shaw said.

"Yeah, don't ever'one?" Pogue replied.

"In fact, my particular grievance is not with

Falcon MacCallister, but with his kinsman, Duff MacCallister."

"Duff MacCallister? I've never heard of 'im."

"It is my understanding that Duff and Falcon will be together, so I cannot hunt for one without hunting for the other."

"You goin' after them, are you?" Pogue asked.

"Yes."

Pogue grunted what might have been a laugh. "Just the two of you?"

"And you, if we can come to some arrangement," Malcolm said. "I think three of us might be enough."

"Malcolm, let me ask you somethin'," Shaw said. "Didn't you tell me that they was three of you tried to take on Duff MacCallister?"

"Yes."

"And what happened?"

"He killed the other two," Malcolm said. "But that was an unusual circumstance. That's not likely to happen again."

"Wait a minute," Pogue said. "You're tellin' me that three of you wasn't enough to take on this here Duff feller, but you think three of us would be enough for Duff and Falcon? Mister, I ain't sure three is enough for Falcon alone, let alone iffen he has someone with him. And this here Duff feller you are talkin' about don't seem like he's goin' to be too easy his ownself."

"I thought you said you said you were as good as Falcon MacCallister."

"I said I might be," Pogue said. "But you done brought up someone else, and that changes it a bit. You said somethin' about comin' to an arrangement with me," Pogue said. "Does that mean you'd be willin' to pay me?"

"Aye."

"That's good. But I'm not goin' to get myself kilt by goin' up against Falcon MacCallister and this other feller you're talkin' about. You can't spend money if you're dead. We're goin' to need some more people."

"I don't have enough money to pay for any more people," Malcolm said.

"Mister, there's lots of folks that want Falcon dead. Onliest thing is there ain't none of 'em got the sand to go up ag'in him alone. But if there was to be a bunch of us all gathered together, they wouldn't be scared and more'n likely we would get the job done. And it wouldn't cost you nothin' 'cept what you are goin' to pay me."

"The only problem is, Falcon is not the one I am interested in," Malcolm said.

"That don't matter none. Iffen they are together like you say, you ain't likely to get one of 'em, without you get the other," Pogue said.

"Do you think you could find such men?" Malcolm asked.

"I can find 'em. I know lots of people that would like to see Falcon MacCallister dead. Hell, the problem ain't goin' to be in findin' 'em, it's goin' to be in decidin' which ones to take and which ones to leave."

Malcolm thought about it for a moment, then he nodded. "All right. Round up the men."

"We ain't talked about gettin' paid yet."

"Suppose I pay you twenty-five dollars?" Malcolm suggested.

"Fifty," Pogue countered.

Malcolm fought hard to suppress his smile. He would have been willing to pay up to one hundred dollars.

"Twenty-five now, and twenty-five when the job is done," Malcolm suggested.

Pogue held out his hand. "Give me the money."

As Malcolm counted it out, Pogue started giggling.

"What is so funny?"

"I was goin' to say ten dollars, 'till you come with twenty-five. When you said that, I figured I could maybe get fifty. You don't know it, Mister, but you got took."

"You're just too smart for me," Malcolm said. "Now, if you would, please start rounding up some more men."

"You would'a give him more, wouldn't you?" Shaw asked after Pogue left.

"Perhaps."

"I mean, you give me a hunnert."

"We'll keep that between ourselves, won't we?" Malcolm asked.

"Hell, yeah, you think I want Pogue knowin' I'm gettin' more money than he is?"

"I think he would not be too pleased with that," Malcolm said.

Scotland—Donuun in Argyllshire

Sheriff Angus Somerled read the letter the postmaster brought him. It was another letter from Duff MacCallister, intended for Ian.

Dear Ian,

I am writing to inform you that it has become necessary for me to leave New York. Alexander and Roderick Somerled came to New York in the company of Rab Malcolm. They came upon me in the theater one night after everyone else had left. It was their intention not to arrest me, but to kill me. In the ensuing encounter I bested them, killing both of the sheriff's sons. The deputy ran into the night, but I take no solace in thinking that my troubles are over.

As I have now dispatched all three of Somerled's sons, I have no doubt but that he will make every effort to kill me, and feel that, for my own safety, as well as the safety of Andrew and Rosanna, my kinsman, I must leave. I am writing this letter from the railroad depot. From here I shall journey to a place in Colorado which bears the name MacCallister. There, I will meet with the brother of Andrew and Rosanna. His name is Falcon, the selfsame name of a distant ancestor whose blood runs in both of us.

I think often of Skye, you, and the town of Donuun. With prayers for your continued health, I remain,

Duff MacCallister

Sheriff Somerled folded up the copy of the letter and drummed his fingers on the desk for moment or two. Then he got an atlas of the United States and looked up Colorado. He put his finger on the town of MacCallister, between Red Cliff and Wheeler, in Eagle County.

"You think you are safe, do you, Duff MacCallister?" Somerled said aloud. He pulled his pistol from his holster and held it for a long moment, thinking of his three sons, all dead because of Duff MacCallister.

Then, putting his pistol back in the holster, he took out a piece of paper and wrote out his resignation. He had sent Malcolm to America to deal with MacCallister, but so far all he had done was get his two sons killed. The old adage "If you want something done, do it yourself," resonated with him. He was going to America to find Duff MacCallister, and he was going to kill him.

Chapter Sixteen

MacCallister Valley—Falcon's homeplace

"You Americans have tremendously large breakfasts," Duff said as he split open a biscuit and laid a piece of fried ham between the halves. His plate showed the residue of three eggs and home fried potatoes.

"That may be so, but you seem to be up to the task," Falcon said.

Duff laughed as he took a bite of his ham biscuit. "I didn't say that I didn't approve. I was just commenting."

"I eat a big breakfast when I can," Falcon said, "because I'm not always certain I will get to eat again on that day."

"Seems reasonable enough to me," Duff said.

"Didn't you tell me that you bought a pistol?" Falcon asked.

"Aye, that I did. I bought an Enfield Mark 1."

"Enfield is it? Hmm, I've heard of Enfield rifles. I didn't know they made a pistol."

"Quite a good one, actually," Duff replied.

"Do you have a belt and holster set?"

"Oh, I do indeed," Duff said.

"I tell you what. After breakfast, suppose you strap on your pistol and we'll go outside for a little shooting?"

"I think that would be splendid."

When Duff stepped outside a few minutes later, he was wearing a pistol belt with bullets in every loop. The holster was in front, just over his right leg.

"Why are you wearing your holster like that?" Falcon asked.

"'Tis the way I wore it in the regiment."

"No, no, pull it around to your side."

Duff did as directed.

"And let it hang low. Look at my gun. When my arm is hanging normally by my side, my hand is even with the pistol grip. See?"

Duff made the necessary adjustments.

Falcon began the task with some reservation because he feared that the job of teaching Duff to use a pistol might be more than he could handle. But he knew, also, that if Duff was going to survive his time in the West, he was going to have to be prepared for it.

"Let's see what you can do," Falcon said. He pulled his pistol and pointed at a nearby tree. "You see those three little limbs sticking up there? I'm going to shoot the one in the middle."

Falcon fired, and half the twig flew away.

"Now you try it."

Duff fired, and the rest of the twig was blasted from the tree.

Falcon squinted, then looked over at Duff. "What did you do? Miss your twig and hit that one by mistake?"

"No, I didn't miss at all," Duff said. "I thought that was the twig you wanted me to hit."

"Can you hit one of the others?"

"Which one?"

"Your choice."

Duff fired twice, the shots coming so close together that it sounded almost as if it were one sustained roar. Both of the other twigs were cut by his bullets.

"Damn," Falcon said. "You'll do just fine."

"I'm afraid I don't have the skills necessary to make a rapid extraction though," Duff said.

Falcon had to think for a moment until he realized what Duff was saying. Then he laughed. "You mean a quick draw," he said.

"Aye."

"Let me tell you something about quick draws," Falcon said. "Half the people who can draw faster than you, can't shoot. They depend upon their speed, then just blaze away, hoping they can hit what they are shooting at. Being able to hit your target is much more important than being able to get your pistol out first."

"You said half the people," Duff said. "That means that the other half can draw faster than I can, and can also hit their target."

"You might think that," Falcon said. "But there is still another consideration. If you are going to draw on someone, you must be prepared to kill them, and you must be prepared to do so without the slightest hesitation."

"I would imagine that one would not draw upon another if he did not want to kill him," Duff said.

Falcon shook his head. "And that is where you would be wrong. It takes a lot of resolve to kill a man. Most will hesitate for just a second trying to fortify themselves to the task at hand. And that hesitation can be fatal. You have killed before, in self-defense, yes. But sometimes the question of self-defense might be a blurry line. Could you do it then?"

"When I was in Egypt I killed men for no other reason than that they were wearing a uniform different from my own," Duff said. "As far as I know they were good men, family men, husbands, fathers, sons, and brothers. But I didn't think about any of that. The only thing I thought of was my duty."

On the morning they were to leave for Cheyenne, Morgan MacCallister arrived at the homestead driving a buckboard. Falcon tossed his saddle and saddlebags into the back of the buckboard, then tied Lightning, his big bronze stallion, onto the back. He had made arrangements to ship Lightning up to Cheyenne on the same train he and Duff would take. Morgan put his bagpipes and sea bag into the back.

"Duff, as you are my guest, you ride up front in the seat with Morgan," Falcon invited. "I'll sit back here."

"Are you sure? I'm as comfortable in either place," Duff replied.

"I'm sure. Besides, this will give you and Morgan an opportunity to visit," Falcon said as he crawled into the back of the buckboard.

"I appreciate the kind gesture," Duff said. He climbed into the buckboard and sat beside Morgan.

"So how have you two gotten along?" Morgan asked as he snapped the reins against the back of the team.

"Splendidly," Duff said. "I feel much closer than a fifth cousin."

"Fifth cousin? Is that what we are? Fifth cousins?"

"Yes, our nearest relative is five generations ago."

Morgan laughed. "Would that be once removed or something?"

Duff laughed as well. "It is admittedly, quite distant," he said.

Toots Nelson was standing on the depot platform when they arrived, and upon seeing Duff, he made a big show of pulling his cane closer to his body.

"Young man, I do hope you have no intention of using my cane to subdue another fleeing ruffian."

"Your bat is safe from me, sir," Duff said.

Duff presented a much different appearance today than he did on the day he arrived in MacCallister. On that day he had worn striped trousers, a white shirt, a frock coat, and a bowler hat. Today he was wearing blue denim trousers, a wine-colored shirt, a broad-brimmed Stetson hat, boots, and a belt with bullet loops, holster, and pistol.

"However, I should not complain. Thanks to your heroics, I got my name in the newspaper," Toots said. "And every time someone's name appears in the paper, they are one step closer to immortality."

"Immortality?"

"Well, not in the flesh, my good man," Toots said. "But it is by newspapers that we chronicle the sojourn of mankind here upon earth. Why, with your name in the paper, it is quite possible that someone one hundred years or more from now will read your name and, for that moment, you are alive again, if only in the mind of the reader."

"I suppose that is so," Duff said, not really knowing where to go with this conversation.

Falcon laughed. "Don't let Toots climb too far into your mind, cousin. He is a—what is it you call yourself, Toots?"

"I am a gentleman out of time, a frustrated poet whose words of wit shall never receive the accolades they deserve."

"But it's my understanding that you have never actually written anything," Morgan said.

"The fact that I have not written anything does not mean I am not a poet," Toots said. "I am afraid, however, that that is a concept few men can actually grasp."

"I have no trouble with it," Duff said.

"Oh? You mean that you can accept that I am a poet, even though I have not written one word of poetry?" Toots asked.

"Aye," Duff replied. "After all, a drum is a drum, whether someone beats upon it or not."

Toots smiled broadly, and nodded his head. "Morgan, my good man," he said. "You should heed your cousin, for he is a man of uncommon genius."

The whistle of the arriving train broke up the conversation as Falcon hurried to make arrangements for his horse. Duff took his sea bag from the back of the buckboard, and Morgan, with a good-bye wave, drove away.

Duff walked toward the train. The next chapter of his adventure was about to begin.

Denver

Rab Malcolm was a structured man who didn't like to be in any situation that wasn't well thought out in advance. He had tried to tell the Somerled brothers that going to the theater after Duff Mac-Callister without a plan wasn't a good idea. But, even though Sheriff Somerled had told his sons that Malcolm would be in charge of the expedition, the Somerled brothers had insisted upon having their own way. As a result of that insistence, their hasty actions had gotten them both killed.

After agreeing to be a part of Malcolm's entourage, Pogue found six more men who were willing to join in pursuit of the MacCallisters. Their motivation was to find and kill Falcon MacCallister, but as Falcon and Duff would probably be together, Malcolm had no problem with the arrangement.

Being the kind of man he was, Malcolm found out as much as he could about each of the men who had joined him.

Clyde Shaw had been his first recruit, and had come west with him on the train. Shaw was in his early thirties, a sometime cowboy, sometime handyman, and sometime rustler. He had been fired from his last job because the rancher for whom he worked suspected Shaw of stealing ten head of cattle and selling them for ten dollars apiece.

"It ain't so much that you stole from me," the rancher told him, "as it is that you sold the beeves for only ten dollars apiece. That makes it harder for an honest cowman to get a fair price."

Pogue (Malcolm still didn't know if that was his first name or last name), was one of the ugliest men Malcolm had ever seen. He had seen Pogue in action when he shot and killed the man named Gentry. He since learned that Pogue had done some time in the Colorado Prison at Cañon City, the result of a failed bank robbery. The bank robbery failed because Falcon MacCallister happened to be in the bank at the time. Pogue killed another prisoner while he was incarcerated, but had beaten the charge because it had been self-defense. Malcolm didn't have any idea how many men Pogue had killed, but if he was to succeed in finding and killing Duff MacCallister he would need someone with the ruthlessness of a man like Pogue.

The other six men were Liam Pettigrew, Asa Moran, the brothers, Carter and Johnny Hill, and two men, McKenna and Garcia, who, like Pogue, had given only the one name. All six men had reason to want to go after Falcon MacCallister, and while none of them had the courage to try it alone, they welcomed the opportunity to do it as part of a larger group. Pettigrew, reputed to have killed nine men, was the most dangerous of the group, and Malcolm considered not taking him because of that. On the other hand, he wasn't that eager to tell Pettigrew that he didn't want him.

Asa Moran was the smallest member of the group. Swarthy, with dark brown eyes, black hair, and beard, he was almost rodentlike. Moran had served five years in prison because of Falcon MacCallister.

Carter and Johnny Hill were brothers who had once ridden with Nance Noonan, but were away when Falcon MacCallister went on a killing rampage in revenge for the killing of his father. Their other brother, Pen, wasn't so lucky and was killed by Falcon. Now they wanted to kill him.

McKenna and Garcia's reason for going after Falcon MacCallister was more business than personal. Martin Mueller, the father of Clete and Luke Mueller, had put up a reward of $1,000.00 to anyone who would kill Falcon MacCallister to avenge Falcon's killing of his two sons.* No one but McKenna and Garcia knew of the reward, and they had no intention of telling anyone else about it. Once Falcon MacCallister was killed, they would claim the reward, no matter who killed him.

And they would throw in the killing of Duff Mac-Callister as a bonus.

"Tell me about this man Duff MacCallister that you are after," Pettigrew said. "Is he anything like Falcon MacCallister?"

"I can't answer that, because I know nothing of Falcon MacCallister," Malcolm said. "I will say, though, that even if he were alone, Duff MacCallister would

*Slaughter of Eagles

present a most formidable adversary. He has killed five men that I know of, and has often bested his opponents, even when placed in the most precarious of circumstances."

"What makes you think he will be with Falcon MacCallister?"

"Falcon is his cousin, and he came west specifically to be with him."

"All right, I don't mind killin' this feller Duff for you, as long as I get a shot at Falcon."

"Do you have any idea where they are?" Moran asked.

"No, I'm afraid I don't. I was hoping that I could find someone out here who might help me find him."

"MacCallister," Johnny Hill said.

"Yes, MacCallister, that's who we are after," Malcolm replied.

"No, I mean MacCallister the town. It's named after Falcon MacCallister's old man, and there's a whole heap of MacCallisters that live there, includin' Falcoln hisself," Johnny Hill said. "And if this feller Duff is with Falcon, then that's more'n likely where we are goin' to find him."

"Yes, that's right," McKenna said. "I recollect now that there is a town by that name."

"Then that is where we shall go," Malcolm said.

"We ridin', or we goin' by train?" Shaw asked. "'Cause if we're ridin', I ain't got no horse and you don't neither."

"We'll go by train."

"That's fine," Pettigrew said. "Only thing is, the MacCallisters ain't likely to be a standing right alongside the railroad tracks, which means we're goin' to have to have our horses with us when we get there."

"All right," Malcolm said. "Shaw and I will buy a couple of horses, then we will ship all of them on the train along with us."

"Señor, where you goin' to get the *caballos*?" Garcia asked.

"I beg your pardon. The what?"

"*Caballos*, uh, horses. Where will you get them?"

"I don't know. The stable, I suppose. Where does one ordinarily get horses?"

"I can get you two horses, with saddles, I think, for one hundred dollars."

"Where?"

"You don't need to worry. I can get," Garcia said.

"All right. Get them, and have them here at the depot in time to ship them with us when the train leaves."

Two hours later, Garcia showed up with two horses, complete with saddles.

"Better you put these horses on the train *rapido*, I think," Garcia said.

Malcolm was reasonably sure then, if he had not been before, that the horses were stolen. But they looked like good animals, and this search was beginning to eat into his funds, so it was better to pay one hundred dollars for horses without bills of sale than it was to pay up to four hundred dollars for two horses with bills of sale.

Thus it was that nine men, well mounted, well armed, and with a common purpose in mind, boarded the train in Denver for the town of MacCallister.

Cheyenne

As Duff and Falcon journeyed by train to Cheyenne, Duff read of the city in his copy of *Williams Pacific Tourist Guide*.

MAGIC CITY OF THE PLAINS

516 miles from Omaha; elevation, 6,041 feet, Cheyenne is at present the most active and stirring city on the entire line. Cheyenne is well laid out, with broad streets at right angles to the railroad and has an abundant supply of pure water.

Travelers will here take a dinner in comfortable style at one of the best kept hotels between the two oceans. It is a good place to rest after a tiresome journey, and it will pay to stop a few days and enjoy the pure air and genial sun in this high altitude. The Inter-Ocean Hotel is owned by the railroad company and is 150 feet long by 36 feet wide, with a wing 25 feet square. It is two stories high, the upper floor being well furnished with sleeping rooms for guests.

The first place Falcon and Duff went after arriving in Cheyenne was the land office. A small bell attached to the top of the door tinkled as it was pushed open. The land clerk, a very thin man with white hair and glasses, was sitting at a table behind the counter that separated his area from the front.

"Yes, sir, can I help you gentlemen?" he asked, looking up as Duff and Falcon entered.

"I have come to file a claim on some land," Duff said.

"And you are?"

"MacCallister. Duff MacCallister."

"Have you picked the land out yet, Mr. MacCallister?"

"I have not. I have just arrived on the train."

"Well, then, welcome to Wyoming. It is always good to get new people in the territory. What do you say you come back here and we'll take a look at the map and find some property for you?"

Falcon and Duff both stepped around the counter, then up to the wall whereupon was attached a large map. The map was of Laramie County, which stretched from the Colorado border more than halfway up the eastern part of Wyoming.

"Now here is a piece of land you may like, Mr. MacCallister," the clerk said. "It is quite near the town of Chugwater. The land is situated between the Little Bear and Bear Creeks, starting at the confluence of the two creeks and extending for three quarters of a mile to the west, bordered on the north by the Bear and on the south by the Little Bear."

"Do the creeks have water year around?" Duff asked.

"Very good question, Mr. MacCallister, and the answer is, yes, they do. And the land between the two streams is gently rolling grassland, so it is ideal for farming or ranching. You can homestead six hundred and forty acres of federal land and two thousand acres of Wyoming territorial land. And, as it is free range there with no adjacent claims, it means you will have an additional ten thousand acres of grazing land available to you."

"What do I have to do to make this come about?" Duff asked.

"Just sign these forms, then occupy and improve the land," the clerk replied. "It is vital that you improve it."

"And that means?"

"You must build and occupy a structure."

"I shall be in need of a horse," Duff said as he signed the papers the clerk put before him. "Have you any suggestions?"

"Beeman's Barn sells horses," the clerk said. "You might start there."

The clerk took the application form from Duff, examined it, then pulled a pre-printed form from his desk. He signed it with a flourish, then picked up a stamp, inked it, and pressed the stamp onto the form. Then he pulled out a second form and did the same thing.

"This is a provisional deed to the six hundred and forty federal acres," he said. He handed the second form to him. "And this is a provisional deed to the two thousand acres of Wyoming Territory land."

"Provisional?"

"The land is yours in all respects," the clerk said. "Provisional just means that if you abandon the land in the first five years, it reverts back to the government. But if you occupy it for that whole time, it is yours without reservation."

Duff took the documents, looked at them, then smiled at Falcon. "How quickly I have improved my lot from pauper to landowner," he said.

"Welcome to America."

"I believe I am going to like my new country."

"My name is Depro. Dennis Depro. If you have any questions about your land, feel free to call on me," the clerk said.

"Mr. Depro, ye have my gratitude, sir," Duff said.

Chapter Seventeen

Falcon had brought his horse on the train to Cheyenne, but Duff was without a mount. Since the only way to the land he had just claimed was by horseback, it was necessary for him to buy one. Taking the land clerk's advice, Duff walked down to Beeman's Barn, a large livery that sat at the end of the street. The two men stepped inside the barn through the big, open, double doors. It was considerably darker inside the barn as it was illuminated only by the sun that spilled in through the doors, or slashed down through the cracks between the wide, unpainted boards. There were little bits and pieces of hay drifting down from the overhead loft, and the barn was redolent with the pungent aroma of hay and horseflesh and horse droppings.

"Yes, sir, can I do somethin' for you gents?" a man asked, coming toward them from the back of the barn. He was wearing bibbed coveralls over a red flannel shirt and had the stump of a pipe clenched between his teeth.

"Are you Mr. Beeman?"

"I am."

"Mr. Beeman, I should like to make the purchase of a horse," Duff said.

"You are a foreigner, ain't you?"

"Have you an ordinance against selling horses to foreigners?"

Beeman laughed. "No, sir, none at all. Your money is as good as anyone else's money." Suddenly the expression on his face changed. "I mean, you will be using American money, won't you?"

"I thought I might effect the purchase with Japanese yen."

"Say what?"

"I am teasing you, Mr. Beeman. Of course I will use American money."

Beeman's smile returned. "Then in that case I reckon we can do business. I have a horse that you might be interested in. Wait here and I'll bring him to you."

Beeman walked out into the corral and Falcon called out to Duff, "He has saddles and rigging here. You might take a look."

"Aye, it's for sure I'll be needing such," Duff said.

Duff picked out a saddle, saddle blanket, saddlebags, and bridle and had them pushed to one side when Beeman came back in, leading a horse.

"I think you'll like this one," Beeman said.

Duff began examining the horse, not only with his eyes, but with his hands. After a moment, he shook his head.

"No, this animal is too fat," he said. "There is a crease down his back, you can't even feel his ribs, and his withers are fat. This one won't do."

"Would you like to step out back and look for another one?" Beeman invited.

"Aye, thank you."

Duff and Falcon walked to the rear of the barn with Beeman and looked out over a gathering of about thirty horses. Duff saw one that he liked and pointed to it. "That one," he said. "The golden one."

"Gary! Bring the palomino over!" Beeman shouted to one of his employees.

Gary, a boy still in his teens, led the horse over. It stopped and stood quietly as Duff examined it. The horse was just over sixteen hands high, and Duff saw a lot of intelligence and a bit of whimsy in the horse's eyes. As he had before, he began running his hands over it.

"This is more like it," Duff said. "His back is flat, you can't see his ribs but you can feel them, the withers are rounded, and the shoulders and neck blend smoothly into the body. I'll take this one."

"Yes, sir, I'll get the bill of sale ready," Beeman said.

"You know horses," Falcon said to Duff as the two waited for Beeman to return with the bill of sale.

Duff chuckled. "We do have horses in Scotland," he said. He began saddling the horse with the saddle he had selected.

When Beeman returned with the bill of sale for the horse, Duff negotiated for the saddle as well and, fifteen minutes later, rode out of the barn on his own horse.

"We'll have to go to the general store and get some supplies," Falcon said. "But before we do that, how about dropping in at the saloon for a drink?"

"That sounds like a fine idea," Duff replied.

Both men now mounted, they rode down the street to find a saloon. Duff stopped when he saw the sign hanging in front of one of the buildings. He stared at it, dealing with a lot of memories and feelings as he did so.

WHITE HORSE

Falcon, at first not realizing that Duff was no longer riding alongside him, rode on for another few feet before he noticed that he was riding alone. He stopped and turned around to look back toward Duff. Duff was staring at the sign.

"Is something wrong?" Falcon asked.

Visions of the White Horse Pub, Ian McGregor, his friends, and especially Skye, were dancing in Duff's head.

"No," Duff said. "Nothing is wrong."

"Is the White Horse all right with you?"

"Aye, 'tis fine with me." Duff clucked at his horse and rode up alongside Falcon, keeping pace with him for the last few yards.

The two men dismounted in front of the saloon and tied off their horses at the hitching rail out front. Duff had his sea bag tied to the horse's saddle, but he took the bagpipes in with him. When they pushed through the swinging doors they saw a saloon that was filled with people, mostly men, and a piano player who was grinding away at the back of the room. There were half a dozen bar girls flitting about the room, carrying drinks to one table, taking orders at another, and flirting with the customers at still another table. Duff and Falcon stepped up to the bar.

The bartender was wearing a low-crown straw hat with a band that read: ASK US ABOUT OUR BITTERS.

"What can I do for you, gents?" the bartender asked.

Duff set the bagpipes on the floor beside him. "I'll have an ale," he said.

"I'm sorry, we have no ale. But we have a fine, locally brewed beer."

"Beer it will be, then," Duff said.

"I'll have a beer as well," Falcon said.

"Coming right up," the bartender said, jovially, as he grabbed two mugs and held them under the spigot of the beer barrel.

"'Tis not at all like the White Horse," Duff mumbled after he got his beer and looked around.

"I beg your pardon?"

"This place," Duff said, lifting the beer mug and moving it by way of encompassing the saloon. "It has the same name as the pub I frequented back in Scotland. 'Twas owned by the father of my fiancée and 'twas there that my Skye worked."

"Maybe we shouldn't have come in here," Falcon suggested. "I would not want to be causing you any discomfort from unpleasant memories."

Duff waved his free hand dismissively. "'Tis only the name that is alike and nothing more," he said. "And any memory of Skye is a pleasant one."

Falcon set his beer down on the bar. "I need to step out back to the privy for a moment," Falcon said. "I'll be right back."

Duff nodded, then turned his back to the bar and perused the place as he took his first swallow.

"Hey, you!" a man yelled toward Duff and Falcon.

"What's that ugly-lookin' thing you got a' layin' on the floor beside you?"

Duff looked over toward the loud-mouthed man. He was sitting at a table near the cold stove, and he had long hair and a beard. He was the perfect example of the cowboy figures Duff had read about in *The Williams Pacific Tourist Guide.*

"Tell me now, sir, and would it be me ye are addressing?" Duff asked.

The man saw Duff looking at him. "Yeah, I'm addressin' you. You see anyone else standin' up there with what looks like an ugly pile of horse apples layin' on the floor beside him?" He laughed at his own joke.

"*Och*, then 'tis me you are addressing. And would you be for tellin' me, what is the nature of your query?"

"What the . . ." the bearded man replied. He looked at the man sharing the table with him. Like his questioner, the man was gruff looking, but with shorter hair and no beard. "Billy Ray, you want to tell me what the hell this feller just said to me?"

"Well, Roy, it sounds to me like he wants to know what you are askin' him."

Roy turned back to Duff. "What I'm a' wantin' to know is, what the hell is that thing that's a' layin' there on the floor beside you?"

"Pipes."

"Pipes? What do you mean pipes? It don't look like no pipe I ever have seed."

"I suppose I should have said bagpipes."

"A bag of pipes? So, what you are sayin' is, you have come in here carryin' a bag full of pipes."

Duff turned back to the bar.

"Hey, Mister, don't you be a' turnin' your back on me when we're havin' a conversation," Roy said.

This time he shouted the words in anger, and that caused everyone in the saloon to stop their own conversations and to look on in curiosity at the discourse between the two men. Even the piano player stopped and the last discordant notes hung in the air.

Duff turned to face him again. "I'm sorry, but when I engage someone in conversation, I have to assume they are possessed with a modicum of intelligence, or at the very least that they are sentient. You don't seem to enjoy either of those qualities."

Roy's face drew up in an expression of total confusion. He looked at Billy Ray.

"What the hell did he just say?"

"I believe he is funning you," Billy Ray replied.

"Are you funnin' me, boy?" Roy asked, turning back toward Duff.

"By funning, I take it you want to know if I am teasing you?"

"Yeah. You tryin' to tease me? 'Cause I don't take too kindly to folks that try and tease me."

"Then, Roy, ye may put your mind at ease. I don't tease people that I don't like. And though I have just met you, you have made reproachful comments about my pipes. I have heard the call of the pipes when engaged in deadly combat, so I dinnae take kindly to those who pass disparaging remarks about something that is so dear to my heart. So, for that reason, if for no other, I don't like you."

"You're a foreigner, ain't ya?" Roy asked.

"Aye. I am Scot."

"I didn't ask you your name. I asked you iffen you was a foreigner."

"When I say I am Scot, I'm not telling you my name. I'm telling you my nationality. I am from Scotland. You do seem to have some difficulty in speaking English, don't you?"

"I know'd you wasn't American," Roy said. "What are you doin' here? You're a long way from home, ain't you?"

"On the contrary, I am quite close to home. I've just arranged for a parcel of land near here," Duff said. "So, Roy, it looks as if you and I are going to be neighbors. And because of the inauspicious meeting, I do not think we could ever be friends, but I think we should at least make an effort to get on with each other."

"You think that, do you? Well, you know what I think? I think you should go back to Scotland."

"I've no plans to go back to Scotland."

"You ain't goin' to like it here," Roy said. "You're goin' to find a lot more people like me, who don't cotton to strangers. Especially strangers who come from some foreign country."

"I appreciate your concern, Roy, I really do, but I fully intend to stay here," Duff said. He took another swallow of his beer, but he didn't take his eyes off Roy.

"I see you're wearin' a gun. Are you very fast with it?" Roy asked.

"I cannot answer that question with certainty, as I have never had to make a rapid extraction of my pistol. So if you are asking if I would be very proficient in that particular act, I think I would have to say that, in all probability, I am not."

"Mister, I don't even know what the hell you are talking about," Roy said. "Why don't you talk in plain English?"

"He says he ain't very good," Billy Ray said.

"Ain't very good, huh?" A humorless smile spread across Roy's lips. Roy stood up, stepped away from the table, and let his arms hang loosely by his sides. That was when Duff saw that Roy was not only wearing a pistol, he was wearing it low, as Falcon had instructed him to do.

"Well, Mister, you're goin' to have to get good just real fast, 'cause I'm callin' you out," he said.

"Now I must confess that it is I who am confused. I have no idea what calling me out means."

"It means I'm goin' to give you a chance to draw your pistol ag'in me. Me'n you's goin' to settle this little disagreement we got."

"I have no desire to engage you in a gunfight," Duff said.

"What if I put a bullet in that bag of pipes you got there? Would that give you a desire to draw?"

"Oh, I don't think I would like that very much," Duff said.

"Well, that's what I'm a' goin' to do," Roy said. "I'm goin' to put a bullet right through that bag of pipes, and then I'm a' goin' to put a bullet right through you."

As Roy's hand dipped toward the pistol in his holster, Duff threw the beer mug at him, hitting him in the nose.

With a cry of pain, Roy interrupted his draw and put his hands to his nose, which was now bleeding.

"You son of a bitch! You bloodied my nose!" Roy shouted in anger. Once more his hand dipped toward his pistol, but as he started his draw this time, Duff, who immediately after tossing his beer mug had drawn his own pistol, pulled the trigger, putting a bullet through Roy's hand.

"Ayiieee!" Roy shouted, jerking his hand back. "I thought you said you wasn't good."

"I said I could not draw quickly, I did not say that I could not shoot," Duff said. "I am, in fact, considered to be a rather superior marksman with a handgun."

"I wouldn't if I were you!" Falcon called loudly. "Drop it!"

Looking toward Falcon, who had just come back in, Duff saw that he was holding a gun in his hand. He also saw that Billy Ray had drawn his own pistol. At Falcon's call, Billy Ray dropped his pistol to the floor.

"That's more like it," Falcon said. "Piano player?"

"Yes, sir."

"I'm sorry about this, I was very much enjoying your piano music. But I'm going to have to borrow your piano for a while."

"Borrow my piano? Whatever do you mean?"

"Open up the back."

With a look of confusion on his face, the piano player did exactly as Falcon asked.

"Now my friend and I came in here for a nice, quiet drink. It's too late for it to be quiet, but we can still have the drink. Only, I don't want to worry about any of the rest of you getting the idea that you might want to shoot one of us. So, this is what I want you to do. All of you, bring your pistols up here and drop them into the back of the piano."

"What? Are you crazy? I ain't goin' to do that!" one of the other men in the saloon said.

"You have three choices, my friend," Falcon said.

"You can either bring your pistol up here and drop it in the back of the piano like I asked you to, or you can walk out of here right now."

"That's only two choices," Billy Ray said. "What's the third choice?"

"The third choice is I'll kill you where you stand," Falcon said, coldly.

"Damn, Billy Ray, I think he means that," one of the others said.

Grumbling, every customer in the saloon, one by one, walked up to the piano and dropped his pistol into the back.

"Hey, I can't play the piano now!" the piano player complained. "How'm I going to make my tips?"

Falcon pulled out a twenty-dollar bill. "This ought to cover your tips for the rest of the day."

"Gee, Mister. Thanks," the piano player said.

Chapter Eighteen

Cheyenne

Duff's room overlooked the street from the top floor of the Inter-Ocean hotel, a three-story brick building on Central Avenue. Though still fully dressed, Duff lay in bed, using the bedside lantern to provide enough illumination for him to read in his guidebook about the area he was going to homestead.

These plains have an average width of forty miles, and are one hundred miles in length. They comprise an area of over two and a half million acres and are regarded as one of the richest grazing areas in the country.

When Duff thought of the vast distances he had encountered here in America and compared it with Scotland, he couldn't help but be amazed. He had left behind two hundred acres and that was considered a very large holding. With a mere stroke of his pen, he would now control twenty-six hundred acres, with access to another ten thousand acres. The sheer size of it boggled his brain.

When someone knocked on his door, Duff put the book down on the bedside table, then walked over to the door. Opening it, he saw Falcon standing in the hall.

"No," Falcon said, shaking his head. "Don't ever do that."

"Don't ever do what?"

"Don't ever open the door like that," Falcon said. "Always ask through the closed door who it is. Never stand behind the door while you are inquiring, and open it only partially until you are satisfied with whoever is on the other side."

"That seems a bit much, doesn't it? Am I to check under my bed for goblins as well?"

Falcon chuckled. "Goblins can't hurt you. But somebody like this fella, Roy, you met today can."

"Do you think Roy might come knocking on my door?"

"I think it is entirely possible that he might," Falcon said. "Do you have any idea how many people there are out there who want me dead?"

"I would have no idea how many, nor any idea as to why they might want you dead," Duff replied.

"I don't know exactly how many, either," Falcon replied. "But there are an awful lot of them."

"Even so, by your own admission it is you that they want dead. You, not me."

"Uh-huh, I wish that was right, but the truth is, you are in as much danger as I am."

"I have made no enemies, unless you are talking about Roy. And that was but a chance encounter."

"It is chance encounters like that that make enemies," Falcon said. "But even if you had not run into him, you would still be in danger."

"And why is that?"

"Didn't you say that this sheriff from Scotland sent people to New York to kill you?"

"Yes."

"Do you think he will give up?"

"No. Though he has no idea where I am."

"It has been my experience that when someone hates enough to want to kill, they have ways of finding out where you are. And, without regard to the sheriff, you are in danger for another reason."

"What reason would that be?"

"I hate to say it, but it is because your name is MacCallister," Falcon said.

"*Och*, so if I'm to look over my shoulder for the rest of my life, I'm to blame you?"

"I'm afraid so."

"You did not knock on my door merely to give me an object lesson, did you, Falcon?"

"What? Oh, no. It's nearly supper time. I thought you might like to go grab a bite."

"Grab a bite," Duff said, chuckling. "What quaint sayings you Americans have."

"*Och*, 'tis quaint indeed," Falcon replied, perfectly mimicking Duff's accent.

Duff laughed out loud. "Well, pardner, let me just grab my hat, and we'll mosey on down to grab a bite," he said, perfectly imitating Falcon's Western twang.

Falcon laughed as well. "I think I'm bringing you along, cousin. Pretty soon you'll fit right in."

* * *

Roy Jameson was still angry about what had happened in the saloon earlier today. The doctor had bandaged his hand, but it still hurt. And he wasn't sure that he would ever have as fast a draw as he once had. Because Roy was someone who made his living by selling his expertise with a gun, this could wind up affecting his livelihood.

He had no intention of letting that go without doing something about it. It was more than just revenge. And as long as that Scottish bastard was free to wander around the streets of Cheyenne, it would diminish his value as a hired gunman.

Roy had once waited for three days for the opportunity to kill someone. He had drunk tepid canteen water and eaten jerky, fighting off mosquitoes, ticks, and fleas while he waited along a trail that he knew his target would take. And he had no personal investment in that killing—it was just a job.

He did have a personal stake in this one. That foreign, funny-talking son of a bitch had put a hole in his hand. So if he had to wait outside for three days until he got a chance at the Scot, then so be it. It was a wait he would do, willingly.

Roy had been here all afternoon, standing in the opening between the apothecary and the leather goods store. Both establishments were already closed, so nobody was curious about him being here and, as darkness began to fall, he couldn't be seen anyway. He reached up to put his hand on the wall, then winced with pain as it caused the wound to hurt.

"Son of a bitch!" he said aloud, jerking his right hand back from the wall and rubbing the wound gently with his left hand. "Scotsman, you are goin' to die," he said. "Yes, sir, you are goin' to die."

As it grew darker, the tone and tint of the town changed. The daytime resonance of a town at work, the rolling of freight wagons, the ring of the blacksmith's anvil, the chatter of commerce, was replaced by the nighttime sounds of a town at rest and relaxation: piano music and laughter from the saloons.

The dining room of the Inter-Ocean hotel was brightly lit with gas lanterns and well decorated with preserved and mounted heads of antelope, deer, elk, mountain sheep, and buffalo. Meat from these creatures was featured on the menu, along with pork and beef.

It was a popular eatery, not only for the guests of the hotel such as Duff and Falcon but for many of the citizens of the town as well. Tonight it was full, as nearly every table was occupied. As was Falcon's habit, he and Duff took a table in the back corner.

"You'll have to try the buffalo," Falcon suggested. "It is very good."

"Have you ever taken a buffalo?" Duff asked.

"Taken? Yes, I've eaten it often."

"I meant, have you hunted the buffalo?"

"Oh. Yes, I have. But the buffalo are getting very scarce now. I fear we have about hunted them out. During the building of the railroad they hired hunters to provide meat for the workers, and there was almost wholesale slaughter. And that's a shame. They are really magnificent animals."

"I should like to see one in the wild."

"I imagine you will on your land," Falcon said. He took in all the other animal heads. "All these as well."

Duff and Falcon both ordered pot-roasted buffalo with potatoes, onions, and corn on the cob.

"This is an ear of corn, isn't it? How does one eat it?"

"Like this," Falcon explained, spreading butter on the corn, then adding salt and pepper. He picked it up and began biting the corn off.

"My word," Duff said. He followed suit, took a bite, then smiled. "It is quite good," he said.

"Stay here long enough, you'll learn to eat properly," Falcon teased.

After supper, Duff declared that he would like to take a walk around town to have a look.

"I'll come with you," Falcon ordered.

Duff held up his hand. "There's no need," he said. "I mean, I'm not trying to stop you, if you genuinely want to come with me. But don't feel that you must."

"All right," Falcon said. "I tell you what. Take your walk around town, then if you feel like it, drop into the White Horse. We'll have a drink together before we turn in."

"I would enjoy that," Duff replied.

The night air felt good as Duff strolled along the board sidewalk. He could hear piano music from the White Horse. Then, as he walked farther, that piano faded out and he heard another piano from a different saloon. Most of the buildings along the street were dark as the businesses were closed, but there were at least six brightly lit buildings, every one of them a drinking establishment.

As he reached the end of the sidewalk, he could hear the sounds from the houses that were close in. A baby was crying somewhere, a dog was barking, and he heard the loud, complaining voice of a woman berating someone. He assumed it was her husband.

He crossed the street here, and then started back down on the sidewalk on the other side, his boots clopping loudly on the wide plank boards. Toward the middle of town there were a few greenish-glowing gas streetlights, and from the saloons, light spilled through the front windows and doors to project clearly defined gleaming squares on the walk and out into the street.

He heard the clopping sound of a horse coming toward him, but he couldn't see it as yet. Then the horse passed under the first street lamp and he saw a rider, wearing a duster, slumped in the saddle. He watched the horse until it passed through all the lighted area, then disappeared into the distant darkness.

Roy Jameson saw him when he passed under the first street lamp. He was too far away now, but he was coming closer. He pulled his pistol, wincing with the pain of grasping the handle. The pain was bearable, in fact, almost welcome, as it underscored what he was about to do. He cocked the pistol, then braced it against the wall. Just a few more steps now, and he couldn't miss.

Duff saw a glint of silver light on the boardwalk and looking down, saw that it was a coin. He bent down to pick it up.

Concurrent with the sound of a pistol shot, he felt the air pressure of a bullet passing but an inch above him. Had he not bent over for the coin, the bullet would have hit him in the head. Pulling his pistol, he instinctively fell, then rolled off the walk into the street. A second shot hit the walk, plunging through the board, but sending out a little shower of splinters into his face.

This time Duff was able to see the flare of the muzzle flash, so he knew where the shot had come from. Keeping as close to the ground as he could, Duff inched forward on his stomach, his movement shielded by the elevation of the walk. When he reached the first watering trough, he moved over to get behind it.

Now, with his position improved, he looked back toward the gap between the two buildings where he had seen the muzzle flash. It was much darker there than out on the walk itself because the buildings blocked out the street lamp. It was so dark that Duff wasn't even sure that whoever had shot at him was still there. He was going to have to smoke him out, and there was only one way to do that.

Cocking his pistol and taking a deep breath, he stood up.

"Here I am," he called.

As he hoped he would, his adversary, whoever it

was, stepped out onto the walk with a scream of rage. He fired at Duff, and Duff returned fire. Duff saw the man drop his gun, then grab his chest. He fell back against the wall, then slid to the ground.

By now several people had come into the street. The first to approach him was wearing a badge on his vest, and it flashed in the light as he approached with a gun in his hand.

"Drop your gun," the lawman called.

"Aye," Duff said, dropping his pistol as ordered.

A hearing was held the next morning in the courthouse to determine the circumstances surrounding the shooting incident on Central Street the night before, resulting in the death of Roy Jameson. The Honorable Anthony Keller, judge of probate, was presiding. Billy Ray Rawles was the first to testify.

"This here foreign feller shot Roy in the hand yesterday for no reason at all. So it ain't no surprise to me but that he decided to finish the job," Billy Ray said. "If you ask me, it's murder, pure an' simple and I think the son of bitch ought to be took out to a tree and hung." He pointed to Falcon Mac-Callister. "And this here feller was in cahoots with him. Yesterday, after the foreigner shot my friend in the hand, this here man pulled his gun and made ever'one in the whole saloon put their guns into the piano."

"In the piano? I don't understand."

"He made the piano player open up the back of his piano and had us all drop our guns down inside."

"Is that right, Mr. MacCallister?" the judge asked Falcon.

"It is, Your Honor," Falcon said.

"Why did you do that?"

"I thought it might stop any further gunplay."

The judge stroked his white beard, then nodded. "You may be right," he said. "Do you have anything further to add, Mr. Rawles?"

"Only that there ain't no doubt in my mind but what my friend Roy was kilt for no reason at all."

"Thank you, Mr. Rawles," Judge Keller said.

Rawles was the only witness who testified on behalf of Roy Jameson. Every other witness testified as to how Roy Jameson had baited Duff MacCallister and had, in fact, drawn first.

The real clincher came, however, when Dingus Murphy testified. Murphy had been hired by Elliot Sikes, owner of the leather goods store, to clean it up after closing. He had heard the first shot. Moving to the window to see what was going on, he witnessed the entire event and gave a very cogent and believable account.

When all had testified, including Duff, Judge Keller rendered his decision.

"I find this killing to be in all ways justifiable. No charges will be filed and Mr. MacCallister is free to go."

Chapter Nineteen

MacCallister, Colorado

It was as disreputable a group of men as had ever stepped down from the train in MacCallister. All were rough looking, and those who were at the depot for one reason or another moved away from them. After the horses were off-loaded, Malcolm asked the others to wait for a moment while he went inside to inquire of the stationmaster where they might find Duff MacCallister.

"Duff MacCallister?" the stationmaster said. He shook his head. "Mister, this town is full of MacCallisters, but I don't recollect any of them by the name of Duff."

"Sure you do, Pete," Toots said. "He was the man who used my cane to subdue Stripland when the brigand tried to steal Mrs. Rittenhouse's purse, don't you remember? It was written up in the paper."

"Yes, of course, I remember that. I guess I just never heard his first name, though now that I think about it, I believe I did hear that he is a cousin to our MacCallisters."

"He is a foreigner," Toots said. He looked more closely at Malcolm. "You are as well, I suspect. You sound just like him."

"Aye, we are from the same town in Scotland, Donuun in Argyllshire, it is."

Toots smiled. "Well, now I can see why you are trying to find him. It is always good to meet a fellow countryman when one is traveling in a foreign country," Toots said. He held up his cane. "I confess that I picked up the habit of carrying a cane when I was in London."

"Yes, the English do that," Malcolm said. "Now, about Duff MacCallister."

"Your friend isn't here," Toots said.

"I thought you said that he was."

"He was here, yes, but he and Falcon left a few days ago."

"Would you be for knowing where they went?"

"No, I don't have any—no, wait. I think it was in the newspaper article."

"Newspaper article?"

"Yes. The one about me."

Pete chuckled. "As I recall, Toots, your name is mentioned one time."

"That's all it needs," Toots said. "One hundred years from now someone will read that article and know that I was here to make my mark."

"Where can I get a copy of this paper?" Malcolm asked.

"I have some copies back here. They are five cents apiece."

Malcolm took a nickel from his pocket and handed it to the stationmaster, who gave him a copy of the paper.

"This is the story," Toots said, pointing to the article on the front page of the paper. "You'll find my name, Toots Nelson, in the story."

"Thank you," Malcolm said. "I shall read it with interest." He stepped back outside.

"Did you find out where he is?" Shaw asked.

"I think I'm about to," Malcolm said as he began reading.

Quick Action Foils Purse Thief

On Thursday previous, shortly after the arrival of the morning train, George Stripland, a known outlaw, attempted to ply his evil avocation upon the innocent person of Mrs. Emma Rittenhouse.

Snatching her reticule, the nefarious Mr. Stripland attempted to effect his getaway by depending upon swiftness of feet to carry him to safety. But to the detriment of Stripland, the benefit of Mrs. Rittenhouse, and the approval of the law-abiding people of MacCallister, a visitor from Scotland foiled his escape.

Duff MacCallister, a cousin to Falcon and the many other MacCallisters who reside in our fair town and valley, snatched the polished cane from the hand of Toots Nelson and with unerring accuracy, launched the stick in such a way as to cause it to become entangled in the feet of the fleeing thief. Stripland fell to the ground, whereupon Mrs. Rittenhouse's purse was recovered and the brigand taken into custody.

This newspaper has learned that Duff

MacCallister is more than a mere visitor from Scotland and has, indeed, immigrated to America. He and his cousin Falcon departed the city recently en route to Cheyenne, Wyoming Territory, where Duff MacCallister intends to homestead land and begin the life of a rancher.

Long an admirer of the MacCallisters, from the one whose statue now graces our fair city and after whom our city is named, to his noble sons: Jamie Ian, Matthew, Morgan, and Falcon, his daughters, Kathleen, Megan, and Joleen, and of course, Andrew and Rosanna, whose stars shine in a much broader universe, this editor wishes Duff much success.

"Back on the train," Malcolm ordered.

"Back on the train? What for?" Pettigrew asked. "We've just got the horses saddled, and I've had about enough train ridin'."

"You want MacCallister?"

"Yeah, I wouldn't be here if I didn't."

"He's not here," Malcolm said. "He's in a place called Cheyenne, Wyoming."

"Damn," Moran said. "That's a long way from here."

"Then best we get started," McKenna said.

"Right," Malcolm said.

"This ridin' a train around all the time is goin' to get expensive, ain't it?" Carter Hill asked.

"Why should that matter to you, since I am paying for the tickets?"

Carter Hill chuckled. "Yeah, you are, ain't you?

I just said that so's you know that we ain't none of us goin' to be payin' for it."

Cheyenne

Once more Duff and Falcon boarded a train, but this time their trip would be a short one. It was only twenty-four miles to Tracy. There they would leave the train, then go by horse for the fifty miles to Chugwater. Though they checked their baggage and their horses, Duff, as he had before, carried the bagpipes with him, for fear they would be damaged by mistreatment in the baggage car.

As soon as they were settled in their seats, Duff opened his book and began reading.

"I've seen you reading that book before. What is it about that it holds your interest so?" Falcon asked.

"It is the *Williams Pacific Tourist Guide*," Duff said. "It is filled with information about the West and all the towns you might visit. I was just reading about Chugwater. Here, read this."

Duff handed the book to Falcon, and Falcon began to read.

VALLEY OF THE CHUGWATER

The Chugwater Valley is about 100 miles long. It has been for many years a favorite locality for wintering stock, not only on account of the excellence of the grass and water, but also from the fact that the climate is mild throughout the winter. Cattle and horses thrive well all winter without hay or shelter. The broad valley is protected from strong cold winds by high walls or bluffs. The soil everywhere is fertile, and wherever the surface can be irrigated, good crops of all kinds of cereals and hardy vegetables can be raised without difficulty.

In this valley and near the source of the Chugwater, are thousands of tons of iron ore, indicating vast extent and richness which can be made easily accessible whenever desirable to construct a railroad to Montana.

"Where did you get this book?" Falcon asked after reading the passage Duff had just pointed out to him.

"I bought it at the depot in Omaha when I changed trains," Duff said. "It has been a source of invaluable information."

Falcon chuckled.

"What is wrong?"

"The railroads have a vested interest in settling the West as quickly as they can," Falcon said. "The more people there are out here, the more the demand for transportation, not only of people, but of goods."

"Would you be for suggesting now that the information is all false?"

"No, I'm not saying that it is all false," Falcon said. "I'm not even saying that it is mostly false. I am saying, though, that they are going to make all of their descriptions sound as inviting as they can."

"Is the land good for cattle or not?"

"Yes, I'm sure it is. And, I'm sure that the mountains will make the winters somewhat more bearable by blocking the worst of the north winds. But don't make the mistake of thinking that the winter will be mild because, cousin, it will not be."

"I hold no such illusion," Duff said.

Though they had only twenty-four miles to travel, they had taken passage on a local, so it made stops at Archer, Hilsdale, and Burns. At Burns, they were shunted onto a side track so the express could come through. Duff watched through the window as the express train, traveling at full speed, barreled through the little town, smoke pouring from the stack, steam streaming from the actuating cylinders, the big driver wheels spinning so fast as to be a blur.

Not until the express had passed through did the local resume its own journey, once more moving out onto the track that it shared with all the other trains. Duff knew that only precise scheduling and perfect timing allowed such a thing. He shuddered to think what would have happened if they had not been shunted off to a sidetrack at just the right time.

It was a ten-mile run from Burns to Tracy and they made that final ten miles in just over half an hour, arriving in Tracy nearly two hours after they departed Cheyenne. At Tracy, Duff and Falcon disembarked and retrieved their baggage and horses. Saddling their horses, they started north, following the map that had been provided by the land office in Cheyenne. The first creek they crossed was identified on the map as Spring Creek. Checking the area around them, they saw a mesa rising in the west. They found the mesa, which though unnamed, did appear on the map, so they were certain they were on the right course. It was late afternoon when they reached Little Bear Creek. Crossing it, they stood at the junction of Little Bear and Bear creeks. According to the map given him by the land clerk, they were now standing on Duff's land.

"What do you say we camp here for the night?" Falcon suggested. "We can go into Chugwater tomorrow."

"Cousin, I have never heard more agreeable words," Duff said as he swung down from his horse. Reaching around, he began massaging the cheeks of his butt.

Falcon chuckled. "A little sore, are you?"

"A little," Duff said. Then, he chuckled as well. "Maybe more than a little."

Back in Scotland, Duff had owned horses, and he rode frequently, not only to manage his property but also when he went into town. But the distances in Scotland were nothing like the huge, open, almost endless plains of the American West. They had come thirty miles just since leaving Tracy, and Duff had never sat a saddle this long. There had been little conversation during the ride, the silence of the ride interrupted only by the clank of the bit in the horses' teeth, the dry clack of horse hooves on the rocky ground, and the creaking of the saddle as Duff shifted his weight, trying to find a more comfortable position.

Despite the weariness of the ride, Duff had to confess that he had never seen more dramatic or inspiring scenery. To the west lay a long purple range of mountains, which the map identified as the Laramie Range. There were other elevations as well, though many were not specifically identified on the map.

They let their horses water, which both animals did eagerly. Afterward, they ground-tethered their horses and the horses immediately began to crop the grass, eating hungrily.

"That's a good sign," Falcon said. "If the horses like the grass, cattle will."

"Aye," Duff replied. "The water and the grass are good here, I think."

"Have you named your horse?"

"I've been thinking about it, and I believe I have come up with a name."

"What?"

"I'm going to call him Sky."

"After Skye, good idea," Falcon said.

"Aye, but being as the horse is male, I'll leave off the 'e' in his name. Still, it will remind me of her."

Falcon walked over to Duff's horse and rubbed it behind the ears. "Hello, Sky," he said. "How do you like your new name?"

A covey of quail flew up in front of them, and Falcon smiled. "Cousin, how do you like your quail? Grilled, or cooked in a pan?"

"I've never eaten the critters," Duff replied. "Though I've taken my share of grouse."

"Well, quail is as good eating as grouse, but they are a mite smaller. I reckon we're goin' to have to have two apiece to make a meal of them."

"How do we hunt them?"

"Easterners use shotguns," Falcon said. "But I use a pistol."

"A pistol?"

"You've never hunted grouse with a pistol?"

"I don't think I have."

"It wouldn't matter if you had. Grouse are bigger and easier to hit, so there's no sport in it. Fill your hand, cousin. Let's get us some supper."

Falcon and Duff stood about twenty yards apart, then started walking through the grass. Duff was the first person to flush a quail. With a loud fluttering of its wings it darted up in front of him. Duff fired, missed the first shot, and fired again. On his second shot he saw a little puff of feathers fly out as the bird tumbled and fell.

"Ahh, what's wrong? It took you two shots," Falcon teased. As he was calling out to Duff, one flew up in front of him, but because he was teasing Duff, his bird got away before he could shoot.

"Did I misunderstand the concept here?" Duff called back. "It was my understanding that we were to shoot the birds, not let them fly away."

Falcon laughed good-naturedly. "You got me on that . . ." Before he could finish his sentence two more birds flew up in front of him and he took them both. Even as he was looking back at Duff for affirmation, a second bird flew up in front of Duff. He got this one in one shot.

Chapter Twenty

Comfortably fed with grilled quail, and with his thirst satisfied by the cool, sweet water of Bear Creek, Duff watched the play of color on Laramie Peak as the sun dipped behind the range. The sun was gone, but a painter's palette of color filled the western sky, from gold, to pink, to purple.

"What do you think about your place?" Falcon asked.

"I think this could make me forget about Scotland," Duff replied.

The two men talked until the fire burned out, until not one glowing ember remained. Then, under a canopy of stars that was more magnificent even than they had been at sea, Duff spread out his bedroll and, to the music of the babbling creeks, the thrum of frogs, and the hooting of owls, he drifted off to sleep.

* * *

"Oh, Duff, I love it here," Skye said. *"This would have been such a wonderful place for us to raise our children."*

"Skye! What are you doing here?"

"I am here because you are here. For the rest of your life, wherever you are, that is where I will be. Was I not with you on the ship? Did you not hear my voice in the wind? Did you not see my face in the sea?"

"I miss you, Skye. I miss you so much."

"I know, my dear. But don't you know how it is here? We are never really apart. All you have to do is think of me, and I will be there, just on the other side of your memory. For you, it is reminiscence, but for me it is real. I will be reliving it."

"Skye," Duff said. *"Skye."*

"Skye?"

Duff sat up in his bedroll, reaching out into the darkness for his Skye, but she wasn't there.

For just a moment Duff felt an overwhelming sense of emptiness, then he knew he had only been dreaming. Or was it a dream? It seemed so true, so physical that it was hard to think of it as surreal. What had she told him? That she would always be just on the other side of memory?

He heard Falcon snoring and he looked over toward the other bedroll. Falcon was sound asleep, and Duff was glad. This dream was very personal and he wanted to keep it that way.

Falcon had come with Duff not only to be with him as he filed for his land but also to help him build the cabin he would need in order to "improve" his holding. So they spent the next morning and into the afternoon scouting the area, first determining the perimeters of his land, then deciding where best to build the cabin. Duff wanted it right at the confluence of the two creeks, but Falcon cautioned him that when the snow in the mountains melted, there would be a runoff and the creeks would be in freshet stage.

"You are likely to wake up one morning knee deep in water," Falcon said.

"Aye, you are right. 'Twould be a big mistake to put it right here."

They found a place on some elevated ground, at least thirty feet higher than the creek but close enough to it that it would be a ready source of water.

"When we come back from town, we will lay out the dimensions of the cabin, right here," Duff said. They didn't leave for town until early afternoon, but it did not take them long to finish their ride, for Chugwater was but ten miles from Duff's land.

Duff's initial view of the town was not all that reassuring. At first it seemed little more than a part of the topography of the land they were riding through: hillocks on the horizon, mostly the same color as the earth from which the clumps emerged. As they drew closer though, the hillocks and clumps began to take shape and he saw that they were not a part of the desert but were a town.

The buildings, consisting mostly of adobe brick and ripsawed unpainted and weathered boards sat festering in the sun. A sign as they entered the town reflected either the hyperbole of an overenthusiastic town booster or his sarcasm.

Welcome to Chugwater, W.T.

population 205

The jewel of Chugwater Valley

The town was not served by a railroad, but as they rode in, Duff saw a stagecoach sitting at the depot, the six-horse team standing quietly in their harness. The driver, with a pipe stuck in his teeth, was sitting in his seat, his feet propped up on the splashboard in front of him, his arms folded across his chest. He appeared to be grabbing a few moments of rest, totally indifferent to the depot personnel who were loading passengers' baggage on top of the coach and into the boot.

The passengers were waiting alongside the coach: three men, two women, and a child. One of the passengers who had just gotten off the stage was a woman, whom Duff guessed was in her twenties. She was quite pretty, with blond hair and blue eyes. She brushed a fall of hair from her forehead, then flashed a smile toward Duff as he rode by. He touched his hand just above his right eye and dipped his head toward her.

"Pretty, isn't she?" Falcon asked as they rode on.

Duff was surprised by the comment. He was riding behind Falcon and had no idea that Falcon had even noticed the brief and silent exchange.

"Aye," Duff said. "She is."

"What do you say we get the dust out of our mouths?" Falcon suggested, pointing toward one of the more substantial looking of the buildings. It was a saloon bearing the unlikely name of Fiddler's Green.

"Aye, 'tis a good idea, I would say," Duff replied.

Dismounting in front of the saloon, Duff and Falcon spent the first few seconds slapping themselves to get rid of the dust and raising a cloud around them.

"I'll bet you've never seen this much dust before," Falcon said.

"Not since Egypt," Duff said.

Falcon chuckled. "Yeah, now that you mention it, I suppose there is a little dust in Egypt."

There was a drunk passed out on the steps in front of the place, so Duff and Falcon moved to one side so they could step directly up onto the porch from the sun-baked ground. They pushed through the swinging bat-wing doors, and because the inside of the saloon was illuminated only by the light that streamed in through dirty windows, they had to stand there for just a second to allow their eyes to adjust. Duff noticed that Falcon had automatically moved away from the door and placed his back against the wall, so he did the same thing.

Compared to many of the saloons Duff had seen since coming west, Fiddler's Green was fairly nice looking, surprisingly so because the town seemed so remote. There was a mirror behind the bar, bracketed by shelves that were filled with scores of bottles of various kinds of liquor and spirits. A sign on the wall read: "GENTLEMEN, KINDLY USE THE SPITTOONS."

The sign was either obeyed, or the saloon proprietor was particular about cleaning, for the floors were remarkably free of any expectorations. There was a piano at the back of the room, but nobody was playing. A young boy, no more than twelve or thirteen, Duff believed, was sweeping the floor with a big push broom. That validated Duff's belief that the saloon owner was fastidious.

As Duff and Falcon approached the bar, Duff saw a brass foot rail and he made use of it, welcoming it because lifting his leg somewhat did seem to ease a bit of the ache he was feeling in his back as a result of the long ride of the last two days.

"What'll it be, gents?" the bartender asked, sliding down the bar with a towel tossed across his shoulder. The fact that the towel was relatively clean spoke volumes about the class of the establishment.

"Two beers," Falcon said.

"And I'll have the same," Duff said.

The bartender laughed. "You boys seem to have worked up a thirst."

"Long ride," Falcon said.

"Where'd you boys come from? Not that it's any of my business," he added quickly, holding up his hand to indicate that they didn't need to answer.

"I take your question as friendly discourse and have no problem with answering," Duff said. "Especially since we will be neighbors and I expect to visit your establishment from time to time. We rode up from Cheyenne."

"That is a long ride," the bartender said as he drew the four beers. Then holding the mugs by their handles, two in each hand, he set them in front of Duff and Falcon. Both men pulled out two nickels apiece, but the bartender took only one nickel from each of them.

"First beer to a first-time visitor is free," he said.

"That's very neighborly of you," Falcon said.

Both Falcon and Duff turned up their mugs and

drained them without pause. Then, both finishing about the same time, they put the empties down.

Duff wiped his mouth with the back of his hand. "That one was for thirst," he said as he picked up the second mug. "This one is for taste."

This time he took only one sip before he put the mug down again.

"Do you serve food here?" Falcon asked. "Or do we need to find a restaurant?"

"Bacon, beans, biscuits," the bartender replied. "The biscuits ought to be pretty good. I was just back in the kitchen and they are about ready to come out."

"What do you think, Duff?"

"I'm not likely to get haggis, taties, or neeps, so bacon, beans, and biscuits will do just fine."

"You're from Scotland," the bartender said with a broad smile. "I thought I recognized your accent."

"Ye have a good ear for accents," Duff said.

"Not really. But my wife's parents are from Scotland, so I am familiar with the brogue. And with haggis, taties, and neeps. Though I have to tell you, I can't stand the stuff." He stuck his hand out. "If we're going to be neighbors, as you say, we may as well get acquainted. The name is Johnson, Biff Johnson."

"Duff MacCallister," Duff replied.

"Duff? Hmm, Duff and Biff, we shouldn't have any trouble remembering our names," Biff said.

Duff chuckled, then turned toward Falcon. "This is my kinsman, Falcon."

"Yes, Falcon, I thought I recognized you," Biff said, shaking Falcon's hand.

"Do we know each other, Biff?" Falcon asked.

"It's been a while but . . ." Biff paused in mid statement. "You don't remember me, do you?"

Falcon shook his head. "I'm sorry, friend, I can't say that I do remember you."

"I'll let you think about it for a while," Biff said. "I believe it will come to you."

"Biff," Duff said. "I don't believe I've ever heard of that name."

Biff chuckled. "Not likely that you would have. My real name is Benjamin Franklin Johnson. But that was too long a handle so folks started calling me B.F., and, somehow, that became Biff. What about eats? Do you want what we have?"

"We'll take it," Falcon said. Scooping a couple of boiled eggs from the large jar that sat on the end of the bar, he handed one to Duff. Then the two of them took the boiled eggs and their beer to a nearby table. It didn't take long for one of the bar girls to approach them.

"Hello," she said, smiling her greeting at them. "My name is Lucy."

Lucy was tall, raw-boned, and full-breasted. She had wide-set, blue-gray eyes, high cheekbones, and a mouth that was almost too full. "Have I seen you two in here before?"

"Not likely, we just got into town," Falcon answered.

Duff stood up and pulled a chair out for her by way of invitation.

"My, aren't you the gentleman though?" Lucy asked. "Most of the time someone just kicks the chair out with their foot and expects me to be all grateful that they have invited me to sit down."

"*Och*, I could never do such a thing," Duff said.

"Oh, my. What a lovely accent."

Duff held the chair until Lucy was seated, then she let out a long sigh. "If you hadn't invited me to sit down I may have anyway. I've been on my feet all day."

"No big thing, you're a whore so you'll be on your back all night," a big man from the next table said. He laughed heartily at his joke, though no one else in the saloon did.

"Pig Iron, you got no call to be saying something like that," one of the other patrons said.

Duff saw the hurt reflected in Lucy's eyes and, without saying another word, he stepped over to the table of the man who had made the rude comment.

"'Tis thinking, I am, that you'll be wanting to apologize to the lady for that intemperate remark," Duff said.

"Ha! You want me to apologize to a whore? In a pig's eye, I will."

"Then I'll be asking you, with all due respect, to move to another table," Duff said.

By now all conversation in the saloon stopped as everyone looked over to see the confrontation between Duff and the man called Pig Iron.

Pig Iron stood up and smiled at Duff. It was not a smile of humor.

"I heard you tell the bartender that you was goin' to be movin' here, so you may as well learn now to mind your manners around ole Pig Iron."

Suddenly, and unexpectedly, Pig Iron took a swing at Duff, but Duff ducked under it easily. Then, with the extended fingers of his left hand, he jabbed hard at a point in the upper abdomen just below where the ribs separated. It had the effect of knocking the breath out of Pig Iron, and with a wheezing *whoosh*, he stepped back and fell into his chair gasping for breath.

"Don't worry, friend, you will regain your breath," Duff said. "Sure and I could follow that up with a blow that would render you unconscious. But I think you are uncomfortable enough as it is, and I've nae wish to make enemies so quickly in my chosen place of abode. So let us just agree that this episode is over. Do I have your agreement on that?"

Pig Iron was still struggling for breath, and because it was impossible for him to actually talk, he nodded.

"Good. Next time we meet, may I suggest a more convivial exchange?"

Pig Iron nodded again, and Duff returned to the table.

"Damn," Falcon said with a big smile. "You'll have to show me that trick sometime."

"Nothing to it," Duff said. He put his fingers on Falcon's solar plexus and made a slight jab. The jab was very gentle, but was enough to show Falcon what a hard jab would do.

"I'll have to remember that," Falcon said.

Pig Iron got up and left the saloon as Biff Johnson was bringing a drink for Lucy, even though the girl hadn't ordered.

"He must know your brand," Duff said as he paid for the drink.

"That's not hard. One glass of tea is pretty much like any other glass of tea," Lucy said with unaccustomed candidness. She picked it up and held it toward Falcon and Duff in a toast. The two men laughed and touched their beers to her glass.

"Well, 'tis an honest lass ye be about me paying whiskey prices for your tea," Duff said.

"Honey, if everything we drank really was whiskey, we'd all be drunk before mid-afternoon," Lucy explained.

"Get down!" Falcon suddenly shouted and reacting quickly and without question, Duff dived from his chair onto Lucy, knocking her down and falling on top of her. By the time they reached the floor, he heard the roar of a gunshot, not a pistol, something bigger.

Falcon fired back as Pig Iron pulled the trigger on the second barrel of his twelve-gauge shotgun. Duff saw Pig Iron grab his chest, then fall back. Looking over toward Falcon, he saw a smoking pistol in Falcon's hand.

"Annie! Oh, my God! Annie!" a woman screamed.

Duff rolled off Lucy and looked over at the table near the back of the room. One of the bar girls was lying on her back, her chest red with blood. Everyone in the room ran to her, but they saw as soon as they arrived that there was nothing they could do.

Lucy began crying quietly.

"I'm sorry, lass, I'm truly sorry," Duff said softly.

Lucy turned and leaned into him, and he held her as she cried on his shoulder. He pulled her more tightly to him, realizing that it was the first time he had held a woman, any woman, in his arms since his Skye had been killed.

Chapter Twenty-one

Pig Iron was taken back to the Davis Ranch where he worked, and there he was buried. Annie, whose real name turned out to be Matilda Ann Gilbert, was buried in the town cemetery at Chugwater. The entire town turned out for the funeral and for the burial. Biff Johnson, upon learning that Duff not only had bagpipes, but could play them, asked if he would play "Amazing Grace." Duff agreed to play it, and when he showed up at the cemetery, he was wearing the kilt of the Black Watch, complete with the *sgian dubh*, and the Victoria Cross.

The townspeople gathered around the open grave as the Reverend E. D. Sweeny of the Chugwater Church of God's Glory gave the final prayer.

"Our Lord and Savior who is ever mindful of all our sins knows that we all fall short. And it might be said of our sister, Matilda Ann Gilbert, that she fell further than most, but those who knew Matilda Ann know that if she was sinful of the flesh, she was saintly of heart. We know that it is Your way to be forgiving, oh Lord, and we ask You to be forgiving of your daughter and to receive Matilda Ann into your bosom. Amen."

Reverend Sweeny nodded at Duff and he inflated the bag. The first sound was from the drones. Then, fingering the chanter, Duff began playing the haunting tune, the steady hum of the drones providing a mournful sound to underscore the high skirling of the melody itself. It was beautifully played, and by the time he finished, there were many who were weeping.

After the interment, Falcon and Duff, who was still wearing his kilts, invited Lucy to have lunch with them.

"If we can have it at Fiddler's Green," she said. "I know that Biff had the cook do something special today to honor Annie."

"That's fine with me," Falcon replied. "Duff?"

"Aye. I can think of no place I'd rather be right now," he said.

When they returned to Fiddler's Green, it was draped in black bunting. A sign on the front said, "IN MEMORIAM, MALTILDA ANN GILBERT, OUR ANNIE."

Biff brought the meal to the table: roast beef, mashed potatoes, green beans, and freshly baked bread. When Duff and Falcon attempted to pay for it, Biff held out his hand and shook his head.

"No. This is for Annie," he said. "But, if you don't mind, I'll be taking my dinner with you as well."

"We don't mind at all," Duff said. "'Tis welcome company you'll be."

"I left my plate on the bar. I didn't want to presume," Biff said. He stepped back to the bar, then returned with his own plate.

"Tell me, Biff, why do you call this place Fiddler's Green? Have you fiddlers who play here from time to time?" Duff asked.

"Colonel MacCallister, suppose you tell him about Fiddler's Green. I know you know what it means."

"Colonel MacCallister?" Falcon looked across the table at Biff for a moment, then he smiled and snapped his fingers. "You are Sergeant Johnson! You were with Custer at Ft. Lincoln!"

Biff smiled and nodded his head. "I knew you would remember it," he said. "I was in D troop with Benteen."

"No wonder you call this place Fiddler's Green."

"I still don't know what it means," Duff said.

"It's something the cavalrymen believe," Falcon said. "Anyone who has ever heard the bugle call 'Boots and Saddles' will, when they die, go to a cool, shady place by a stream of sweet water. There, they will see all the other cavalrymen who have gone before them, and they will greet those who come after them as they await the final judgment. That place is called Fiddler's Green."

"Do they really believe that?" Lucy asked.

"Why not?" Falcon replied. "If heaven is whatever you want it to be, who is to say that cavalrymen wouldn't want to be with their own kind?"

"I like the idea," Duff said.

"Many is the time we went into battle with the promise to a friend to be waiting at Fiddler's Green," Biff Johnson said. "I've many friends there now, waiting for me, and I've no doubt but that Custer and his brother Tom and Captains Calhoun and Keogh are there now."

"And Isaiah Dorman," Falcon added.

"Custer's black scout," Biff said. "That's right; he was a friend of yours, wasn't he?"

"He was indeed."

"'Tis a good thing to hold on to," Duff said. "I've many friends of my own who were killed in battle. Perhaps they have found their way there as well."

"If they were good men, warriors who died in battle, you need have no doubt about it. My lads will invite them over, to sit and visit," Biff said.

"I hope they behave like gentlemen when they see Annie," Lucy said.

"You need not trouble yourself, Lucy," Biff said. "All in Fiddler's Green are gentlemen."

"Tell me what you knew about the lass we buried this morning," Duff said.

Biff shook his head. "I'm sorry to say that I know very little about her. She came into town on the stagecoach one day, came straight here from the stage depot, and asked me for a job. She was attractive and had a good sense of humor. The men liked her. I was glad to see that the whole town turned out for her funeral, but I wasn't all that surprised. We are very isolated out here, and to a degree each one of us is dependent upon the other."

"She was from Memphis," Lucy said. "She had married into one of the wealthiest families there, but she was raped one night while her husband was out drinking. The rapist was one of her husband's friends, but her husband blamed her and said he couldn't live with her anymore because she was soiled. So she decided that if she was going to have the name, she would have the game. She came here with the specific intention of becoming a soiled dove."

"I thought it might be something like that," Biff said. "All of you girls had lives before you came here. I've never tried to find out, because I've always thought that you deserved some privacy."

"We know that, Mr. Johnson. And we appreciate you respecting us in that way."

After they finished eating, Duff and Falcon went down to the R. W. Guthrie Lumber and Building Supplies Company. There, they were met by the owner, a short, stout man with a round face and a somewhat oversized nose. Guthrie took Duff and Falcon out into his lumberyard to show them what he had.

"Yes, sir," he said. "I've got everything you might need to build a house, from the studding, to the outside planking, to the inside walls and floor. I've got the roof trusses, the roof shingles, doors, and windows. I've got all the nails you will need."

"That is good to know," Duff said.

"I even have some building plans if you would like to see them."

"I've no wish for something grand. I want to build a one-room cabin."

"How large?"

"It need not be too large," Duff said.

"We have plans for one that is fifteen by twenty feet. That will give you three hundred square feet of living space. How does that sound to you?"

"It sounds just right," Duff said.

"Good, then we'll start gathering up what you need. Where will you be building this cabin?"

"On my ranch, or what is going to be my ranch," Duff said. "It is ten miles south of town at the junction between the Bear and the Little Bear creeks."

Guthrie looked surprised. "Did you say at the junction of the Bear and Little Bear? You are really going to try and settle there, are you?"

"Try? What do you mean by try?"

"Nothing, nothing at all," Guthrie said. "That's really quite a nice piece of land out there. It's just that . . ."

"Just that what?"

"Well, sir, that's where the Little Horse mine was."

"Little Horse mine?"

"Yes, it is an old, abandoned gold mine that was dug by the Spanish more'n a hunnert years ago. There was stories told about it. Some Cheyenne Injuns brought in some gold nuggets to a trading post that they say had been in the tribe for a long time. It was supposed to have been played out, but about ten, maybe fifteen years ago it is said that a man named Elmer Gleason found gold in the mine. He showed up in Denver with a bagful of gold nuggets tryin' to sell the mine, but he didn't have no proof that he had got the gold at the Little Horse Mine. There's all kinds of stories as to where he might have got the gold; some say he picked it up in the Black Hills, some say he got it California during the gold rush of forty-nine. At any rate, nobody bought the mine and Gleason never come back. There don't nobody know if he is dead or alive, 'cause there ain't nobody heard anything from or about him since that time. But most folks think maybe he come back to the mine and died. They never found him, but they found a mule, its bones picked clean by buzzards and such. They figure he was kilt, and the critters dragged his bones off."

"Killed? By who?" Duff asked.

"Don't nobody know that," Guthrie said. "And that's part of the mystery, 'cause you see, there was a couple of fellas, Lonnie Post and Sam Hodges, who went out there to see if there was any gold to be found, and the next thing you know, both of them turned up dead.

"By that time folks was gettin' just plumb skittish about goin' out there, gold mine or no gold mine. But Arnold Brown said the whole thing was foolish, and if there was some gold out there, he intended to go find it."

"Don't tell me," Duff said. "Mr. Brown turned up dead as well."

"Don't nobody know. Didn't find a skeleton or nothin' like that, but ain't nobody ever heard from him since then. And there ain't nobody gone out there since. They say the place is hainted. 'Course, I ain't sayin' that I believe in haints, you understand. But that is what they say. Some say it wasn't the Spanish, that it was Injuns that first found the gold, but they was all kilt off by white men who wanted the gold for themselves. But what happened is, after the Injuns was all kilt, they become ghosts, and now they haint the mine and they kill any white man who comes around tryin' to find the gold. Now, mind, I don't believe none of that. I'm just tellin' you what folks says about it."

"Where is this mine, anyway? We didn't see anything that looked like a mine," Falcon said.

"Didn't you say you was betwixt the Bear and the Little Bear creeks?" Guthrie asked.

"Yes."

"Well, sir, that mine is just south of the Bear in a butte that you see there. The butte is called Little Horse Butte. It ain't all that high, a hunnert feet or so, and it's flat as a table on top."

"Aye, I remember seeing that," Duff said.

"The mine is dug into the west end of that butte. You can't see it from a distance I'm told, but if you get right up close, you can see it real clear."

"That's quite an interesting tale," Duff said.

"But it ain't goin' to stop you from goin' out there, is it?" Guthrie asked.

"No, sir."

Guthrie chuckled. "I didn't think it would scare you away. I heard how you handled Pig Iron, and then how he come back in blazin' away with his shotgun. And I heard how you kilt him, Mr. Mac-Callister," he said to Falcon.

"I'm afraid I had no choice," Falcon said.

"Don't get me wrong, Mr. MacCallister. I sure ain't puttin' no blame on you. They ain't likely to be nobody that'll blame you for it. Truth to tell, and near 'bout ever'one will say this, Chugwater Valley is a heap better off without him. But, I know you didn't come in here for all this palaverin'," Guthrie said. "You decided what you want to do, Mr. MacCallister?"

"How much will it cost me to buy enough material to build a cabin?" Duff asked.

"You're wantin' the one that's fifteen by twenty?"

"Yes."

"Would you be wantin' a front porch to it? And roof over it, so's you can sit in the afternoon out of the hot sun?"

"That might be nice," Duff said.

"I can sell you ever'thin' you are goin' to need, supplies and tools, and I'll ship it out there for you, too—it's goin' to take two wagons at least—for . . ."—Guthrie began figuring on a piece of paper—"a grand total of one hunnert and three dollars and fifty cents," he said.

"It will take two wagons?"

"Yes, sir, I think so. We might be able to get it all on one wagon, but it would put quite a strain on the wagon and the team."

"No, two wagons are fine. But I shall have some additional purchases to make and 'tis wondering I am if there might be a little room on one of the wagons."

"If we use two wagons, there will be plenty of room," Guthrie said. "You'll be goin' over to the mercantile, I take it, so just tell Fred, he's the owner, Fred Matthews, just tell him to get in touch with me. I'll see to it that your stuff gets on one of the wagons."

"Thank you. When I make my additional purchases, I shall so inform the merchant," Duff said.

Reaching into his pocket, Duff pulled out a wad of money, then began counting it out.

"How soon can you get the material out to my site?" he asked.

"I can have it all out there by noon tomorrow," Guthrie replied.

"Good. Please do so."

"Yes, sir," Guthrie said as he picked up the money. "It has been a pleasure doing business with you."

"I have fifty cents in change," Duff said.

"Yes, sir, don't you worry, I wasn't goin' to forget that."

From the Guthrie Lumber and Building Supply, they went to the Chugwater Mercantile, a large store that had a sign out front boasting that they sold "GOODS FOR ALL MANKIND."

"You're the fella that played the music for Annie's funeral, aren't you?" Fred Matthews, the proprietor said.

"Aye."

"That was some kind of pretty, real mournful, like it should be for a funeral. That instrument you used, a bagpipe?"

"Bagpipes, though often we just call it pipes."

"Yes, sir, well, I've heard of them things, but this is the first time I ever actually heard one played. Has kind of a strange sound to it. Don't get me wrong, it's real pretty, but it is kind of strange sounding."

"I agree that the music the pipes make is quite unique."

"Unique. Yes, sir, I reckon that's what I'd call it, too. Unique."

Here, Duff bought the things he would need to furnish the house. He bought a potbellied wood-burning iron stove that would serve both for warmth and as a cookstove. He bought an iron skillet, two pots, a coffeepot, a water bucket and a dipper, and two plates, two cups, and two sets of flatware. He also bought a washbasin, a small table, two chairs to go with the table, and a rocking chair and footstool. Finally, he bought a Winchester .44-40 lever action repeating rifle, six boxes of .44-40 cartridges, a double-barreled Greener shotgun, and six boxes of twelve-gauge shotgun shells.

"Would you be for having any .47-caliber ammunition?" Duff asked.

Fred Matthews stroked his chin for a moment. "Mister, I not only don't have any of that, I don't think I've ever even heard of .47 caliber. Don't know as they make such a thing."

Duff pulled a round from one of the bullet loops on his belt and showed it to Matthews. "This is a .47-caliber bullet," he said.

"What sort of gun would use such a bullet?" Matthews asked.

Duff pulled his pistol and showed it to him. "This is an Enfield Mark 1," he said. "I'm told that it is the weapon of choice for the Royal Canadian Mounted Police."

"Is it now? The Royal Canadian Mounted Police? Well, in that case, I expect I'll be able to find some. I don't have it now, but I will put some on order for you."

"You have my gratitude, sir."

"How do you plan to get everything out to your place?" Matthews asked.

"Tomorrow Mr. Guthrie will be taking all the building supplies I need out to my place. He has agreed to let me ship additional purchases on one of his wagons."

"Fine, I'll see R.W. and get it all set up with him."

"I'll be taking the rifle and the shotgun with me," Duff said.

"Of course."

While Duff was busy making his purchases at the mercantile, Falcon had been over at the general store, buying food they would need over the next several days. He came out of the store with two large cloth bags that he draped over his horse, just forward of Lightning's saddle.

"Did you get everything all taken care of?" Falcon asked.

"Everything will be delivered tomorrow," Duff said.

"Well, then all we have to do is ride out there and wait for it."

They had ridden for at least two miles before Falcon brought it up. "Are you going to do it?" he asked.

"Am I going to do what?"

"I think you know what I'm talking about. I just want to know if you are going to do it."

"You are talking about the mine, aren't you? The gold mine."

"Yes, I'm talking about the gold mine. Are you going to check it out?"

"I thought I might."

Falcon laughed out loud. "Well, I must say, you would have disappointed me if you had said otherwise."

"Do you think there is anything there?" Duff asked.

"Now I don't know what you are talking about," Falcon replied. "By anything there, are you talking about ghosts? Or are you talking about gold?"

"I'm talking about the gold."

"What about the ghosts?"

"Let them get their own gold," Duff said.

Falcon laughed.

They made the ride from town in just over half an hour. Then, after taking care of the horses and the supplies they brought with them, they used the cabin plans Guthrie had given them and began laying out the outline where the house would be. They did that by use of the engineering stakes and string Duff had also purchased at Guthrie's Building Supply.

By sundown, the cabin was well laid out, including the place where the porch would be. They cooked bacon over an open fire and had that with a can of beans for their supper. By then it was too late to check out the mine, and Duff didn't want to go to the mine the next day either, because he didn't want to take a chance on being gone when his supplies and building materials were delivered.

It had been a tiring day, and Duff was asleep within minutes of stretching out on his bedroll. Falcon was asleep just as quickly, and added to the sounds of the night creatures were the soft snores of the two sleeping men.

Chapter Twenty-two

Cheyenne

The Bucket of Blood Saloon was the least attractive of all of Cheyenne's saloons. The bar consisted of nothing but boards stretched across two upright and empty beer barrels. It served only two types of drink, beer and a local whiskey that got its color and taste from rusty nails. The women who worked there were on the bottom rung of their profession, tired and scarred by rough treatment and dissipation.

The Bucket of Blood drew habitual drunks and the denizens of the town, and it was here that Malcolm and the men who were with him had gathered. They came because it was cheap and also because nine men traveling together would garner less attention here than they would in one of the more socially acceptable saloons. Malcolm was ill at ease here. He found the bad whiskey, unsightly interior, and scarred women to be off-putting.

"How much money do you have?" Pettigrew

asked Malcolm. The men were gathered around two tables in the back of the Bucket Of Blood saloon.

The question not only surprised Malcolm, he was a little frightened by it.

"Why do you ask?"

"You're spendin' a lot of money for train tickets and the like. The reason I ask is I know how we can pick up some more money."

"How?" Moran asked.

"By goin' to where the money is."

"Pettigrew, you ain't makin' no sense a'tall," Carter Hill said. "What do you mean, by goin' to where the money is?"

"Well think about it, Hill. Where do folks keep their money?"

"A bank," McKenna said. "You're talkin' about holdin' up a bank, ain't you?"

"Finally figured it out, did you? Yeah, I'm talkin' about holdin' up a bank. As long as we've got this many people together, it would be an easy thing to rob a bank."

"We haven't gathered together to rob a bank," Malcolm said.

"I know what we have come together for," Pettigrew said. "I'm just saying that it would be a shame not to take advantage of us all bein' together like this."

"Pettigrew is right," Johnny Hill said. "With this many men, there couldn't no bank in the country stop us from just walkin' in and cleanin' it out."

"I am an officer of the law," Malcolm said. "How can you expect me to go along with something like this?"

"You ain't a officer of the law in this country," McKenna said.

"And unless I misunderstood you, you are plannin' on killin' this here Duff MacCallister fella when you find him," Carter Hill said. "That will be against the law."

"Here's the thing, Malcolm. We're goin' to hold up this bank and you can be with us and share in the money, or you can stay out of it and don't get anythin' at all," Pettigrew said.

"I've never held up a bank before. I wouldn't have any idea how one would go about doing such a thing."

"Hell, there ain't nothin' to it," Pettigrew said. "All we got to do is keep a few men posted outside while the rest of us go inside and tell the teller to empty the safe."

Malcolm drummed his fingers on the top of the table for a moment. "How much money is one likely to get in such a thing?"

"In a town like this, if we didn't come away with ten thousand dollars I'd be some surprised," Pettigrew said.

"Ten thousand dollars?"

"At least."

"If we hold up the bank, we will have to make a rapid exit from town, will we not?"

Pettigrew chuckled. "Only if you don't want to get strung up," he said.

"All right, I'll go along with it on one condition. We came here to find MacCallister. If we are required to make a hasty exit, we are not likely to find out anything about him. I think we should make sufficient inquiries to satisfy our quest before we engage in anything like robbing a bank."

"That ain't goin' to be no problem," Pettigrew

said. "We're goin' to have to check out the bank first anyway. Goin' into a bank to hold it up before you know what you are gettin' yourself into ain't that smart of a move anyhow."

"Ten thousand dollars," Malcolm said. He smiled. "All right, gentlemen, you may consider me a participant in this endeavor."

Chugwater Valley

It was early afternoon by the time the two wagons arrived at the place Duff had chosen to build his cabin. As there were two men on each wagon, it did not take long for Duff, Falcon, and the four freight men to unload all the material. Less than an hour after they arrived, all the lumber, tools, and furnishings were lying on the ground near the staked-out area for the cabin, and the wagons, empty now, were heading back to Chugwater.

Both Falcon and Duff had done building before, so they worked well together, getting the floor down. After the floor was down, they placed the support posts at the four corners, then additional posts between the corners until, finally, they had the basic part of the house framed up. By that time it was dark, so they spent one more night under the stars, though they promised each other that by the next night they would be inside.

The next morning they had the roof trusses up by mid morning, and two of the walls closed in by noon.

"Here's an idea," Duff posed. "The floor is down.

Let's move all this stuff in now and finish building around it."

"Good idea," Falcon replied. "Where do you want the stove? We'll need to know so we know where to vent the chimney through."

"Right here, right in the middle," Duff said. "I believe this to be the most efficient location for providing heat this winter."

"You are probably right," Falcon said.

The stove was very heavy, but both Duff and Falcon were strong men and as all the walls had not been erected, they did not have too much difficulty in getting the stove in position.

Once everything was inside, they resumed work on building the cabin. As they had promised each other, they spent the night inside, throwing their bedrolls out on the floor. They were finished with everything but the porch. The next morning, they added the porch.

"Now, Duff, you have a ranch," Falcon said as the two men sat on the front porch, eating a meal of bacon and fry-bread (Falcon showed Duff how to make it), and drinking coffee. "What are you going to name it?"

"I have been giving that some thought," Duff said. "I think I will call it Sky Meadow."

"An outstanding name," Falcon said. "Yes, I think it fits the place."

"However, it is my understanding that in order to be a rancher one must have livestock," Duff said. "And as you may have noticed"—Duff took in the wide expanse of his property with a sweep of his hand—"I have no livestock."

"Ahh, what do you want a bunch of cows for

anyway? They are ignorant brutes and they just tie you down," Falcon said.

Duff laughed. "Perhaps you have a point. But one can scarcely be a rancher without livestock. How am I to acquire the cattle I shall need?"

"Don't worry about it. I can lend you enough money to get started," Falcon said. "You can pay me back when you can."

"You have already been too generous with your time, Falcon. I have no intention of making a demand on your finances as well."

"Cousin, I don't want you to take this wrong because it isn't that you are not trustworthy," Falcon said, "but I don't think you are going to find a bank that will lend you the money. If you are indeed going to start ranching you will, as you have pointed out, need cattle, and in order to buy cattle you will need money. Where else will you get it, if not from me?"

"Good question. However, there may be a solution, if . . ." Duff paused in mid-sentence, held up his finger and smiled at Falcon.

"If there is gold in the mine," Falcon said, completing the sentence for him. "You do know that it is highly unlikely that there is really anything there. It is probably all just a story and we'll just be wasting our time."

"Exactly. Shall we go have a look?"

Falcon chuckled. "Yeah, but we had better take a lantern," Falcon said. "You don't have to go very far down into one of those things before it gets so dark you can't see your hand in front of your face."

"A lantern and a pickaxe," Duff said.

"Aye, sure'n 'twould be a shame to go into the

mine with nae a pickaxe," Falcon said, mimicking Duff's accent.

"You'd better stick to American English," Duff said, laughing. "And 'tis a shame, too. Our mutual grandfather would be rolling in his grave now to hear how his descendants have brutalized the mother tongue."

It took half an hour to find the mine entrance because it was shielded by an outgrowth of sagebrush. But when they did find the opening, they were gratified to see that it was tall enough and wide enough to allow both of them to enter while fully erect. Both men were carrying full canteens. In addition, Duff was carrying a lantern and a pick. They got no more than one hundred feet into the mine before it became dark enough that it was necessary to light the lantern.

The lantern threw out a wide bubble of golden light that reflected back from the walls and showed a long, black tunnel before them. The two men walked for several minutes, then Duff called for them to stop.

"What is it?" Falcon asked.

Duff walked over to the wall and held up the lantern. Something in the wall glittered back in the light.

"I'm going to pick here for a while and see what turns up," Duff said.

Setting the lantern down, Duff began using the pickaxe on the wall. Each time he struck, large chunks of shale would tumble down from the wall. As he continued to strike at the wall, the tailings piled up on the floor of the mine, and Falcon got on his knees to sift through them, looking for any sign of color.

"Have you found anything?" Duff asked.

"No, not yet. Wait, there might be something here. . . ."

Duff turned to look at Falcon and when he did he saw a frightening apparition behind him. A two-legged creature covered with hair and with wild eyes was holding a large rock in both hands, about to bring it crashing down on Falcon's head.

"Look out!" Duff yelled and, reacting quickly, Falcon leaped to one side as, with a loud scream, the creature brought the rock down.

Thanks to Duff's warning the rock missed Falcon, but the creature lifted it over his head again, and with gleaming red eyes came toward Duff. Duff used the head of the pickaxe to knock the rock out of the creature's hands. With another bloodcurdling scream, the creature turned and ran, disappearing into the dark tunnel of the mine as if able to see in the dark.

"Are you all right?" Duff asked.

"Yes," Falcon said, standing up and brushing himself off.

"What on earth was that?" Duff asked.

"I don't know. Maybe Mr. Guthrie's haint?" Falcon replied.

"'Twas no ghost, for it was something physical."

"A bear, maybe?"

"I don't know about American bears, but I've never seen a bear in Europe that could use his hands like this one did."

"Whatever it was, I think we know what happened to the men who were killed here," Falcon said.

"Aye, that's for certain," Duff replied.

"Are you going to continue to look for gold?"

"Sure'n you aren't thinking I'm going to be frightened off by a ghost, are you? Especially since it isn't a ghost."

"If we are going to continue to work in here, I have an idea," Falcon said.

"What?"

"We have some string and engineering stakes left over from building the house. We can bring them here. . . ."

"Aye, and stretch a tripwire across the passage to give us warning when the beast returns," Duff said. "'Tis good thinking, cousin. We've already shown that, whatever or whoever it is, it can be fought off. We need only to be alerted to its presence."

Cheyenne

When Malcolm stepped into the land clerk's office, he saw a wall that was covered with a huge map of Laramie County, Wyoming. Beneath the map were several cabinets, filled with drawers. The land clerk, a very thin man with white hair and glasses, was sitting at a table behind the counter that separated his area from the front.

"Yes, sir, what can I do you for?" the land clerk asked, chuckling at his whimsical transposing of the words.

"My name is Rab Malcolm. I was told by my kinsman that he would be filing on some land here in Wyoming, and it is my hope that you would have a record of such."

"Well, if he filed here I will have a record," the land clerk replied. "I keep a very tidy office and can tell you the name of everyone who has filed for land in Laramie Country for the last six years. What would be the name?"

"MacCallister. Duff MacCallister."

"Ah, yes, I should have known by your accent. You sound just like him. And you are in luck, he did indeed file here a short time ago."

The clerk walked back to the long row of cabinets, opened one of the long drawers, and pulled it out.

"MacCallister," he said, speaking to himself. "Hmm, Kelly, Kilmer, Logan, Lynch, Mabry—here it is. MacCallister."

The clerk pulled the card out and looked at it. "Yes, he applied for Section 280417."

"And where would that be?"

"I'm sorry. I just gave you the map coordinates and for sure it would mean little to you if you didn't have a map. If you would step back here, I'll show you where it is."

"Thank you," Malcolm said as he pushed through the little swinging half-door that stretched between two sections of the counter and walked back to the map.

"It's about fifty miles north of here, at this point, where Bear and Little Bear Creek join. Do you see?"

"Aye, and would ye be for having a smaller map available that I could use?"

"Are you filing for land? Because we provide maps, free gratis, for anyone who is applying for land."

"I'll not be applying for land," Malcolm said.

"In that case, I'll have to charge you fifteen cents for the map."

"I'll take it."

Chapter Twenty-three

New York—Castle Garden Immigration

The steamship *Neckar* was built by Caird & Co, Greenock, Scotland, for the White Star Lines, and was launched on the 11th of October 1873. It displaced 3,122 tons; had a straight bow, 1 funnel, 2 masts; iron construction, and screw propulsion. The service speed was 16 knots, and the ship had accommodations for 144 passengers in first class, 68 in second class, and 502 in steerage. Angus Somerled, who was no longer the sheriff of Argyllshire County, took his passage in second class, which lacked some of the amenities of first class, but was far superior to steerage, wherein the passengers were loaded like cattle.

After two weeks in transit, the *Neckar* was met by two tugboats that nudged the big ship into anchorage at an island off the southwest tip of Manhattan Island. His first view of the United States was a huge round building, so large that nothing could be seen beyond it. This was Castle Garden, and as he followed the other passengers down the gangplank, he saw that the roped-off walkway led all the passengers through a great double door over which hung the sign: UNITED STATES IMMIGRATION.

Once inside, to Somerled's annoyance, there was an area marked specifically for first-class passengers. The remaining area had a sign that said: SECOND CLASS AND STEERAGE.

Somerled greatly resented being herded in with all the steerage passengers, many of whom had not bathed for the two weeks onboard the ship and now smelled of vomit and body odor. No doubt the vermin were coming to America, certain that they would find fame and fortune in the new country. Somerled wanted to tell them that if they were paupers in Europe, they would be paupers in America.

A small boy, clutching the hand of his mother, whose face was drawn and tired from two weeks in steerage, was looking at Somerled.

"Boy, what are you staring at?" Somerled barked in a voice that was more severe than normal because of his frustration over being processed with the unwashed minions of steerage.

Tears sprang to the boy's eyes and he turned toward his mother, wrapping his arms around her leg and burying his face in her gray, shapeless dress.

"Sir, I'm sure he meant no harm. He is just a young child."

"Teach him some manners," Somerled said, roughly.

A moment later, Somerled was in customs and his luggage was being gone through. The customs officer saw a pistol, and looked up at Somerled.

"I don't know what you have read, sir, but not

all Americans are Wild West cowboys. And most of those who do own guns do not carry them."

"I've no intention of carryin' the weapon," Somerled said, though his response was a lie. He had every intention of carrying his pistol.

The customs officer nodded, then searched through the rest of the luggage to make certain Somerled was not bringing anything into the country that might violate customs or require a tax. After customs, the immigrants were sent to various areas for processing, depending upon their language.

Somerled stood in line at the ENGLISH ONLY counter until he reached the front.

"Your name?"

"Somerled. Angus Somerled."

"John, this one is for you. Another Irishman," the clerk called to one of the other men.

"I'll have you know, sir, that I am not Irish," Somerled said with as much dignity as he could muster. "I am Scot."

"Irish, Scot, it is all the same to me," the clerk said. "I handle only people from England. Mr. Patterson will take care of you."

Somerled moved over to the next space, where a man wearing a green visor looked up at him.

"Where are you from?"

"Scotland, Donuun in Argyllshire."

"Were you gainfully employed while you were in Scotland?"

"Aye, and was a man of respect, too."

"What was your occupation there?"

"Why do you need to know?"

"We can't have people in our country who are

unable to take care of themselves. We have to know that you can find gainful employment."

"I was the sheriff."

"Ah. Well, we have a lot of Irish in the police force. I suppose you could get a job there."

"I don't intend to stay here. I am in pursuit of a criminal who fled to the United States."

"What is the criminal's name? If he came through Castle Garden, perhaps we will have a record of him."

"His name is Duff MacCallister."

"Did he come this year?"

"Aye. 'Twas near three months ago now."

The clerk turned the pages in the large ledger book and ran his fingers down a list of names. Finally he shook his head.

"I've no record of him coming through here."

"'Tis my thinking that he would not have come through here."

"That's impossible. If he came to America, he had to come through here."

"Do all ships stop here?"

"All ships that come to New York do. That is, all passenger ships. There is no such requirement for merchant vessels."

"What is Colorado?" Somerled asked.

"Do you mean where is Colorado?"

"Where and what? Is it a city?"

The immigration clerk laughed. "You people come to America and you know nothing about us. Colorado is a state. It is in the western part of America, many miles from here."

"How would one go about getting there?"

"Well, you don't just go to a state. You must

choose a town or city within the state. For example, Denver."

"Denver is in Colorado?"

"It is."

"What sort of conveyance goes to Denver? Does one reach it by boat?"

"Ha! One would have a most difficult time reaching it by boat," the clerk said. "Seeing as there is no water that goes there."

"Then how does one reach it?"

"By train, of course. Unless you want to go by wagon or coach, but if you choose to go that way, you will be an awfully long time in transit. Your best move would be to go to Grand Central Station and secure your tickets there."

"Tickets?" Somerled asked. "You mean I must purchase more than one ticket?"

"Yes. There isn't one train line that makes the entire trip, so you will have to purchase tickets for every train. But you can buy all you need at Grand Central, which will give you a ticket on every rail service between here and Denver."

"Thank you."

"Next," the clerk called.

Cheyenne

In order to more closely examine the bank, Rab Malcolm stepped up to the teller's window with five hundred and fifty-seven dollars in his hand, which was all the money he had remaining from the amount that had been sent to him by Somerled.

"Yes, sir?" the teller said, smiling obsequiously at him.

"My good man, I should like to make a deposit in your bank." Malcolm had never in his life used the term "my good man," but he had heard some of the wealthier lairds use it, and he thought that it, along with his natural accent, would impress the teller.

"Yes, sir, we would be glad to open an account for you," the teller replied. He pulled a book of forms over to him, picked up a pen and started to write. "What is your name, sir?"

"The name is Malcolm. Rab Malcolm." Almost as soon as Malcolm told him his name, he realized that he should not have given it. But he was not known here, so it might be all right. It wasn't something he was going to worry about.

"And how much money do you wish to deposit?"

"Here, let's not be in such a hurry," Malcolm said.

The teller looked up from the book of deposit slips with a questioning expression.

"I beg your pardon, sir? Is something wrong?"

"How safe is this bank? What I'm asking is, suppose I put my money in here and someone robs the bank?"

The bank teller laughed. "Oh, sir, I assure you, you will never have to worry about anything like that happening."

"Oh? Why not?"

"Mr. Snellgrove?" the teller called.

A rather rotund man with a bald head, round face, pudgy nose, and eyes enlarged by the glasses he was wearing looked up at the call. Like the bank teller, he was wearing a three-piece suit.

"Yes, Mr. Lisenby?" Snellgrove asked.

"This gentleman wants to make a deposit with us."

"Very good," Snellgrove said. "I am sure you will be pleased with our bank, sir. All of our customers are."

"I'd like you to show me around," Malcolm said. "I want to see just how safe my money would be in here."

"Oh, it will be quite safe, I assure you."

"Aye, but I'm from Scotland, and if you know anythin' about we Scots, it is that we are very frugal people with our money. Could you show me some of the features that you say will keep my money safe?"

"I would be glad to. Suppose you step back here," Snellgrove invited as he reached down and released a latch that opened the Dutch door to allow Malcolm access to the back part of the bank. "Right this way."

Snellgrove led Malcolm to the side, where sat a very large, heavy-looking, steel safe.

"It is called an American Standard," Snellgrove explained, standing proudly in front of the big safe. The heavy door was painted light green, while the trim and lettering were in gold. "The door is four-inch-thick steel, and it is locked by four steel bars, each two inches in diameter. In addition, the tumblers are absolutely silent so that no one can pick the lock."

"Could one breach the door with dynamite?" Malcolm asked.

Snellgrove laughed. "If someone attempted to blast the vault open with dynamite all they would do is destroy the building. The safe would remain impervious."

"That must be a very strong safe," Malcolm said.

"It has to be strong," Snellgrove replied. "As of this morning we have on deposit." He paused and called over to Lisenby, "Exactly how much money do we have?"

"Eighteen thousand, nine hundred, twenty-seven dollars, and forty-six cents," Lisenby replied with a smirk of pride that he could quote to the penny the amount of money deposited with the Cheyenne Cattlemen's Bank and Trust.

"That's a lot of money," Malcolm said.

"Yes, it is. And now, how much money will you be depositing with us?" Snellgrove asked.

"I don't know, I need to think this over for a while," Malcolm replied.

Snellgrove smiled. "Very well, Mister—uh— I don't think I heard your name."

"Malcolm," Lisenby said. "His name is Rab Malcolm."

"Mr. Malcolm, once you consider the security of our bank, I'm sure you will wish to become a customer," Snellgrove said.

"Thank you for the information," Malcolm said. "I will make my decision shortly as to whether or not I will entrust my funds to your establishment."

Sky Meadow

Duff and Falcon had been working the mine for three days, and though they had not made a significant find, they had found enough color in the tailings to make their effort worthwhile. Last night, examining the nuggets they had recovered, Falcon estimated that they had at least one hundred dollars' worth of gold.

"If we keep getting these results, you will get enough money to build your herd," Falcon said.

"Aye, and that is my intention," Duff replied.

The creature that had appeared on their first day in the mine did not reappear until late on their third day. This time, though, they were ready because they heard it when something hit the tripwire causing the empty tin cans to rattle.

"Did you hear?" Falcon asked.

"Aye."

"Get ready."

Duff picked up the lantern and moved it about fifty feet back toward the entrance. Doing so left them in the dark, but that was part of their plan. Falcon had a looped rope ready, and when the creature passed them, Falcon stepped out behind, then threw the rope out in a wide loop. The loop fell down over the creature and Falcon jerked the rope back, tightening the loop, which had the effect of securing the creature's arms by its side.

The creature let out a bloodcurdling scream as Duff leaped out behind him to knock him down. The creature struggled, but Duff and Falcon were too strong, and within a moment Falcon had looped the rope around him enough times to have both his arms and legs restricted. The creature continued to scream for the whole time.

"Get the lantern, Duff, let's see what we have here," Falcon said.

Duff hurried back to get the lantern. Then he returned and held it up as Falcon turned the creature over.

"I'll be. It's a man," Falcon said.

The man's hair hung down to his waist and he had a full beard. He was wearing clothes made of wolf skin and his fingernails were long and curled.

"Of course, I'm a man! What did you think I would be?" the man replied in a gravelly voice. "Turn me loose!"

"So you can try to kill us again?" Falcon asked.

"I wasn't tryin' to kill you. I was tryin' to scare you away."

"Like the three men you killed?"

"I only kilt two."

"There were three, Elmer Gleason, Lonnie Post, and Sam Hodges."

"Is that what their names was? They never told me."

"Why did you kill them?"

"I kilt 'em 'cause they tried to kill me. They wanted me to show 'em where the gold was, and when I wouldn't do it, they pointed a gun at me and said they was goin' to shoot me. I got away from 'em, and when they come after me, I kilt 'em. Then I dragged their bodies outside as a warnin' to anyone else as might come around."

"What about Elmer Gleason? Did he try to kill you, too?"

The man laughed, a high-pitched, insane cackling laugh. Then he stopped laughing and stared at Duff and Falcon, his eyes gleaming in the light of the lantern. "What are you doin' here?" he asked. "You got no right in here. This is my home."

"Sure'n you aren't for sayin' you live here, in this mine, are you?" Duff asked.

"Yes, I am a-sayin' that. Now I want you to turn me a' loose and get out of here."

"How do you live? What do you eat? What do you drink?" Falcon asked.

"Bugs, rabbits when I can catch 'em, such wild

plants as can be et. And they's a pool of water back
a-ways."

"What is your name?" Duff asked.

The man laughed again, the same, high-pitched
insane laugh as before. "You already know my
name. You done said it."

"What do you mean we've already said it?"

"I'm the feller I didn't kill."

"Mister, you've been in this mine too long,"
Falcon said. "You aren't making any sense at all.
What do you mean, you are the man you didn't kill?"

"Wait a minute," Duff said. "I think I know what
he means. Are you trying to tell us that you are
Elmer Gleason?"

"I ain't tryin' to tell you nothin', sonny," he said. He
laughed again. "I'm a' doin' it. I am Elmer Gleason."

Chapter Twenty-four

Cheyenne

"I think it would be ill advised of us to arrive at the bank simultaneously," Malcolm said.

"What?" Asa Moran asked.

"He means don't all of us show up at the same time," Carter Hill said.

"Why not?" Pettigrew asked.

"Because if all of us ride up to the bank together, then dismount and enter the bank simultaneously, it cannot help but arouse suspicions," Malcolm explained.

"I think he's right," McKenna said.

"All right. So how are we going to do it?" Pettigrew asked.

"We won't ride up to the bank at all. Shaw, Pogue, McKenna, and Johnny Hill will be with me. We will come up Central from the south, then dismount about four buildings away and walk to the bank. Pettigrew, you, Moran, Carter Hill, and Garcia, will come down Central from the north, and you will also stop about four buildings away from the bank.

"Pettigrew, you and I will go into the bank first, but since we will be approaching from different directions, it will not appear that we are together. I will go to the table and start filling out a slip as if I am about to make a deposit. Pogue, you, Shaw, and McKenna will come together from the south; Moran, and Garcia will come down from the north. That will give us seven men inside the bank at the same time, certainly enough to take care of business. Johnny Hill will hold the horses from the south group; Carter will hold the horses from the north group. When you two see the last one of us enter the bank, both of you come riding toward the bank and stop out front, holding the horses. After we get the money we will make our exit from the bank as rapidly as possible, mount our horses, and ride away."

"That sounds like a real good plan," Moran said.

"I would add something to it," Shaw said.

"What would you add to it?" Malcolm asked.

"I think as we ride out of town we ought to be shooting."

"Certainly if we are shot at, we should return fire," Malcolm said.

"No, I ain't talkin' about just returnin' fire. I mean we should just start shootin' at anybody and ever'body."

"Why would you suggest such a thing?" Malcolm asked.

"You want to get away, don't you?" Pettigrew asked.

"Yes, of course."

"Then Shaw is right. If we start shootin' up the

town on the way out, there ain't nobody goin' to think about shootin' us. Only thing they're goin' to be thinkin' about is not gettin' kilt. Near 'bout ever'one is goin' to just try and find 'em a place to get out of the line of fire."

"All right," Malcolm said. "This is your country, I shall defer to your suggestion."

When Malcolm and the others rode into town the next morning, approaching as planned from opposite ends of Central Avenue, Cheyenne was in the middle of its mid-morning commerce cycle. At the Wyoming Freight and Transport Company, three wagons were backed up against the loading dock taking on freight that had come into town by train, but would have to be delivered to the various destinations by wagon.

A boy of about sixteen was sweeping the front porch of Dunnigan's General Store. A dog that lay sleeping on the porch made no effort to move, nor did the boy make an effort to move him.

There were two Chinese women doing laundry outside Wo Ching's Laundry and they were carrying on a spirited conversation in their own language.

A man was standing on the porch roof of Sikes' Hardware store, painting the false front.

Malcolm dismounted in front of White's Apothecary, then started walking toward the bank. He saw Pettigrew approaching the bank from the other side. Arriving at the bank door simultaneously, they went inside without acknowledging each other. Malcolm stepped up to the table, while Pettigrew, holding a twenty-dollar bill, went up to the teller's window and stood in line as if waiting to make change. There were four other customers in the bank, three men and one woman.

The others came as planned. When all seven were in the bank, Malcolm nodded at Pettigrew, who nodded at the others. Pettigrew drew his pistol, which was the signal for all to draw their weapons.

"Ever'body put their hands up!" Pettigrew yelled. "This is a bank holdup!"

"Oh, my!" Lisenby said.

"Open that safe!"

"I don't know the combination," Lisenby said. "Only Mr. Snellgrove knows."

"Who is Snellgrove?"

"He isn't here."

"You are lying, Mr. Lisenby," Malcolm said. "That gentlemen is Mr. Snellgrove."

"Mr. Malcolm, you?" Lisenby said, surprised by Malcolm's comment. "You are with them? But, you were going to make a deposit."

"I decided I would rather make a withdrawal," Malcolm said, laughing at his own joke.

"How the hell does he know your name?" Pogue asked.

"It's quite simple, Mr. Pogue. I told him my name," Malcolm said, purposely using Pogue's name.

"That was a dumb thing to do," Pogue said.

Malcolm looked over at Snellgrove. "Mr. Snellgrove, I appreciated the guided tour you provided for me yesterday. Now, if you would be so good, sir, please open the safe for us."

"No," Snellgrove said.

Pettigrew pointed his pistol at Snellgrove. "Open the safe, or I'll kill you."

"What would that accomplish?" Snellgrove asked. "If I am dead, then no one will be able to open the safe."

"You're right," Pettigrew said. He pointed his pistol at one of the male customers. "Open your safe or I'll kill this man here."

"I have no intention of opening the safe."

Pettigrew pulled the trigger. The pistol boomed and smoke poured out of the end of the barrel. Even before the smoke drifted away, the customer was lying on the floor of the bank with a bullet in his heart.

"God in Heaven, man!" Snellgrove shouted. "You murdered him!"

"No, Mr. Snellgrove, 'tis you who committed the murder," Malcolm said. "You didn't pull the trigger, true enough, but you were given the opportunity to cooperate with us, and you refused to do so. That sealed the man's fate."

"How can someone like you be in league with people like this?" Snellgrove asked. "You aren't like them."

"I would advise you to cooperate," Malcolm said. "My friend does seem quite determined to see you open the safe."

"No."

Pettigrew pointed at one of the other men.

"No, please, I beg of you!" the man said. "I have a wife and children."

Pettigrew looked over at Snellgrove. "Did you hear what he said? He has a wife and children. You want to be responsible for another one of your customers gettin' killed?"

"No, please!" The man pleaded. He got down on his knees.

"Maybe your customers don't mean anything to you," Pettigrew said. "I reckon I'm shootin' the wrong people. Maybe I should kill your friend here." He pointed the pistol at Lisenby.

"No, wait!" Lisenby said. "I'll open the safe for you!"

"You will open the safe? I thought you didn't know the combination," Malcolm said. "Tsk, tsk, Mr. Lisenby. It would appear that you lied to us."

"That's what Mr. Snellgrove told me to say if anything like this ever happened."

"Lisenby, don't do it!" Snellgrove said.

"Mr. Snellgrove, I'm not going to die for twenty dollars a week," Lisenby said.

With shaking hands, Lisenby walked over to the safe and began turning the combination. It took only a few turns, then the big vault door swung open.

"Very good, Mr. Lisenby," Malcolm said. He produced a cloth bag from under his jacket and handed it to Lisenby. "Now, if you would be so good, please put all of your money in here."

"Lisenby, you are fired!" Snellgrove said.

"I can get another job, Mr. Snellgrove," Lisenby said as he began dropping bundles of cash into the bag. "I can't get another life."

When the bag was full, he handed it to Malcolm.

"Thank you," Malcolm said. He looked over at Snellgrove, who was seething with anger as he stared accusingly at Lisenby.

"Mr. Snellgrove," he said. "Would you kindly step into the safe, please?"

"What! What do you mean, step into the safe? What are you talking about?"

"I know that 'tis a Scottish brogue I have," Malcolm said. "But I'm for certain that you understood me. Step into the safe."

"You don't understand," Snellgrove said. "I could smother in there!"

"Aye, you could indeed," Malcolm said. "Unless Mr. Lisenby opens the safe door in time to let you out. Oh, but, wait. He can't do that, can he? You just fired him."

"Get in!" Shaw said gruffly, grabbing Snellgrove by the shoulders and shoving him toward the open door of the safe.

"Lisenby, get me out!" Snellgrove called out in terror as Shaw shoved him into the safe. "You aren't fired! I take it back, you aren't fired!"

The safe was large enough to hold Snellgrove, but barely.

"Mr. Lisenby?" Malcolm asked.

"Yes, sir?"

"Don't let him out until we have left."

"Yes, sir."

Just as the outlaws reached the door, the man on his knees, the one who had begged for his life, drew a pistol from some unseen place and fired.

"Uhnn!" Garcia grunted loudly. The bullet hit Garcia in the back, just to the left of his right shoulder blade. He stumbled, but did not fall. McKenna grabbed him and, helping him stay on his feet, half walked and half dragged Garcia through the front door.

Pettigrew, with a shout of anger, turned his pistol and shot the customer who had shot Garcia, hitting him in the forehead. The customer fell back with his eyes open and unseeing.

"What happened?" Johnny Carter shouted as he held his hand down for the other riders to grab the reins.

"Garcia got shot!" McKenna called back. "Shaw, help me get him into his saddle!"

With Shaw and McKenna on each side of him, Garcia was able to climb into the saddle. After that the others mounted as well.

"Yee-ha!" Pettigrew shouted as they started out of town. He began shooting. "Shoot away, boys!" he called. "Shoot everything that walks, slithers, or crawls!"

With pistols blazing, and the townspeople running, the nine bank robbers thundered out of town, though, not without shooting down two more citizens.

St. Louis

Under the cavernous dome of St. Louis's Union Station, the sounds of the many trains moving in and out of the great car shed were a distant, rumbling echo that one could not only hear but feel in the stomach. Angus Somerled was two days out of New York and, according to his schedule, three days from Denver.

As he waited for his train, he visited the newsroom, where several papers were on display. He read with amusement the advertisements for Extract of Buchu, guaranteed to cure headaches. Then, next to the newspapers, he saw a book entitled

Falcon MacCallister and the Desert Desperados.

The name Falcon MacCallister jumped out at him, for that was the kinsman of Duff MacCallister. Somerled picked up the paperbound book and opened it to a random page.

Falcon stood at the opening to the canyon wherein Dangerous Dan and his villainous compatriots had gathered after the daring train robbery they perpetrated on the Express. They thought they had escaped all pursuit, but they were wrong. With the eye of an eagle and the cunning of a fox, Falcon followed, unerringly, the trail of the nefarious band until—suddenly— a shot rang out!

"That is far enough, Falcon MacCallister. Take one more step and it is at your peril, for surely, with six of us and but one of you, the outcome of a fight may be foretold!" The voice of he who called was none other than that of Dangerous Dan himself.

Falcon was in great danger for, as Dangerous Dan had correctly spoken, he was but one against an armed and desperate band of six. But Falcon was nothing if he was not a man of great courage and coolness under pressure. He gathered himself to hurl back a defiant response to the challenge issued by Dangerous Dan.

"Dangerous Dan, I do not fear you, nor the evil associates who are in your company!" Falcon called back. "For my cause is just, and I have the strength of many. I call upon you to surrender, or face judgment from the bullets of my Colt .45!"

Looking up toward the huge chalkboard, Somerled saw that his train had arrived on track number seven. He started to put the book back, but decided to buy it. If Duff MacCallister was, indeed, in league with Falcon, then it would be to his advantage to learn as much about him as he could.

With the book in hand he passed through door that had a sign overhead reading: TO TRAINS.

There were several trains under the huge car shed, some leaving, some arriving, and some backed in to discharge or to take on passengers. The shed captured the smoke and steam so that it burned his nostrils as Somerled walked up the long brick ramp between the trains. Stepping up into his assigned car, he settled down to read his book.

He had been traveling for two days by fast train, and yet he had two days remaining before he reached a place called Denver, Colorado. One could cross Scotland by train in but half a day. He had had no idea how large this country of America was until he arrived here.

Chapter Twenty-five

Sky Meadow

Elmer Gleason, bathed, shaved, his hair cut, fingernails trimmed, and wearing some clothes Duff had provided, sat on the porch drinking a cup of coffee.

"I forgot how good coffee was," he said.

"How long has it been since you have had a cup?" Duff asked.

"I don't know," Gleason said. "I don't know what year this is."

"It is 1887," Duff said.

"1887? Well now, I'm goin' to have to do some ci-pherin' here," Gleason said. He counted on his fingers and mumbled to himself. "I reckon it's been eleven years."

"And you've lived in that mine all those years?" Falcon asked.

"Purt' much," Gleason answered. "Some years ago I spent some time with the Cheyenne Injuns. I even married me one of 'em, but she died when she was birthin' our youngin', and the youngin', he up and died a couple days later. So I left. I wandered around a bit, then come back to the mine. Not sure when that was, but I know I spent six, maybe seven winters there."

"Mr. Gleason, you said you killed Lonnie Post and Sam Hodges in self-defense," Falcon said. "What about Arnold Brown? Did you kill him in self-defense, too?"

"I never heard of a feller named Arnold Brown," Gleason said. "Who is he?"

"According to Mr. Guthrie, he is a man who went out to the mine to look for gold, and has never been heard of since."

Gleason laughed. "So that was his name," he said. "There was a feller come out there not too long after I kilt them two men. But I scairt him off and he never come back."

"How much gold did you find?" Duff asked.

"I ain't found much more than you have found," Gleason said. "But I know it's there, I can smell it." Gleason laid his finger alongside his nose.

"But in all the years you spent there, you never found it," Duff said.

"That don't mean it ain't there."

"Why didn't you file on it?" Falcon asked.

"I never got around to it," Gleason replied. "Now you're a' tellin' me that this here fella owns it." He pointed to Duff.

"He does own it," Falcon said. "He filed a claim on this land and all its environs."

"That there word, 'environs.' That means he owns the mine?" Gleason asked.

"Yes."

"Well then, there ain't much more I can do, is there?"

"You can sell the mine to me," Duff said.

"What do you mean I can sell it to you? Didn't you just tell me you already own it?"

"Yes, but that doesn't mean you have no claim whatever. You were here first."

"I wasn't first. It was either the Spanish or the Injuns that was first."

"When you tried to sell it before, how much did you ask for it?"

"I wanted five hunnert dollars," Gleason said. He chuckled. "But I couldn't get nobody interested in it."

"Suppose I give you two hundred dollars, and twenty percent of anything the gold mine ever makes?" Duff suggested.

"Why would you do that?"

"Because I am more interested in getting a ranch started than I am in poking around in a mine, and this way you could keep looking. Only, you would be working for me, and you wouldn't have to eat bugs, rats, and the like."

Gleason laughed. "I don't mind tellin' you that sounds pretty good to me."

"We'll build you a cabin down by the mine," Duff said. "You can live there, and, anytime I am gone, you can keep an eye on the ranch."

Gleason smiled broadly, then he spit in his hand and held it out. "Sonny, you got yourself a deal."

Duff looked at the extended hand, then looked at Falcon. Falcon laughed. "If you want to close the deal, shake his hand."

Duff started to extend his own hand.

"Un-huh," Falcon said. "You have to spit in it."

"My word," Duff said. "Ye Americans be quaint people indeed." He spit in his hand, then grasped Gleason's in his.

Tie Siding, Wyoming

The pain in Garcia's wound had eased somewhat and a warming numbness set in. Garcia was thankful for the numbness because it allowed him to stay in his saddle as they rode away from the bank holdup. But he had lost a lot of blood and was getting weaker and dizzier with every passing moment. By the time they rode into the tiny town of Tie Siding, Garcia was barely able to stay in his saddle.

"Hey, Malcolm, Garcia's not going to make it if we don't find a doctor pretty soon," McKenna said. McKenna was riding alongside Garcia as well as leading Garcia's horse, because Garcia needed to hold on to the saddle pommel with both hands just to keep from falling off.

"He'll be all right. He was just hit in the shoulder," Pettigrew said.

"No, he ain't goin' to be all right if we don't find us a doctor soon to patch him up," McKenna said. "He's a' bleedin' like a stuck pig."

"Maybe we can find a doctor here," Malcolm suggested.

"We don't have time," Pettigrew said. "You know damn well they've got a posse together by now."

"We rode outta town headin' east," McKenna said. "We're west of town now. It's goin' to take 'em a while to figure out that we swung around and come back to the west. And I'm tellin' you, Garcia can't go on much longer if we don't get him a doctor."

"Hell, as much blood as he's lost, he's probably goin' to die anyway," Pogue said. "Seems to me like takin' him to a doctor just to have him tell us that Garca is goin' to croak is a' goin' to slow us down more."

"Pogue, what kind of thing is that to say?" McKenna asked.

"Yeah, well, I'm with Pogue," Pettigrew said. "I don't plan on gettin' myself caught by the law 'cause I'm wastin' my time tryin' to save a Mex who is more than likely goin' to die anyway, no matter what we do."

"I'm with McKenna," Carter Hill said.

"Me, too," his brother, Johnny, said. "What if it was you that was shot?"

"If it was me, I wouldn't be complainin' about it," Shaw said.

"If you notice, Shaw, he isn't complaining," Moran said.

"We'll find a doctor," Malcolm said.

"If it was up to me, I'd just leave him there," Shaw said.

"We're going to stay with him," Malcolm said.

"Anyway," McKenna said. "Maybe we can get somethin' to eat there."

"How we goin' to get somethin' to eat?" Moran asked.

"More'n likely the doctor is married," McKenna said. "We'll have his wife fix us some food."

"What if she doesn't want to?" Johnny Hill asked.

Pettigrew laughed, a sharp, evil-sounding laugh. "I think we can talk her into it," he said.

It was early, just before noon, as Malcolm and the others rode through the street. Tie Siding was a quiet, sleepy little town with very few people out in the street, and even fewer who paid any attention to their presence. Malcolm saw a boy of about seventeen painting a fence. Separating from the others, he rode over to him.

"Good morning, lad," he said as pleasantly as he could.

The young man didn't reply vocally, but he nodded his head at Malcolm, then looked by him at the other eight riders.

"Are you fellas cowboys lookin' for work?" the boy asked. "'Cause if you are, you ain't likely to find nothin' here. Mr. Lyman Byrd, he owns a ranch twixt here 'n Walbach and I was ridin' for 'im, but he let a bunch of us go last month. Said he couldn't afford to keep us on."

"'Tis grateful I am, lad, for your report on the availability of employment, but our quest is to find a doctor."

"We ain't got no real doctor here, 'cept for Dr. Tillman, and he's an animal doctor is what he is. But seein' as we ain't got no doctor, well, he sometimes treats folks, too."

"And where is he domiciled?"

"What?"

"Where may I find this doctor?"

"Oh, he has a house that's about a mile out of town." The boy pointed. "Just keep on a' goin' that way 'till you run out of buildings and houses, then keep on a' goin' some more till you'll come to a white house on the right side of the road. It's got a sign out front that has a picture of a horse on it. That's in case you can't read the words that say veterinary doctor."

"Thank you, lad, you have been most helpful," Malcolm said. He rode back to join the others.

"Did you find a doctor?" McKenna asked.

"In a manner of speaking," Malcolm replied.

"What does that mean?"

"It means I found a doctor," Malcolm said without going into further detail.

Following the directions the boy gave him, Malcolm led the men to the doctor. His office, which was also his home, was a low, single-story building that sat at least a hundred feet back from the road. A wisp of wood smoke rose from the chimney, carrying with it the aroma of frying pork chops.

"This is it," Malcolm said.

"Wait a minute, what do you mean this is it?" McKenna asked. "Can't you read? This here is a veterinarian."

"There are no physicians available, but according to the lad in town, the veterinarian also treats people," Malcolm said.

"But an animal doctor?"

"What choice do we have, McKenna?" Moran asked.

"Yeah," McKenna replied. "I reckon you are right."

"Before we ride up there, take a good look around," Malcolm said. "Make sure there is no one in sight."

The saddles squeaked as the riders twisted to look around. "There is no need for all us to go inside," Malcolm said. "I'll go in with Garcia and McKenna. The rest of you move around behind the house. I don't want anyone riding down the road and getting curious as to why so many horses are here."

"Wait a minute," Pogue said. "I thought we was goin' to get somethin' to eat here."

"Yeah," Pettigrew said. "That's the only reason I come. I sure don't care nothin' about the Mexican. He can die as far as I'm concerned. But I ain't a' goin' to wait around outside iffen there is a chance we can get us somethin' to eat inside."

"All right, Johnny, you and your brother take all the horses around back. The rest of you can come in with us."

"What about us gettin' somethin' to eat?" Johnny asked.

"We'll bring something out to you," Malcolm said. "Let's go." Malcolm clicked to his horse and they rode up to the front of the house, then dismounted.

That is, all but Garcia. Now too weak to dismount on his own, he sat in his saddle until McKenna and Moran helped him down from his horse. The Hill brothers took the horses, then moved them around back as the remaining seven men stepped up onto the doctor's front porch.

Malcolm didn't bother to knock, he just pushed it open. McKenna and Moran helped support Garcia as they walked into the house.

"What the . . . ? What is this?" the surprised doctor asked, looking up from a chair where he was reading the newspaper. His wife was standing at the stove frying pork chops, and she looked around in alarm as well.

"Doctor, please forgive us for startling you," Malcolm said. "We were doing some target shooting a bit earlier, and one of our number was inadvertently shot. 'Tis wondering, I am, if perhaps you could patch him up so that we may complete our journey."

"And maybe while you're at it, your woman could fix us somethin' to eat," Pettigrew suggested.

"My woman?"

"That one there, standin' over by the stove," Pettigrew said.

"She is my wife."

"Yeah, that's what I said. Have her cook us somethin' to eat. Them pork chops smells pretty good."

"You do know, do you not, that I am a veterinarian? I'm not a people doctor. What makes you think I could take care of your friend?"

"Animals, people, they are pretty much the same when they get a bullet in 'em," Pettigrew said. "I've seen bullets get took out of a horse and I've seen bullets get took out of people. Looked pretty much to me like there wasn't no difference."

The doctor looked at the men for a long moment. "You weren't taking target practice, were you?" he asked. "Are you outlaws on the run?"

"What if we are?" Malcolm asked. "Doesn't the Hippocratic Oath say that you have to treat him anyway?"

"I told you, I am a veterinarian. I don't take the Hippocratic Oath. That is for physicians," the doctor said. He sighed and ran his hand through his hair. "Never mind, take him over to the bed and let me take a look at him."

Moran and McKenna lay Garcia on his back on the bed.

"Where was he shot?"

"In the back, just inside the shoulder blade, I think," McKenna said.

The doctor opened Garcia's shirt. "That's not good," he said.

"What?"

"The bullet didn't go all the way through him. It's still inside. I need you to turn him over so I can have a look. And do it carefully. It is going to be quite painful for him."

With help from McKenna and Moran, Garcia was turned over, but the doctor was correct in suggesting that it would be painful, and Garcia grimaced as they moved him.

"Well, he's lucky in one thing," the doctor said. "I don't think there's any festering. But, I expect he has lost a lot of blood, and like I said, the bullet is going to have to come out."

"Hell, why bother?" Pogue asked. "He's goin' to die anyhow, ain't he?"

"Probably," the doctor agreed. "But it's not an absolute. I can at least try."

"You want to waste your time on him, go right ahead," Pettigrew said.

Turning, Pogue saw the doctor's wife standing close by. "Lady, I ain't seen you put no more pork chops in that skillet," he said.

"I don't have any more pork chops," the doctor's wife answered, her voice quivering with fear.

"Well what have you got?"

"Fix them some bacon, Pearl. We've got a whole slab of bacon," the doctor said.

"Is bacon all right?" Pearl asked.

"Hell, bacon is fine. Just get to cookin' it," Pogue said.

"I have a basket of fresh eggs, maybe two dozen or more. I can scramble them. And I have a couple of loaves of bread I baked yesterday, if that's all right. I had no idea there would be so many to feed."

"Woman, quit talkin' so much and get to cookin'," Shaw said.

"And, don't forget," Malcolm added, "there are two more outside."

"Actually, whenever my husband doctors a person, I have to help. I'll cook you some food as soon as he is through attending to his patient."

Pogue pulled his pistol and pointed it at Garcia, who, by now, had passed out.

"Well hell, if that's all that's stoppin' you, I can take of that. I'll just shoot the son of a bitch now and get it over with."

The doctor stepped between Pogue and Garcia. "If you shoot him, you're goin' to have to shoot me, too," he said.

"Hell, that's all right by me," Pogue said easily.

"And me," Pearl said, stepping in front of her husband.

"I don't have no problem with that, either," Pogue said, and he cocked his pistol.

"No, Pogue," Pettigrew said. "You ain't goin' to shoot either one of 'em."

Malcolm, who had been surprised by the sudden turn of events, was glad that Pettigrew had spoken up. He didn't want to shoot the doctor and his wife, but it wasn't because of any sense of compassion. He knew that if they did kill the doctor and his wife, the entire territory would be after them. He wondered for a moment how he had gotten himself into this position. He had come to America to deal with one man, and though he had no real police authority, he did have some cover for what he was doing because Duff MacCallister was wanted back in Scotland. That was before. Now, he was an outlaw pure and simple, a bank robber, a party to murder, and in league with the most disreputable bunch of men he had ever known, or even heard about.

Malcolm was supposed to be in charge, but was he? He knew that he had no wish to challenge these men—especially Shaw, Pogue, or Pettigrew. He was glad that, on this issue at least, that of not killing the doctor and or his wife, Pettigrew was on his side.

Pogue looked at the defiant doctor and his equally defiant wife for a moment longer, then he eased the hammer back down. "All right, have it your way. McKenna, you fix the food."

"Why me?"

"Why you? 'Cause you're the one that was so determined to get Garcia to a doctor. Now, fix the damn food like I told you to."

Pogue's voice was cold and demanding.

"All right, all right," McKenna mumbled.

"Doc, you got yourself a brave woman there," Pogue said. "She's pretty, too. Makes a fella wonder how someone like you ever managed to come up with a woman like that."

When the doctor didn't answer, Pogue smiled at both of them, then left them and walked over to join the others. By now McKenna had carved off several pieces of bacon and they were twitching and dancing in the frying pan.

The doctor slapped Garcia in the face.

"Here, what did you do that for?" Moran asked.

"I have to wake him up," the doctor said. "I have

to give him some laudanum. He's goin' to need it when I start probing for the bullet."

Garcia opened his eyes, and the doctor held the bottle to his mouth.

"Drink this," he said.

Garcia took the liquid, then closed his eyes again.

"Help me get his shirt off, Pearl."

The doctor and his wife removed Garcia's shirt. Then the doctor picked up a long, slender instrument and began probing for the bullet. As the doctor and his wife worked on Garcia, the others began to eat the bacon and scrambled eggs McKenna had cooked for them, totally unconcerned with the ordeal Garcia was going through.

"Mr. Moran, would you be for making a couple of bacon and egg sandwiches and taking them out to the Hill brothers?" Malcolm asked Moran when he saw that Moran was finished eating.

"All right," Moran said as he went about his task.

"How are you progressing, Doctor?" Malcolm asked, calling over to the bed where the doctor and his wife were busily attending to Garcia.

"We are doing quite well, thank you. The bleeding has stopped, and digging for the bullet hasn't initiated any new hemorrhaging."

"Good. Continue with your task."

For the next several minutes the doctor and his wife bent over the unconscious form of the wounded outlaw, talking quietly between themselves, using words that none of the men could understand. "Good, I was worried about secondary atelectasis, but despite the bullet insult, I don't think the lung has collapsed," Dr. Tillman said.

"I don't think so, either," Pearl said. "He seems to be aspirating normally."

After what seemed like several minutes, the doctor announced that he had successfully removed the bullet and he dropped it with a clink into the pan of warm water. The bullet lay in the bottom of the pan with tiny bubbles of blood rising to paint a swirl of red on the water's surface. None of the eaters seemed particularly interested in his announcement.

"So, you're finished up, are you, Doc?" Pogue asked, coming over to stand by the bed.

"I've got the bullet out."

"Good, hurry up and get him patched up so's we can put him back on his horse and get out of here."

"Are you insane? If you move him now, it will kill him."

Malcolm came over to join the conversation. "What is going on?" he asked.

"This fool wants to put this man on a horse and leave," the doctor said. "I just told him that he can't do that. If he tries to move him, it will kill him."

"Doctor, you don't seem to understand our situation," Malcolm said. "We must be going. We can't stay around while Mr. Garcia recovers."

"Then, by all means, go. Leave your friend here. I will take care of him until he is recovered."

"And, no doubt, turn him over to the law," Malcolm said.

"Suppose I do turn him over to the law? Isn't incarceration preferable to dying?"

"You ain't never been incarcerated, have you, Doc?" Pettigrew asked.

"Of course not."

"It ain't necessarily preferable," Pettigrew said.

"Come on, Garcia. Get up!"

Garcia blinked his eyes a couple of times, then closed them again.

"He can't even hear you now," the doctor said. "He has passed out."

"Why don't we leave him here, like the doc said?" McKenna asked.

"We can't do that. He knows where we're goin', He might talk."

"Garcia won't talk," McKenna said. "He's a good man, he won't talk."

"We killed two people in that holdup," Pettigrew said. "That means if we get caught, we're goin' to hang. If they tell him they won't hang him if he'll help 'em find us, are you tellin' me he won't talk?"

"We didn't kill two people in the holdup, Pettigrew," McKenna said. "You did."

Malcolm listened to the discussion between the two men and knew that there was only one thing to be done. He knew also that, if he was to maintain the position of leadership among these men, he was the one who was going to have to do it. He walked over to the bed and picked up a pillow, then pushed it down over Garcia's face.

"Here, what are you doing? Stop it! You are killing him!" Pearl shouted. She reached for pillow, but Malcolm continued to press it down over Garcia's face.

"Doctor, do you want your wife to risk her life to save an outlaw?" Malcolm asked, sharply.

"Pearl, come away!" the doctor said.

"But, John, don't you see what he is doing?"

"Yes, he is killing the patient," the doctor said. "But better him than us."

Malcolm smiled. "You have more sense than I gave you credit for, John," he said.

Garcia offered no struggle at all, but Malcolm saw him arch his back slightly, as if trying to breathe. Malcolm held the pillow for at least two more minutes, then he pulled it away.

Garcia's eyes were open but blank, and his face was slightly purple.

"John, if you would, sir, please confirm for me that he is dead," Malcolm said.

The doctor picked up Garcia's wrist and felt for a pulse. There was none. Then he put his hand to the carotid artery. He nodded.

"Mr. Garcia is dead," he said.

Pearl crossed herself.

"Thank you, madam," Malcolm said. "I am sure that Mr. Garcia needs all the prayers he can get."

"I have to hand it to you, Malcolm," Pettigrew said deferentially. "I didn't think you had it in you."

"Let's get out of here," Malcolm said, starting toward the back door.

The others obeyed instantly.

Chapter Twenty-six

Sky Meadow

Falcon was tightening the cinch strap on Lightning as Duff stood by watching.

"You sure you don't want me to stay awhile longer?" Falcon asked. "If this man Malcolm finds you, I might come in handy. Besides, I can help you build the barn."

"Falcon, you have been more than helpful," Duff said. "But the time has come when I must stand on my own. Besides, I've hired Mr. Gleason. As far as any further construction is concerned, I think the two of us can get the job done."

"I'm sure you can as well. It looks like you've made a fine start."

Gleason came out of the house carrying a little cloth bag. He handed it to Falcon.

"This is in case you get hungry on the train," he said. "I baked you somethin'."

"Mr. Gleason, you didn't have to go to all that trouble," Falcon said.

Gleason chuckled. "What do you think, that I

cooked up a rat? I didn't always eat rats and bugs
and such. Before I got the gold fever, I was a belly
robber for Mr. Richard King on his ranch down in
Texas. And I was a good one, if I say so myself. I
cooked you up a batch of sinkers. I think you'll like
them."

Falcon opened the sack and looked down inside.
As the aroma hit him, he smiled. Then he pulled
one of them out and took a bite.

"Uhhmm," he said. "Mr. Gleason, this is delicious. Cousin, if he can't drive a nail for you, he's
worth keeping around just for his sinkers."

"I don't know what a sinker is," Duff said.

"Some people call them doughnuts," Falcon
said. He broke off a piece of the one he was eating
and handed it to Duff. "Try this."

Duff tasted it, then smiled. "Mr. Gleason, I do
hope you didn't give all of them to Falcon."

"Sonny, do you think I don't know where my
bread is buttered?" Gleason said. "I gave him a few,
but I kept most of them back."

Falcon laughed, then swung into his saddle.
"Duff, I think I am leaving you in good hands," he
said. "You know how to get hold of me if you need
me." Slapping his legs against Lightning's sides,
Falcon rode off, throwing a wave as he left.

"He's a good man," Gleason said.

"Aye, I have found that to be so," Duff agreed.

Chugwater

It created some curiosity when eight men rode
into Chugwater together. That was because while
groups of cowboys who were involved in trail drives

often traveled together, this was not the time for a trail drive. Also, news of the bank robbery in Cheyenne had already reached Chugwater by telegraph message. So when Malcolm and the others tied up in front of Fiddler's Green, Fred Matthews, who was standing at the window in the front of his mercantile store, saw them.

"Lonnie," he called to the sixteen-year-old who worked for him.

"Yes, Mr. Matthews?"

"Go down to Marshal Craig's office and tell him that he might want to check in on that bunch of men who just went into Fiddler's Green. I've got a feeling about them."

"Who do you think they are?"

"I think they may be the bunch that held up the bank down in Cheyenne."

"You think they're maybe goin' to rob our bank? I got me near thirty dollars in that bank."

"I don't know," Fred admitted. "But I think the marshal should know about it."

"Yes, sir."

Biff Johnson had just finished tapping a new barrel of beer, and he held a mug under the spigot, then operated it to see if it was working properly. A steady stream of golden liquid flowed from the spigot, so, satisfied that the flow was all right, he shut it off, then took a sip to see if the beer tasted all right. It was necessary that he do that, because the beer came by train from Denver to Tracy, then by wagon from Tracy up to Chugwater, and sometimes it got a little stale. But that wasn't the case now, because this beer was fine.

Biff was putting the mug in a tub of water when he saw the eight men coming into his saloon. Though that wouldn't have been unusual during the cattle season, it was unusual now, and he looked up at them in curiosity.

"Good morning, gentlemen," he said. "Welcome to Fiddler's Green."

"We've ridden long and hard, and we're thirsty," one of the men said. He was a small man, with nostrils so prominent that they reminded Biff of a pig's snout. He chided himself for having such a thought, though. After all, these were customers.

"Well, gentlemen, I have just the thing for thirst. I have only this moment tapped a new keg of beer."

At the marshal's office, Russell Craig, a man in his early sixties, had just poured himself a cup of coffee when young Lonnie Mathers came into his office. "Good morning, Lonnie," the marshal said.

"Marshal, them folks that robbed the bank in Cheyenne is in town," Lonnie said.

Craig had just lifted the cup to his lips, but he brought it down quickly when Lonnie said that.

"What? How do you know?"

"That's what Mr. Matthews said. They's eight folks just rode into town an' they all went into Fiddler's Green. Mr. Matthews said he's sure they was the ones that robbed the bank."

"He said that? He said he's sure?"

"Well, no, sir, not exactly. But he said he believes they might be the ones."

"He *believes* they *might* be the ones," Craig repeated. This time he did raise the cup to his lips.

"Yes, sir."

"All right, Lonnie. You can tell Fred that I will look into it."

"Yes, sir," Lonnie replied. "I'll tell him that."

Marshal Craig watched Lonnie walk back down the street to the mercantile store, then he went over to a hook on the wall and took down his holster and pistol. Strapping the gunbelt on, he pushed through the door of the marshal's office and started toward Fiddler's Green.

Back at Fiddler's Green Lucy and Peggy, the only two bar girls remaining since Annie had been killed, were sitting at a table in the corner having a cup of coffee. It was just ten-thirty in the morning, and their normal work hours didn't start until two o'clock in the afternoon, but they had no place else to go and they often just relaxed and visited with each other before starting to work.

"Peggy, let's get out of here," Lucy said quietly.

"Get out of here? Where do you want to go?"

"I don't care. Anywhere but here. I don't like the looks of this."

"What? You mean all those men?" Peggy asked.

"Yes," Lucy said. "There's something not right about this."

Marshal Craig came into the saloon, then stopped and stood for just a moment inside the door. Malcolm and the men with him looked around at him.

"Liam Pettigrew," Craig said, recognizing one of them. "I thought you were in prison."

"I got out," Pettigrew said.

"So I see. What are you men doing here?"

"Good morning, Constable," Malcolm said. "We have come to find a friend of mine, a fellow countryman."

Upon hearing Malcolm's accent, Marshal Craig's eyes narrowed. The telegram he had received telling about the bank robbery in Cheyenne identified two of the men by name. One was Pogue, no first name available, and one, who spoke with a Scottish brogue, was Rab Malcolm.

"You would be Rab Malcolm, I take it?"

Malcolm looked surprised. "Aye. How do you know that?"

"Son of a bitch!" Pogue shouted. "Malcolm, he knows about the bank robbery, that's how he knows about it!"

Upon hearing Pogue's shout, Marshal Craig went for his pistol, but he was too late. Pogue, Pettigrew, and McKenna all beat him to the draw. Their three guns fired almost as one. Craig pulled the trigger on his pistol, but as he had not brought his gun to bear, the bullet plunged into the floor. Craig fell facedown with three bullets in him.

By now all the other outlaws had drawn their pistols as well, and they stood there holding them at the ready as the smoke from four discharges floated up to form a blue-gray cloud just under the ceiling.

Malcolm turned toward Biff Johnson just as he was reaching for the shotgun that he kept under the bar.

"I wouldn't if I were you," Malcolm said, pointing his pistol at the bartender.

Biff backed away from the bar.

"You killed the marshal," Biff said.

"You saw it, barkeep," Malcolm said. "We really had no choice."

"He was a good man," Biff said.

"Ha!" Pettigrew said. "Well, he's a dead man now."

"Barkeep, I want you to do a favor for me," Malcolm said.

"Why should I do you a favor?"

"Because if you don't do that favor for me, I shall kill one of these ladies," Malcolm said, pointing his pistol toward Lucy and Peggy. "And here is the interesting thing. I am going to let you pick the one that I kill." He smiled at the two women, who had been stunned into silence by what they had just witnessed. "What do you think, ladies? Which one of you will he pick?"

"You can't do that!" Biff said. "I'm not going to choose which one you kill. Are you insane?"

"Insane? No, just curious as to which one you will choose."

"I'm not going to choose either one."

"Never mind, I will choose. And after I kill one of them, if you still won't do the favor, I will kill the other one. What do you think about that? And so, you see, it really doesn't matter which one you would have chosen, because I will kill them both if you force my hand. And if you still won't do the favor, then I will simply kill you and find someone else who will do me the favor."

"What do you want?"

"I want you to go find Duff MacCallister and bring him to me."

"Duff MacCallister? What do you want with him?"

"He is a countryman of mine," Malcolm said.

"Somehow I have the idea that you don't want him for a reunion of old friends."

"Do ye now?" Malcolm said. He laughed. "You are most astute. Now, will you fetch MacCallister for me? Or shall I choose one of these ladies to die?"

"No, no, there is no need for that. I will go."

"Good for you. You have made a wise choice."

"And Falcon MacCallister," Pettigrew added quickly. "Don't forget to bring him along as well."

"Aye," Malcolm said. "Do, please, bring Falcon MacCallister along as well," Malcolm said. "Mr. Shaw?"

"Yeah."

"You have a loud voice. Kindly step out into the street and announce that we have two women as hostages. If anyone comes into the pub, we will kill them. If anyone makes a move toward us, we will kill the women."

"All right," Shaw said.

"I wonder where Biff is going," Fred Matthews said as he saw Biff riding away.

"The marshal, he ain't come out yet," Lonnie said.

"This doesn't look good."

Next door to the saloon was Megan's Dress Emporium. The proprietor and seamstress was Megan Parker, a very pretty young woman. Mrs. Finley, one of her customers, had just finished trying on a dress and was about to leave when Megan held out her hand.

"No, Mrs. Finley, I don't think you should leave yet," she said.

"Oh, dear me," Mrs. Finley said. "What is happening?"

"I don't know, but I don't have a good feeling about it."

At that moment Shaw came out into the street and began yelling at the top of his voice.

"All you people, hear me now!" Shaw shouted. "We just kilt your marshal! We got some business to take care of in this town and we're goin' to stay here till that business is done! Don't nobody come into the saloon! If you do, we'll kill you! Don't nobody make any moves toward us, 'cause we got us two whores in here, and we'll kill them."

"Did he say they killed Marshal Craig?" Mrs. Finley asked.

"That's what he said," Megan replied.

"Oh, my. Poor Gladys."

Sky Meadow

"He is Scottish, you say?" Duff asked.

"He is Scottish, all right," Biff said. "I would recognize the brogue anywhere."

"I'm sure it is Rab Malcolm," Duff said. "He is nothing if not persistent."

"Malcolm, yes, that is his name. I heard the marshal call him that."

"And you say he has men with him?"

"Counting the Scotsman, there are eight of them," Biff said. "One of them asked that I bring Falcon back as well. I think they want him as much as Malcolm wants you."

"Aye, Falcon had spoken of the enemies he has made, and 'twould be like Malcolm's way to recruit others by using Falcon as his bait. But Falcon isn't here. He left yesterday, to go back home."

"What are you going to do?"

"Did ye not say that Malcolm has threatened the ladies if I don't appear?"

"Not exactly. He threatened them as a means of persuading me to come after you," Biff replied. "I have kept my end of the bargain, I have come after you. I think that is all that's needed to keep Lucy and Peggy safe."

"I would not want to count on that," Duff said. "Malcolm is a man with fewer redemptive qualities than a bilge rat. I had better go into town and get this settled, once and for all."

"You forget, he isn't alone."

"I think there will be no problem with the others. 'Tis obvious they want Falcon. They hold no animus toward me."

"Duff, you don't understand," Biff said. "People like that don't have to be angry with someone in order to kill them. They can kill a human being as easily as they can step on a bug."

"He's right, Mr. MacCallister," Gleason said. "You bein' from a foreign country an' all, maybe you don't understand what kind of polecats we have over here. I've known fellas that would as soon kill you as look at you. And this here bunch that's gathered around Malcolm strikes me as that kind."

"If you have another gun, I'll go in with you," Biff offered.

"I'll go as well," Gleason added.

"No, I appreciate the offer, but this is my fight," Duff said.

Chugwater

Back in Fiddler's Green, Malcolm saw that the men with him were taking advantage of Biff Johnson's absence by helping themselves to all the drinks they wanted. Malcolm was sitting at the table with Lucy and Peggy, and he wasn't drinking. And, though he said nothing about it, he was getting concerned that the amount of alcohol the others were consuming would hinder their effectiveness.

"Why do you want Duff MacCallister?" Lucy asked.

"Ye may not know this, lass, but I am a deputy sheriff back in Scotland. And there, he is wanted for murder. That's why I am here."

"You are a deputy sheriff, but you robbed a bank and you just killed our marshal," Peggy said.

"Aye, well, it has gotten a bit—complicated, let us say."

"Who did Duff MacCalliser kill?"

"He killed the sheriff's three sons and two of my friends."

"I don't believe it."

"'Tis of no matter to me, lass, whether you believe it or not."

"You talk just like him," Lucy said. "But you aren't like him."

"What the hell?" Shaw suddenly said, holding up his hand. "Ever'one, be quiet and listen. What the hell is that sound? Do you hear it?"

Everyone stopped talking and, as they did, all

could hear the sound. It was a high, skirling sound, underscored by a constant drone.

"'Tis the pipes!" Malcolm said, standing up so quickly that the chair in which he was sitting fell over with a bang.

"The what?" Pettigrew asked.

"The pipes! MacCallister is playing the pipes! Everyone get into position, he's coming!"

The others moved quickly to get into the positions they had already selected. Malcolm, with pistol in hand, moved to the bat-wing doors and looked out into the street as Pogue and Shaw went about clearing it.

"Get off the street! Get out of the way!" Pogue and Shaw were shouting. "Get out of the street or get shot!"

The pipes continued to play "Scotland the Brave," which only Malcolm recognized as the incitement to battle. The fact that pipes were being used against him gave him a chill, and though he wouldn't mention it to any of the others, it frightened him.

Everyone in town heard the pipes being played, from R. W. Guthrie, to Fred Matthews, to Megan Parker, the beautiful young dressmaker who, as she was disembarking from the coach, had noticed Duff on the first day he came to town. She knew that he was the one playing the pipes, because she had heard him play them at the funeral of one of the bar girls.

At first she felt a little thrill at hearing the pipes being played. But when she saw armed men running everyone off the street, she felt a great sense of apprehension and knew, somehow, that Duff

MacCallister, the handsome young Scot, was the center of all this, and was in danger.

She stood to one side of the big window in front of her shop and leaned over to peek outside. The street was absolutely quiet, except for the sound of the pipes.

Then the pipes fell silent.

Chapter Twenty-seven

Duff let the air out of the bag with one, long, lingering, dying tone. He hooked the pipes on the pommel of his saddle and rode the remaining quarter mile into town. In contrast to the way the town was on Duff's previous visit, this time the street was absolutely empty. He stopped at the south end of Bowie Street, dismounted, and tied Sky off at a hitching rail. Then, as he walked down the middle of the street, he saw Rab Malcolm step out of Fiddler's Green.

"'Twas nice of you to play me a tune before you came in," Malcolm said.

"Pity the man who hears the pipes and is nae a Scotsman," Duff said. "Or who be Scot, but is evil of heart."

Malcolm chuckled. "And would that be me?"

"Aye," Duff replied.

"Where is your cousin? The one they call Falcon."

"He has gone," Duff said. "He stayed long enough

to help me build my house, then he went back home."

"*Och*, and you've built a house, have you? 'Tis too bad you won't live long enough to enjoy it."

"How is this to be?" Duff asked. "Are we to face each other down in the street?"

Malcolm laughed out loud. "Sure'n I think ye may have been reading one of the sensational novels about the American West. Nae, we won't be facing each other down in the street. Well, that's nae entirely true, is it? Ye see, lad, I'll be facing you down, but there won't be anything you can do about it."

Megan was watching from the window of her dress emporium and she saw, right in front of her store, two men lying on the ground behind a watering trough, one at one end, and one at the other. She knew that they were there to ambush Duff, and she wanted desperately to call out to him. But she knew that if she did, they would more than likely shoot her and her customer. She had to do something to let Duff know, but what? How could she warn him?

Duff saw Malcolm turn and give a signal to someone. Another man came out of the saloon, holding a bar girl in front of him. It was Peggy, one of the bar girls who worked in the saloon.

"Recognize this woman? I'm told that she is a friend of the whore for whom you played the pipes at her funeral. Really, MacCallister, you actually debased our national instrument by playing a dirge at the funeral of a whore? Be ye without shame? That is enough to cost you your commission in the Black Watch."

"I've resigned my commission," Duff said.

"Aye, I daresay you have."

Lucy appeared at the bat-wing doors of the saloon. "Peggy!" she called.

Malcolm turned toward the saloon and pointed at Lucy. "Get back inside!" he called.

"Please, let Peggy go!"

"Back inside," Malcolm ordered.

"Let the woman go," Duff said.

"Sure, I'll let the woman go," Malcolm said. He walked back to the saloon, but just before he stepped inside, he turned back to the man who was holding Peggy. "Let her go, Pettigrew."

Pettigrew let Peggy go and she stood there for a moment, looking around as if unable to believe she had been released.

"Peggy, get off the street," Duff called. "Go into the mercantile."

As Peggy started across the street toward the mercantile store, Pettigrew and Malcolm went back into the saloon. Duff didn't like the way this felt. He had a sick feeling in the pit of his stomach and the hair stood up on the back of his neck. He drew his pistol and started running toward Peggy.

"Peggy, get down!" he shouted.

Startled by Duff's sudden shout, Peggy stopped in the middle of the street and looked at him with an expression of confusion on her face. At that moment Pettigrew stepped back out of the saloon and fired.

"No!" Duff shouted, and he saw blood and brain

matter fly from Peggy's head as she fell facedown into the dirt.

Duff fired at Pettigrew and saw the look of shock on Pettigrew's face when the bullet hit him. Duff ran back across the street toward the nearest watering trough and leaped over it, even as the bullets began whining around him.

Megan saw the two men behind the watering trough cock their pistols and start to move toward the edge. If Duff had no idea they were there, they would have the advantage over him. Dare she call out to him?

Then, she got an idea, and she hurried to the back of her shop.

"What is it?" Mrs. Finley asked from behind a trunk. "What is going on out there?"

"Stay down, Mrs. Finley. Just stay down and you'll be all right," Megan said. She unscrewed the knobs that held the dressing mirror on the frame. Then carrying it to the front, she turned it on its side so that it had a lengthwise projection. Holding it in the window, she prayed that Duff would see it.

Once he was safely behind the watering trough, Duff slithered on his stomach to the edge, then peered around it. He looked first toward the saloon to see if Malcolm was going to make another appearance, but the saloon was quiet. Then, looking across the street, he saw a woman in the window of the dress shop. It was Megan, the same pretty woman he had seen step down from the stagecoach the first day he rode into town, and had actually met for the first time at Annie's funeral. At first, he wondered what she was doing there, then he saw exactly what she was doing.

Megan was holding a mirror, and looking in the mirror Duff could see the reflection of two men lying on the ground behind the watering trough that was directly across the street from him. He watched as one started moving toward the end of the trough in order to take a look. Duff aimed his pistol at the edge of the trough and waited.

"MacCallister!" Malcolm called from the darkness of the saloon. "Maybe you do have the right idea. Why don't you come back out into the street, and I will as well. We can face each other down, just as your cousin does. Oh, yes, I know all about your cousin. I have read of him in a dime novel. He must be a most courageous man. What do you say? Just you and I, alone in the street."

"You don't expect me to believe that, do you?" Duff called back.

"Believe what?"

"That it would just be the two of us."

Malcolm laughed. "You think that because I have friends with me, that I may take unfair advantage of you, MacCallister? Alas, that is probably true. Tell me, what does it feel like to know that you won't live long enough to see the sun set tonight?"

All the while Malcolm was talking, Duff was keeping one eye on the mirror and the other on the corner of the watering trough. Then his vigil was rewarded. Duff saw the brim of a hat appear, and he cocked his pistol, aimed, took a breath, and let half of it out. When he saw the man's eye appear, Duff touched the trigger. Looking in the mirror he saw the man's face fall into the dirt, and the gun slip from his hand.

"Carter! Carter!" the man at the end of the trough shouted. Suddenly he stood up. "You son of a bitch! You killed my brother!" He started running across the street, firing wildly. Duff shot one time, and the man running toward him pitched forward in the street.

Duff heard the bark of a rifle. Then he saw someone tumbling forward off the roof of the dress shop. The man had had a bead on Duff, and Duff hadn't seen him. Looking toward the sound of the rifle shot, Duff saw Biff Johnson. Smiling, Biff waved at him, then stepped back behind the corner of Curly Latham's Barber Shop.

There was someone behind the false front of Fiddler's Green, and he fired at Duff. Duff returned fire, but the man had slipped back behind the false front, so he missed. But he kept his eye peeled on the false front and when the man appeared to take another shot at Duff, Duff fired first. The man dropped his gun to the street as he pitched back.

"I'm gettin' out of here!" someone shouted.

"Me too."

Duff saw two more men abandon their hiding places behind the corners of buildings. As they ran across the street, they started shooting toward Duff. He fired back. His bullet caught one of the men high in the chest, and he pitched forward, halfway across the street, falling across Peggy's body. He missed the second man with his first shot, but the next one brought him down.

"Malcolm!" someone shouted. "Malcolm, they's

five of us down! There's only three of us left! Hey, wait a minute! He's shot six times! Ha! He's out of bullets!"

The person who was shouting suddenly appeared from the corner of another building, running across the street toward Duff, shooting as he ran.

"MacCallister!" a voice shouted from behind Duff. Turning toward the voice he saw Fred Matthews. Fred tossed a revolver toward him.

Duff caught the revolver, then turned it around and shot his adversary at point-blank range.

"What the hell? Where did you . . . ?" He fell forward, facedown into the watering trough.

The man's shout that there were only three of them left corresponded with Biff's report that there had been eight of them. That meant that now there were only two. He knew that Malcolm was in the saloon, but he had no idea where the other one was.

"MacCallister, look over here!" Malcolm called.

Looking toward the front door of the saloon, Duff saw Malcolm coming outside. Another man was with him and this man was holding Lucy in front of him. Duff couldn't see that much of him, just about half of his head as he was peeking around Lucy's shoulder.

"Now, Mr. MacCallister, here is how we are going to play this little drama," Malcolm said. "You and I will both raise our pistols toward each other. I will count to three, then we will fire. If you fire before I get to three, Mr. Pogue, here, is going to kill this lady. But"—Malcolm smiled, as he held up a finger—"here is what makes the game even more interesting. When I get to three, Mr. Pogue is going to kill the girl, anyway. That means you are going to have to make up your mind as to whether you want to try and save the whore or shoot me. Not fair I know, but those are my rules."

Duff raised his pistol and shot Pogue, the bullet whizzing cleanly past Lucy and hitting Pogue in the forehead. He dropped like a poleaxed mule.

"No!" Malcolm shouted, shocked at how quickly and cleanly Duff had killed Pogue.

"I'll make my own rules," Duff said.

Malcolm had turned his pistol toward Lucy, but realized, at once, that he had made a big mistake. He tried to bring his pistol back to bear on Duff, but it was too late.

Duff's bullet hit Malcolm between his eyes.

Before he headed back home, the entire town of Chugwater turned out to hail Duff as a hero. Duff had a few people of his own to thank, Biff Johnson for shooting the man off the roof who had a bead on him, Fred Matthews for tossing him a loaded revolver just in time, and Megan Parker, who reminded Duff that Chugwater held a dance, once a month, in the ballroom of the Dunn Hotel.

It was about a ten-minute ride back home, and as he approached, he saw a strange horse tied out front. Dismounting, he was examining the horse when Elmer Gleason stepped out onto the front porch.

"Mr. MacCallister, you have a visitor inside. He is a friend from Scotland."

Duff smiled broadly. Could it be Ian McGregor? He stepped up onto the front porch, then went inside. "Ian?" he called.

It wasn't Ian, it was Angus Somerled. Somerled was standing by the stove, holding a pistol that was leveled at Duff.

"Somerled," Duff said.

"Ye've been a hard man to put down, Duff Tavish MacCallister, but the job is done now."

Duff said nothing.

"Here now, lad, and has cat got your tongue?"

"I didn't expect to see you," Duff said.

"Nae, I dinna think you would. Would you be tellin' me where I might find my deputy?"

"Malcolm is dead."

"Aye, I thought as much. Killed him, did ye?"

"It seemed the thing to do."

"There is an old adage: If you want something done right, do it yourself. I should have come after you a long time ago, instead of getting my sons and my deputies killed."

"That night on Donuum Road, I was coming to give myself up," Duff said. "None of this need have happened. Your sons would still be alive, Skye would still be alive. But you were too blinded by hate."

"We've talked enough, Duff MacCallister," Somerled said. He cocked the pistol and Duff steeled himself.

Suddenly the room filled with the roar of a gunshot—but it wasn't Somerled's pistol. It was a shotgun in the hands of Elmer Gleason. Gleason had shot through the window, and the double load of 12-gauge shot knocked Somerled halfway across the room.

"Are you all right, Mr. MacCallister?" Gleason shouted through the open window. Smoke was still curling up from the two barrels.

"Aye, I'm fine," Duff said. "My gratitude to ye, Mr. Gleason."

Gleason came around to the front of the cabin and stepped in through the front door.

"Seein' as how I saved your life, don't you think me 'n you might start callin' each other by our Christian names?"

"Aye, Elmer. Your point is well taken."

"Sorry 'bout tellin' you he was your friend. But that's what he told me, and I believed him."

"And yet, you were waiting outside the window with a loaded shotgun."

"Yes, sir. Well, considerin' that the fella you went to meet in Chugwater was from Scotland, and wasn't your friend, I just got to figurin' maybe I ought to stand by, just in case."

"Aye. I'm glad you did."

Gleason leaned the shotgun against the wall and looked at the blood that was on the floor of the cabin.

"I reckon I'd better get this mess cleaned up for you," he said.

"Elmer, I'm sure you don't realize it, but you just did," Duff said.

Turn the page for
an exciting preview of

THE LONER: RATTLESNAKE VALLEY

by J. A. Johnstone

On sale now, wherever Pinnacle Books are sold!

Chapter One

Kid Morgan reined his horse to a halt and looked at the bleached white skull on the ground in front of him. He rested his hands on the saddlehorn and leaned forward to study not only the grotesquely grinning skull but also the two long bones laid across each other that accompanied it.

"Skull and crossbones," The Kid muttered. "Pirates."

More than a dozen years earlier, in what seemed now like a previous, half-forgotten lifetime when he had still been known as Conrad Browning, The Kid had read a novel called *Treasure Island*, so he knew about pirates and the symbol from the flags they flew on their ships.

The question was, what was that ominous symbol doing here in the mostly arid landscape of West Texas, hundreds of miles from the sea?

The Kid lifted his head. Keen eyes gazed at his surroundings. A broad valley bordered by ranges of low, brush-covered hills fell away to his left and right and stretched in front of him for at least twenty miles to the east before the hills closed in sharply and pinched it off, leaving only a narrow opening for the trail. Beyond the hills, what appeared to be an endless stretch of sandy wasteland was visible through the gap. Behind The Kid was the pass through which he had just ridden in the rugged gray mountains that closed off the western end of the valley.

In stark contrast to the desert, the mountains, and the scrubby hills, the valley itself was an unexpected oasis of green. A line of trees marked the meandering course of a river that rose from springs in the mountains and flowed eastward, watering the rangeland on either side of it before the desert wasteland swallowed it whole at the far end of the valley. The grass that covered the range might not have been considered lush in some parts of the world, but here in West Texas, it certainly was. Not surprisingly, The Kid saw cattle grazing here and there, hardy longhorns that could not only survive but actually thrive on the graze they found here. A man who had been riding for days through sandy, rocky country that wasn't much good for anything, as The Kid had, would find the sight of this valley mighty appealing.

Except for the skull and crossed bones in the trail that looked for all the world like a warning to keep out.

A tight smile pulled at the corners of Kid Morgan's mouth. Even before the events that had changed his life so dramatically, he had never been the sort of hombre who took kindly to being told what to do. He lifted the reins and heeled the buckskin he rode into motion again.

As he did, movement stirred *within* the bleached skull, visible behind the empty eye sockets. A rattlesnake suddenly crawled out through one of those sockets and coiled on the ground. The vicious buzz of its rattles filled the air as it raised its head, ready to strike. Its forked tongue flickered in and out of its mouth.

The Kid's horse was used to gunfire and the smell of powdersmoke, but the sound and scent of the snake must have spooked it. The buckskin tossed its head, shied away, and tried to rear up.

The Kid's strong left hand on the reins kept the horse under firm control. His right hand brushed his black coat aside and dipped to the Colt holstered on his hip. Steel whispered against leather as he drew the gun, then the hot, still air was shattered by the blast of a shot.

It seemed that The Kid hadn't even taken time to aim, but the snake's head exploded anyway as the bullet found it. The thick body with its diamond-shaped markings uncoiled and writhed frenziedly as the knowledge of its death raced through its prehistoric nervous system. The Kid's lips tightened in distaste as he watched the snake whip around and die.

With his gun still in his hand, The Kid dismounted. He stepped around the snake, which had a grisly red smear where its head used to be. A swift kick from The Kid sent the skull bouncing into some brush. He reached down, picked up one of the long bones, and flung it off in a different direction. The other bone went sailing away with another flick of his wrist.

You shouldn't have done that, a voice seemed to say

in the back of his head. *Whoever those bones belonged to may have been innocent of any wrongdoing.*

The Kid didn't know if the voice belonged to his own conscience—not that he would have admitted to having such a thing after all the men he had killed, justifiably or not—or to his late wife, Rebel. Either way, hearing voices was a sure sign that a person was going mad.

But the revulsion he had felt toward the snake was the last straw. He'd already been a little angry about being warned to keep out of the valley. He had given in to his irritation.

That wasn't a good thing, either. He tried to keep his emotions under control at all times. A man who wanted to live very long in this harsh land couldn't afford to let himself be distracted by hatred or fear or loneliness.

The Kid holstered his gun and turned back toward the buckskin. He was a tall, lean young man, not yet thirty, with sandy hair under a flat-crowned black hat. He wore a dusty black coat over a white shirt, and black trousers that weren't tucked into his high-topped boots. His saddle was a good one, relatively new, and he carried two long guns in sheaths strapped to the horse, a Winchester and a heavy-caliber Sharps. His clothes and gear were a notch above those of the average saddle tramp, but his deeply tanned face and the slight squint around his eyes, that was becoming permanent, spoke of a man who spent most of his time outdoors.

That hadn't always been the case. Once he had spent his days either in an office or a mansion, depending on whether or not he felt like working. As Conrad Browning, he had grown up among the wealthy on Boston's Beacon Hill, had attended the finest academies and universities, had taken his place in the business world, and owned stakes in mines, railroads, and shipping companies. He was rich, with probably more money than he could spend in the rest of his life.

None of which meant a damned thing when his wife was murdered.

So after avenging her death by tracking down and killing the men responsible for it, he chose not to return to his old life as the business tycoon Conrad Browning. Instead, he held on to the new identity he had created in his quest for vengeance, that of the wandering gunfighter known as Kid Morgan, and for months now he had roamed the Southwest, riding alone for the most part, not searching for trouble but not avoiding it when it came to him, as it seemed that it inevitably did.

For a while, a young woman he'd met during some trouble in Arizona had traveled with him, but she had stayed behind in Santa Fe to make a new life for herself while he continued drifting eastward into Texas. That was better, The Kid thought. It was easier not to get hurt when you didn't allow anyone to get too close to you.

He was reaching for the buckskin's reins when a voice called, "Don't move, mister!"

Two things made The Kid freeze. One was the tone of command in the voice, which meant it was probably backed up by a gun, and the other was surprise at the fact that the voice belonged to a woman. He looked over his shoulder and saw her coming out of a nearby clump of boulders. He'd guessed right about the gun. She had a Winchester leveled at him.

"Don't even twitch a muscle," she ordered, "or you'll be damned sorry."

"Take it easy," The Kid began, but the woman didn't. She pulled the trigger and the Winchester went off with a sharp crack.

Just before the shot, though, The Kid heard another wicked buzzing from somewhere very close by. The buckskin jumped and landed running, racing a good twenty yards before it came to a halt. The Kid stayed right where he was, just in case the woman had missed.

She hadn't. When he looked down, he saw a second rattler writhing and jerking in its death throes at his feet. He hadn't seen it slither out from among the rocks bordering the trail, but there it was, and it could have very easily sunk its fangs in his leg.

The woman's shot hadn't been quite as clean as The Kid's, however. Her bullet had ripped away a good chunk of flesh from the snake's body just behind its head, a gaping wound from which crimson blood gouted, but the head was still intact and attached to the body. The mouth was open and ready to bite, and The Kid knew that dying or not, the venom was still there and the creature was as dangerous as ever.

He lifted his foot and brought the heel of his boot crunching down on the snake's head, striking almost as fast and lethally as a snake himself.

He ground his heel back and forth in the dirt, crushing the rattler's head and ending its threat. Then he looked over at the woman, who had lowered the rifle, and said coolly, "Thanks for the warning."

"I shot the blasted thing."

"Yes, but you didn't kill it," The Kid pointed out.

"You know how hard it is to hit the head of a snake when it's moving?"

The Kid smiled and made a casual gesture toward the second reptile carcass that lay on the ground nearby. "Apparently, I do," he drawled.

The woman came forward, looked at the snake The Kid had shot, and frowned. "That first shot I heard?"

"Yeah."

She let out a low whistle of admiration. "Pretty good shooting."

The Kid could have said the same thing about her appearance, as well as her shooting. She was in her early twenties, he estimated, with curly golden hair pulled back behind her head. She wore a low-crowned brown hat with its strap taut under her chin. Her skin had a healthy tan a little lighter in shade than her hair. She wore a brown vest over a white shirt and a brown riding skirt and boots. She didn't look like the sidesaddle type.

She still held the Winchester, and while the rifle wasn't pointed at The Kid, she carried it with an easy assurance that said she could swing the barrel toward him again very quickly if she needed to. Keeping her distance, she asked, "Who are you?"

"The name's Morgan," he replied, not offering any more information than that.

"Why'd you kick that skull off into the brush? The poor hombre it belonged to never did you any harm."

"I know," he said without mentioning that the same thought had occurred to him. "I took it as a warning to keep out of the valley . . . and I don't like being told where I can and can't go."

"A warning is exactly what it was," she said, "and you were foolish to disregard it. But if you were bound and determined to do that, why didn't you just ride around it?"

"I wanted whoever put it there to know how I felt." He paused and studied her. "Was that you?"

She bristled in anger. The Winchester's muzzle edged toward him as she said, "Do I look like the sort of person who'd do something like that?"

"I don't know," The Kid said. "That's why I asked. You're the one who just told me I'd be making a big mistake if I rode on into the valley."

"Well, for your information, I *didn't* put those bones there. I'm not the one you have to worry about. It's—"

She stopped short. Her head came up in a listening attitude. Alarm leaped into her eyes.

The Kid heard it, too. A swift rataplan of hoof-beats that approached too fast for them to do anything. Half a dozen riders swept around a stand of thick brush about fifty yards away and thundered toward them.

Chapter Two

There was nothing The Kid could do except stand his ground. He had five rounds in his Colt, which meant it wasn't possible to kill all six of the strangers if gunplay broke out.

But the young woman was armed, too, he reminded himself, and if she could account for one or two of them, he might be able to get the rest. Of course, he would probably die, too, and so would she, but he believed it was better to go down fighting and take as many of your enemies with you as you could.

Maybe it wouldn't come to that, he thought as the riders reined in . . . although from the looks of this bunch, they were no strangers to killing.

The man who sat his horse a little in front of the others was a big hombre, tall and broad-shouldered with brawny arms. The sleeves of his blue shirt were rolled up over forearms matted with dark hair. More hair curled from the open throat of the shirt. A beard jutted from his belligerent jaw. A gray hat was cuffed to the back of his head. He wore a pair of pearl-handled revolvers. Cruel, deep-set eyes studied The Kid from sunken pits under bushy eyebrows.

The apparent leader was the biggest of the bunch, but the man who rode to his right was almost as large. His slablike jaw bristled with rusty stubble, and a handlebar mustache of the same shade twisted over his mouth. As he took off the battered old derby he wore and used it to fan away some of the dust that had swirled up from the horses' hooves as they came to a stop, The Kid saw that the man was totally bald. The thick muscles of his arms and shoulders stretched the faded red fabric of the upper half of a set of long underwear he wore as a shirt. Double bandoliers of ammuntion crisscrossed over his barrel-like chest. He held a Winchester in his right hand.

To the leader's left was a smaller man dressed all in gray, from his hat to his boots. His size didn't make him seem any less dangerous, though. Those rattlers The Kid had killed hadn't been very big, either, but they were deadly nonetheless. In fact, the dark eyes in the man's lean, pockmarked face had a reptilian look about them. The Kid noted how the man's hand never strayed far from the butt of the pistol on his hip.

The other three men were more typical hard-cases, the sort of gun-wolves that The Kid had encountered on numerous occasions. He didn't discount their threat, but the trio that edged forward toward him and the young woman garnered most of his attention. He'd kill the big, bearded man first, if it came to that, he decided, then the little hombre in gray, and then the baldheaded varmint. Once the three of them were dead, then he'd use what was left of his life to try for the others. He was pretty sure he'd have some lead in him by that point, though.

White teeth suddenly shone brilliantly in the leader's beard as he grinned. "Been stompin' some snakes, eh?" he asked in a friendly voice.

The Kid wasn't fooled. The man's eyes were just as cold and flinty as they had been before.

"That's right," The Kid said. "Looks like you've got some diamondbacks around here."

The man threw back his head and guffawed. As the echoes from the booming laughter died away, he said, "Hell, yeah, we do. Why do you think they call this Rattlesnake Valley?"

"I didn't know they did," The Kid replied with a shake of his head.

"You're a stranger to these parts, eh?" The man looked at the young woman. "You should've warned your friend what he was gettin' into, Diana."

"He's not my friend," she said. "I never saw him before until a few minutes ago."

"Is that so?" The black-bearded giant sounded like he didn't really believe her. His eyes narrowed. "And here I thought your uncle had gone and hired himself a fast gun."

The woman shook her head. "He told you he's a stranger here, Malone. Why don't you let him just turn around and ride away?"

"Why, who's stoppin' him?" The man called Malone grinned at The Kid and went on in an oily tone of mock friendliness, "You just go right ahead and mount up, mister. We wouldn't want to keep you from goin' back wherever you came from."

The Kid had a feeling that if he got on the buckskin and headed back west through the pass, he wouldn't make it twenty yards before he had a bullet in his back. He said, "What if I want to ride on down the valley?"

Malone rubbed the fingers of his left hand over his beard. "Well, I ain't so sure that'd be a good idea. We got all the people we need in the valley right now."

"It's a public road, isn't it?"

"Not exactly. There's supposed to be a marker here so folks will know they're enterin' Trident range, and they'd be better off turnin' around."

"That's not true," Diana said with a sudden flare of anger. "The boundaries of your ranch don't extend this far, Malone. You're claiming range that doesn't belong to you."

He turned a baleful stare on her. "I don't like bein' called a liar, even by a pretty girl like you, Miss Starbird."

The Kid had noticed the brand on the horses the men rode. It was a line that branched and curved into three points. Now he said, "Neptune's trident."

That distracted Malone from the young woman named Diana Starbird. He looked at The Kid again and asked, "You know of it?"

"Neptune was the Roman god of the sea, and he was usually depicted carrying a trident like the one you're using as a brand. The Greeks called him Poseidon."

"Didn't expect to run into a man who knows the classics out here in the middle of this godforsaken wilderness," Malone said.

The Kid didn't waste time explaining about his education. He knew that he and Diana were still balanced on the knife-edge of danger from these men.

And yet there was something about Malone, something about the way he looked at Diana, that told The Kid he didn't want to hurt the young woman. The Kid's own fate was another story, though. He had a hunch Malone would kill him without blinking an eye, if the whim struck him to do so.

"Is there a town in the valley?"

Malone looked a little surprised by the question. "Aye. Bristol, about fifteen miles east of here."

"I need to replenish my supplies, and my horse could use a little rest before I ride on. I'm not looking for trouble from you or anyone else, Malone. Just let me ride on to the settlement and in a few days I'll be gone."

Malone frowned. "Are you sure Owen Starbird didn't send for you?"

That would be Diana's uncle, The Kid recalled. "Never heard of him until now," he replied honestly.

"Well . . ." Malone scratched at his beard and hesitated as if he were considering what The Kid had said.

While that was going on, the little man in gray turned his horse from the trail and started riding around the area, his eyes directed toward the ground as if he were searching for something. After a moment, he found it. He reined in, dismounted, and reached into the brush to pick up the skull. He turned and held it up to show the others.

"Look at this, Terence."

"My marker," Malone rumbled angrily. "Part of it, anyway."

The baldheaded man pointed toward the trail. "Only one set o' fresh tracks comin' from the west, Terence," he said. "And the bones were there earlier. I seen 'em with my own eyes."

Malone glared at The Kid. "That means you disturbed my marker, mister . . . What is your name, anyway?"

"It's Morgan."

Malone smiled, but his eyes were flintier than ever. "Like Henry Morgan, God rest his soul."

Or like Frank Morgan, The Kid thought. But he didn't mention his father, the notorious gunfighter known as The Drifter. He fought his own battles these days, with no help from anyone.

He recognized the name Henry Morgan, though. He had no doubt that Malone was referring to the infamous English buccaneer from the Seventeenth Century who had led a fleet of pirate ships against the Spaniards in the Caribbean and Central America and captured Panama City. The skull and crossbones that had been planted in the trail left no doubt about Malone's interest in pirates and piracy.

"I've been known to let travelers use this trail, Mr. Morgan," Malone went on, "if they can pay tribute. I'm afraid I can't do that with you, though."

"Just as well . . . because I don't intend to pay you one red cent."

Malone's lips drew back from his teeth. "Destroyin' my marker is like a slap in the face, Morgan, and I can't allow you to go unpunished for that. You can go on down the trail . . . but you'll have go past either Greavy"—he nodded to the small, gray-clad gunman—"or Wolfram." A jerk of the bearded chin indicated the baldheaded man. "Guns or fists, Morgan. It's up to you."

Wolfram held up his right hand and opened and closed it into a fist as he grinned at The Kid. He flexed those strong, knobby-knuckled fingers and chuckled.

Greavy's face was cold and expressionless. He was clearly the fast gun of this bunch. The Kid was confident that he could beat Greavy to the draw, but if he did, that didn't mean the others would let him pass. They might just use the shooting as an excuse to kill him.

But if he took on the bruiser called Wolfram and bested him in single combat, that might be different. The rest of them might be impressed enough by such a victory to let him go. More importantly, such an outcome wouldn't expose Diana Starbird to the danger of flying bullets.

And the anger that was always seething not far below the surface of The Kid's mind would have an outlet again.

The Kid looked at Malone and said, "I have your word of honor that if I defeat one of them, you'll allow me to ride on to Bristol?"

"Word of honor," Malone said. He looked at his other men. "You hear that? If Morgan lives, no one bothers him . . . today."

The Kid caught that important distinction but didn't challenge it. First things first. He added, "And Miss Starbird comes with me, either to the settlement or wherever else she wants to go."

Malone frowned. "Diana knows I'd never harm a hair on her head, and none of my men would dare to do so, either. I think the world of her."

"Then you wouldn't want to hold her against her will, would you?"

Before Malone could answer, Diana stepped closer to The Kid and said in a quiet voice, "You don't have to do this on my account, Mr. Morgan. I'll be all right—"

"You don't want to stay here, do you?"

She shot a glance at Malone and his men and admitted, "Well . . . no."

"Then you're coming with me." His words had a tone of finality to them.

"It's mighty confident you are that you're goin' to live through this," Malone said. "Greavy is a talented man with a gun, and I've seen Wolfram break bigger fellas than you in half with his bare hands."

"I'll risk it," The Kid said. He took off his hat and handed it to Diana, who had a worried look on her face as she took it. The Kid didn't want to demonstrate his own gun-handling prowess just yet, since it might come in handy later if he needed to take them by surprise, so he unbuckled his gunbelt and handed it to the young woman as well. Then he stripped off his coat and dropped it on the ground. "I'll take on Wolfram."

The baldheaded man had already figured that out. Grinning, he slid the rifle he carried into its saddle boot and then swung down from the back of his horse. He didn't wear a handgun, but he had a knife sheathed at his waist. He removed the sheath from his belt and tucked it into a saddlebag, then took off his derby and hung it on the saddlehorn.

"I'm gonna enjoy this," he said as he turned toward The Kid, who was rolling up his sleeves while Diana stood there looking more frightened by the second.

"Bust him up good, Wolfram," called one of the other men.

"Yeah," another man added in a raucous shout. "Show him he can't mess with us."

Wolfram started forward, moving at a slow, deliberate pace as he approached The Kid. He was still grinning and flexing his fists. The Kid stood there, arms at his sides, apparently waiting calmly, even though his blood surged at the prospect of battle.

Wolfram charged without warning, swinging a malletlike fist at The Kid's head with surprising quickness, and the fight was on.

Chapter Three

The Kid moved now with the same sort of speed he exhibited whenever he drew his gun. He ducked under the looping punch that Wolfram threw and sprang aside from the bull-like charge.

Wolfram's momentum carried him past his intended victim. The Kid kicked out behind him as Wolfram went by, driving the heel of his boot into the back of Wolfram's left knee. The baldheaded bruiser howled in pain and pitched toward the ground as that leg folded up beneath him.

The Kid whirled toward him, intending to kick Wolfram in the head and finish the fight in a hurry, but he saw to his surprise that Wolfram had slapped a hand on the ground and managed to keep from falling. A supple twist of the big body brought Wolfram upright again, facing The Kid. The lips under the handlebar mustache pulled back in an ugly grin.

"Well, now I know that you're fast, you little son of a bitch," Wolfram said as he began to circle more warily toward The Kid. He limped slightly on the leg that had been kicked. "I won't make that mistake again."

The Kid knew his chances of surviving this fight had just gone down a little since he hadn't been able to dispose of his opponent quickly. But the battle was far from over. True, Wolfram had advantages in height, weight, and reach, but as Conrad Browning, The Kid had been a boxing champion during his college days.

More importantly, his vengeance quest as Kid Morgan and the wandering existence on the frontier that had followed it had taught him to do whatever was necessary to win when he was fighting for his life.

He didn't hang back and let Wolfram bring the fight to him again. Instead, he launched an attack of his own, darting in to throw a flurry of punches. The blows were almost too fast for the eye to follow, and they were too fast for Wolfram to be able to block all of them. A couple of The Kid's punches got through, hard shots that landed cleanly on Wolfram's shelflike jaw and rocked his head back and forth.

Wolfram roared in anger and counterattacked, managing to thud a fist into The Kid's breastbone with staggering force. The impact stole The Kid's breath away and sent him stumbling backwards a few steps.

Wolfram bellowed again—obviously, he was one of those fighters who liked his battles noisy—and surged forward to try to press his advantage. As The Kid gasped for air, he saw the light of bloodlust shining in Wolfram's eyes and knew his opponent thought the fight was just about over.

The Kid went low again, sliding under pile-driver punches that would have broken his neck if they had landed. He threw his body against Wolfram's knees in a vicious block that cut the man's legs out from under him. This time Wolfram wasn't able to recover. He went down hard, his face driving into the dirt.

The Kid rolled and came up fast. He had gotten a little breath back in his lungs. His heart pounded madly in his chest and his pulse played a triphammer symphony inside his skull. He leaped and came down on top of Wolfram, digging both knees into the small of the man's back as hard as he could. Wolfram jerked his head up and yelled in pain.

That gave The Kid the chance to slide his right arm around Wolfram's neck from behind. He grabbed his right wrist with his left hand and hung on for dear life as he tightened the pressure on his opponent's throat. He kept his knees planted in Wolfram's back and hunkered low so that the awkward, frantic blows Wolfram aimed behind him couldn't do any real damage. The Kid forced Wolfram's head back harder and harder and knew that if he kept it up, sooner or later the man's spine would crack.

Wolfram might pass out first from lack of air, though, and he appeared to know it. In desperation, Wolfram rolled over and over. The Kid felt the big man's weight crushing him each time he wound up on the bottom, but he didn't let that dislodge his grip. He clung to Wolfram's back like a tick.

Suddenly, he felt Wolfram's muscles go limp. Either the man had lost consciousness, or he was trying to trick The Kid into relaxing that death grip. The Kid wasn't going to be fooled. The muscles of his arms and shoulders bunched. One more good heave would break the bastard's neck—

A shot crashed like thunder. The Kid's head jerked up. He saw that Malone had dismounted and now loomed over him, blotting out the sun as he aimed one of those pearl-handled revolvers at The Kid's head. Smoke curled from the barrel as a result of the warning shot Malone had fired.

"Let him go," Malone said. "You're gonna kill him. Let him go, Morgan."

"He would've . . . killed me . . . if he could," The Kid said between clenched teeth.

"I reckon that's right, but I've got the gun, and I'm tellin' you to let him go. We been partners too long for me to let you just snap his neck like that."

"You'll keep your word and let me and Miss Starbird go on to Bristol?"

"Aye, go and be damned to you!"

The reluctance with which Malone uttered the words convinced The Kid that he was telling the truth. The Kid eased his grip on Wolfram's throat, then released it entirely. The man's head slumped forward into the dirt. He was out cold, all right, not shamming. But he was still alive. The Kid heard the ragged rasp of breath in Wolfram's throat.

With an effort, The Kid kept his muscles from trembling as he climbed to his feet. He didn't want Malone to see how shaky he felt at this moment. Instead he reached out to Diana as she came closer to him, took the gunbelt from her, and buckled it around his hips. The weight of the holstered Colt felt good to him.

"For your own benefit, you ought to keep movin' instead of stoppin' in Bristol," Malone went on. "There's no place in this valley that'll be safe for you after today."

"Then if I see you or any of your men again, I might as well go ahead and shoot on sight, is that what you're telling me?" The Kid asked.

Malone's lips twisted in a snarl, but he didn't say anything else. He slid his gun back into its holster, then bent to grasp one of Wolfram's arms. Without being told to, a couple of the hardcases dismounted and hurried over to help their boss hoist Wolfram's senseless form back onto his feet. Wolfram began to come to, shaking his head groggily.

The Kid took his hat from Diana and put it on, then picked up his coat, folded it, and stuck it in his saddlebags. The sun was too hot for the garment.

He asked in a low voice, "Where's your horse?"

She inclined her head toward the boulders where she must have been hidden as she watched him kick the skull out of the trail. He figured he hadn't heard her ride up because the echoes of his shot had been rolling away over the hills at the time.

"Go get it," he told her.

"Not yet," she replied. "Not until they're gone."

He understood what she meant. She believed that Malone would be less likely to break his word and try to gun The Kid down as long as she was close by.

She was probably right about that, too. He stood there holding the buckskin's reins in his left hand and kept his right close to his gun while Malone and his men helped Wolfram climb onto his horse. Greavy kept a close eye on The Kid while that was going on. The Kid had a feeling that Greavy sensed the presence of another fast gun. He saw the appraisal and the challenge in the little man's eyes. Greavy was trying to figure out if he could take The Kid.

Once Wolfram was mounted again, Malone swung up into his own saddle and motioned for his men to follow suit. They turned their horses around and started jogging away, following the trail that led through the valley. They rounded a bend and rode out of sight.

"Do you think they'll try to find a place to pull an ambush?" The Kid asked.

Diana shook her head. "Not now. Black Terence keeps his word . . . most of the time."

The Kid glanced over at her and lifted an eyebrow.

Diana waved a hand and said, "I'll explain on the way to Diamondback."

"Diamondback?"

"The ranch my uncle and I own."

"I was headed for Bristol, remember?"

Diana shook her head. "Not anymore. It won't be safe for you. I'm pretty sure Malone has spies working for him in town. Anyway, there are a lot of alleys where bushwhackers could hide."

"You don't owe me anything, if that's what you're thinking," The Kid told her.

Diana let out a snort. "Me owe you anything? It's the other way around, Mr. Morgan. If I hadn't been here, Malone and his men would have killed you. And it was your shot that drew them in the first place. When you saw the skull and crossbones, why didn't you just turn around and ride away?

Don't you know what they mean?" She drew in a deep breath. "They mean death."

The Kid wasn't in any mood to argue with her. "I've seen plenty of it," he said. "Let's get your horse."

"You'll come to the ranch with me?"

The Kid shrugged. "Why not? The main thing I wanted was a chance to rest my buckskin. I reckon I can do that at your place as well as I can in town."

"Better," Diana said. "Our hands will take good care of your horse."

They fetched her mount, a fine-looking chestnut, from the rocks where she had left it. She put her foot in the stirrup and stepped up into the saddle with a lithe grace that didn't surprise The Kid. From everything he had seen so far, he guessed that she had been born and raised out here in West Texas. He knew a Western girl when he saw one. He had married one, in fact, and a pang went through him at the reminder of what he had lost. Months had passed since Rebel's death, but he still reacted the same way every time he thought about her.

As they started along the trail, he kept his eyes peeled for any sign of trouble, just in case Diana was wrong about Malone and his men trying to ambush them. The range seemed peaceful enough, though.

"Where is this Diamondback ranch?" The Kid asked.

Diana pointed to the line of trees that marked the stream's course. "Everything in the valley north of the Severn River is Diamondback range."

"The Severn, eh?" That was the name of a river in England, he recalled, and Bristol, of course, was an English town. He wondered if that meant anything. He had been to England, and while Rattlesnake Valley certainly wasn't as dry and barren as most of West Texas, it was still a far cry from the lush green English countryside.

Diana didn't offer any explanations. She was watchful, too, as if she didn't have complete confidence in her assurances that Malone wouldn't attack them.

"Why the skull and crossbones?" The Kid asked after they had ridden a mile or so. "I know they put it on the labels of liquids that are poisonous, but I never saw anybody use it as a road marker before."

"It's the symbol from the pirate flag," Diana said, telling The Kid something he already knew. "I suppose Malone thinks that it's appropriate."

"Appropriate?" The Kid repeated. He frowned over at her. "Are you telling me that—"

"Black Terence Malone is a pirate," Diana said with a nod. "At least, he used to be, and just because he's not on the high seas anymore, that doesn't mean he's any less of a brigand."